LucyDreams

or

The Unremarkable Life *of* Jeremy Moore

Lucy

or The
Unremarkable
Life *of*
Jeremy Moore

dreams

PAUL E. PIERPOINT

Dedicated to Matt and Jeff.

And so from hour to hour we ripe and ripe,
And then from hour to hour we rot and rot;
And thereby hangs a tale.

Shakespeare, *As You Like It*

Row, row, row your boat

Gently down the stream.

Merrily, merrily, merrily

Life is but a Dream.

—Eliphalet Orem Lyte

It started a year ago. I was imprisoned in a hospital room, encased in bandages and casts, and shackled to the wall with tubes and wires. I was seventy-seven years old and not having a good week. I vaguely remembered I had fallen off my roof while cleaning my gutters. I lay there with the afternoon sun warming one side of my face, the other side buried in fresh mulch. It was a beautiful spring day and I was fucked. I wondered if I was dead. Then I realized I was in excruciating pain. I couldn't be dead if it hurt this much. My shoulder burned; my leg screamed; my chest felt like a knife was stuck between my ribs. I wasn't dead but I was dying. My life flashed before my eyes.

Worst movie ever.

I passed out. The next thing I knew I was staring into a blinding bright light. Now I was sure I was dead and about to finally see what that would entail. Instead, the light was eclipsed by a dark shadow and a masked face came into view. I wasn't dead. I was in a hospital room trussed up like a damn Christmas goose. "He's waking up," I heard from a far distance. "Mr. Moore, can you hear me?" the mask asked.

"Mmnnrrfaah," I replied.

"Good, just relax now. I'm going to give you something to sleep. You'll feel better when you wake up." The room went black.

I woke up with a screaming headache which masked the pain that throbbed through every fiber of my body. I am not good with pain. This was a lot of pain. After a few minutes that felt like hours, the mask reappeared in front of my face. "Good morning, Mr. Moore. How are we feeling today?"

"Mmnnnnrrfah."

"That's good. I'll give you a little something to help you relax." Everything went black again.

After several trips to lala land, I was able to stay awake long enough to figure out where I was. I had a blurry recollection of what happened. I took inventory. OK. So, I didn't die. That was probably a good thing. But I must have done some serious damage. That was definitely a bad thing. I moved my right arm. It hurt but I could bend it. I could wiggle my fingers. That's a good thing. I tried my other arm. Nope, couldn't move anything. Bad thing. Left leg? I felt my toes move under the sheet. Good thing. Right leg? Screaming pain shot through me. Very bad thing. Even in my drugged stupor, I knew it was going to be a long, strange trip to get back to health. Or whatever you call the default physical condition of a seventy-seven-year-old man. I wondered if the effort would be worth it. As Sartre said, life is drained of meaning when you have lost the illusion of being eternal.

Looking back on that time a year ago I'm not proud of myself. I was feeling sorry for myself. Lying there in the misty world of strong opiates, I knew I was well past life's final turn and heading for the finish line. I realized a big chunk of that limited time was going to involve casts, bedpans, and lots of pain. It wasn't fair. Why did this have to happen to me? Life sucks. I was depressed.

Then I met Samantha.

I've wanted to tell Samantha's story for a while. Now, finally, I can. But her story is also my story. Rather, it is the final chapter in my story. So let me tell you our stories. You may want to grab a cup of tea and get comfortable. This could take a while.

Now, where do I start? Well, here's as good a place as any, I suppose…

My Unremarkable Life
1953

It was 67 years ago. Bitter cold wind blew ice crystals across my black goggles while the sun reflected off brittle snow blinding us as we scraped and inched our way toward the summit. We were already higher than any human had ever climbed before. Another climbing team had tried to summit the day before and turned back when their oxygen tanks began to falter just below where we stood now. Today was our turn. The tall beekeeper from New Zealand, the yak herder from Nepal, and I, an heroic Hoosier from Mount St. Anne, Indiana, were determined to succeed where so many had failed before.

We had just conquered the last significant technical obstacle before the final push to the summit. A twenty-foot vertical chimney between a sheer rock wall and an ice face would have been a challenge for most climbers even at sea level. But for the beekeeper at 29,000 feet, it was a mere hindrance to be surmounted and cast aside. He wedged his back against the rock, dug his crampons into the ice, and shimmied his way up through the gap that would forever after be known as Hillary's Step. The powerful Nepali followed up the rope that tethered them together. I scampered up behind. We sat on a small ice shelf for a moment puffing into our oxygen masks as we garnered our strength for the final push.

In the lead, the Kiwi struggled to chop small steps into the steep snow crust with his ice axe. I watched in fascination from below as the big man and the small man steadily worked their way up the ridge toward the peak ahead of us. They were clearly exhausted. Progress was slow. Step—breathe-breathe-breathe. Step—breathe-breathe-breathe. Step—breathe-breathe-breathe. Even with bottled oxygen we faced serious hypoxia as we rationed our supply.

All we could see was the blinding snow and ice immediately in front of us as we inched our way toward the top of the world. Several times we thought we were about to find the peak only to discover it was a false summit and more ridge line climbed high above us. Chopping steps into the ice; moving up one step at a time; pushing towards the greatest mountaineering achievement in history, we carried on.

Finally, as our energy and spirits were beginning to fail, we crested one more summit and before us opened hundreds of miles of sharp, glacier-covered mountains pushing through clouds and spreading from horizon to horizon. The sky was a brilliant blue dome high over the peaks and clouds. We stood on top of the highest mountain in the world. Finally, after decades of failure and too many deaths, mankind stood at the top of Mount Everest.

The beekeeper took a picture of the Nepali standing alone on the peak holding his ice axe victoriously overhead adorned with flags flapping in the harsh wind. Then he turned to me. His face was hidden behind the dark goggles and oxygen mask. His deep blue parka hood was pulled tightly around his face. He looked like a giant insect. Then he said, in a surprisingly tinny voice, "Here, take the toilet seat, Jeremy, and go get a crescent wrench."

I blinked in utter confusion. I stared open-mouth at my hero. Speechless.

"Jeremy!" the bug-man said more forcefully," take this damn toilet seat and get me that wrench!"

As I stared at the face of Edmund Hillary, the goggles and oxygen masked dissolved into the pink, fleshy face of my father. The waves of sharp peaks marching to the horizon morphed into the inside of the little bathroom in our Cape Cod house at 321 Apple Tree Lane, Mount St. Anne, Indiana. I looked down at the Life magazine in my hand, Edmund Hillary and Tenzing Norgay on the cover. Then I looked back at my father.

"Forchissake, Jeremy, wake up. Get your head out of that damn magazine and take this toilet seat!" Alas, I was back in my boring life.

I was ten years old. I was an average kid. Average height, average weight, average intelligence. A solid B-minus student. My waxed flattop haircut looked like the haircut on nearly every other boy in my neighborhood. I wore short-sleeve plaid shirts and grass-stained blue jeans every day. My Keds sneakers were usually untied, laces flapping uselessly around my ankles when I walked or ran.

I had glasses that I hated to wear outside where people could see me. They made me look like a dork. But I loved my glasses when I was in my room doing my favorite thing - reading books about heroes and scalawags living lives of adventure. I loved books about brave men daring fate and living on the edge far from the safety and comfort of the picket-fence world I inhabited. Every night when I read before bedtime I became Jim Thornton mushing my dog team through the Arctic night answering the call of the wild. I became Jim Hawkins drinking grog with peg-legged pirates and digging for gold on Treasure Island. I journeyed with Professor Lindenbrock to the center of the Earth.

The shelves in my room were stacked with paperbacks. My small desk was buried under old issues of National Geographic. I loved the maps that came with each issue. I'd spread them out on my floor and study them like Caesar or Napoleon learning the landscape as they prepared to conquer another part of the world.

Of course, I wasn't a total bookworm. I loved movies, too. Especially the movies with heroic stars who stared death in the face with steely-eyed courage. Gary Cooper in High Noon. Bogey in African Queen, Alan Ladd as Shane. Many Saturday afternoons of my childhood were lost in the front row of the Odeon Theatre eating Good & Plenty candy and staring intently at the big, shining screen.

On summer nights I often climbed out my bedroom window to lie on the slanting roof and think. Fireflies blinked across the yard below. Warm breezes carried the smell of honeysuckle and jasmine. I'd lie there and dream of adventure.

So it was that fateful summer day when the postman delivered our Life magazine with the cover picture of Edmund Hilary and Tenzing Norgay after they had climbed the highest mountain in the world. I was in awe. The whole world was amazed, of course. But I was moved deep inside me. It was so amazing it hurt. I consumed the article like a starving dog on a cheeseburger. I may have drooled while I read. I was transported to Nepal. I was slogging my way up Everest. I was cold and weary and exhilarated. I was also sitting on the floor of our tiny bathroom supposedly helping my father replace the broken toilet seat. The realization deflated me like a scimitar slicing through a Macy's parade balloon. The awareness hurt. My pretend life in books and movies was an adventure while my real life was anything but. It was boring. It was stupid. Not once in my whole life had I ever been shot at. I had never dangled over a cliff or faced down a man-eating lion. I had never discovered a new land or saved anyone's life. My life would make a terrible book. I had never done anything worth reading about.

That is what I was thinking as I took the toilet seat from my father and headed down the steps to the kitchen to get the wrench. Halfway down the stairs my thoughts were broken by a loud gasp from my father followed quickly by a dull thump and splash. I ran back to the bathroom to find my father on his knees with his hands clutching his chest and his head in the toilet - dead as a stump. I stared at his body. I looked at the magazine in my hands. Hillary seemed to be chuckling. I looked back at my father. I yelled, "Mom!" and ran out of the room.

Bartholomew

L ying in my hospital bed sixty-seven years later, those memories were vivid - bright and alive as if they happened yesterday. Of course, I could barely remember yesterday. Hell, I couldn't remember what I had for breakfast two hours ago. I blamed it on the meds. It was two days since the operation. I had some lingering pain issues. Of course, I was still pretty drugged up. But I remembered my life. Or most of it. Some of it anyway. While I was lying on my back staring death in the face from my lawn behind my house a week earlier, my life passed before my eyes. It wasn't the story I wanted it to be back there in 1953, not by a long shot.

As for the operation, they called it a routine procedure. Two titanium plates, eight screws, thirty-nine stitches. A routine procedure to repair a common fracture in the femur of an ordinary man. My other injuries—sprained ACL in the other leg, dislocated shoulder, two broken ribs, punctured lung, severe wrist sprain, and multiple cuts, abrasions, and bruises, probable concussion—were properly treated and left to take care of themselves aided only by some delightful painkillers. The doctor said I'd be stuck in this hospital room for at least another week then another six weeks in rehab in an extended care facility. Then, if I was lucky, I could go home and convalesce for six or seven months until I could maybe, possibly, be healthy enough to "get back to my normal life" whatever the hell that means for an old man.

I lay in my hospital bed, thinking and remembering. Thinking and remembering, it's what old men do when they feel like they're getting close to the last act of the show. But thinking and remembering can wear a guy out. So I pressed the button to raise the head of my bed and stared out the window at a robin perched on a thin twig bobbing slightly in the sun. I wondered if the bird was male or female. How can you tell with robins? I decided I'd have to Google that later. My leg projected from under the thin blanket supported by a padded rest. My gaze drifted from the bird to my toes peeking absurdly from the plastic brace. I was a little embarrassed by the ugly yellow nails. I'd have to see about trying one of those products they were always advertising on late shows that promised to cure toenail fungus. Not that I ever go barefoot. It was just that the glaring imperfection of thick toenails was so damn pedestrian. As I pondered my toes a familiar baritone voice slowly drew my attention. The still handsome face of an old man came into focus beyond my foot.

"They have services that do that, you know. And they're pretty cheap. Mostly Mexican workers…" Bartholomew Cross was my first visitor after the surgery. Good old Bartholomew - never Bart - professional actor who was still looking for a breakthrough part to bring him fame and fortune. Six feet tall with broad shoulders, he still had the body of an athlete. Well, an old athlete. His rugged face had softened over the decades, but his jawline remained sharply defined, his dimples still deep and endearing. He wore an ascot to hide the pockmarked waddle on his neck. His pale blue eyes peered from under slightly sagging lids—bedroom eyes. If a septuagenarian can have bedroom eyes.

Bartholomew was a lifelong friend. One of my three closest friends in the world along with Lyle and Junior. The four of us grew up together and remained friends our long lives. For the last few years since Junior's wife Daisy died we met for breakfast every Tuesday, Thursday, and Saturday morning at the coffee shop in

Lyle's bookstore where we argued and complained, ate yummy pastries, and drank strong coffee. One day while complaining loudly about the smart-phone addictions of young people and the pending collapse of civilization, our teenage barista said we sounded like the Four Horsemen of the Acropolis. After wiping up the coffee we had sputtered out, we decided we liked the sobriquet. Sometimes it felt like we had been around as long as the Acropolis.

"People our age shouldn't be climbing ladders and cleaning gutters." Bartholomew pointed an unlit cigarette at me. "We're not teenagers anymore, you know." He was trying to quit smoking but thought he looked more dashing with a cigarette dangling from his lips or held "European-wise" between his middle and ring fingers, so he usually had an unlit cigarette moving around. I sipped ginger ale from a plastic straw and peered at a small zit on my friend's forehead - a minor imperfection on a face that, even at seventy-seven years old, was strikingly handsome.

"I mean look at what happened. You're lucky you only broke your leg. If you landed on your head, we wouldn't be having this conversation. I'd be at your funeral wondering how you could've been so careless. *A man that apprehends death no more dreadfully but as a drunken sleep: careless, reckless, and fearless.*"

"Let me guess. Shakespeare?"

Bartholomew gave a weary smile. "Of course. Isn't it always Shakespeare?"

A hard rap at the door drew our attention. Dr. Akufo strode into my room like George Patton into an Army barracks. Without a word she commanded the attention of everyone wherever she went. She wasn't tall - maybe five-six - but she moved larger. Her short-clipped black hair was sprinkled through with white. Her piercing brown eyes were framed by sharp crow's feet and heavy, graying brows. Deep lines on either side of her chin gave her mouth a permanent frown. She was a renowned orthopedic surgeon, and she intimidated the hell out of me.

"How are we feeling this morning, Mr. Moore?" she asked, her voice a surprising baritone.

"We feel like shit. We're old and we feel like shit."

"That's progress. Last time I saw you, you weren't feeling anything." Dr. Akufo pulled the blanket from my lap. She deftly pulled back the Velcro straps holding the plastic cast closed and opened the shell exposing my leg all the way up to my hip. Large purple and yellow bruises were stark against the pale pinkish flesh of my age-withered leg. A line of dark stitches wormed up the side of my hip.

"Color looks good. No seepage," She looked at my chart. "No fever. Competent urine output."

"Thank you."

"That's not really a compliment, Mr. Moore. Any pain?"

"Pretty much everywhere."

Dr. Akufo checked the chart again. "We have you on some pretty strong pain medication. But if you feel too much pain, tell the nurse and she'll get you more Percocet." She put the chart down and took another glance at my leg. "Mr. Moore, you can expect to be in that cast for six weeks. It is removable so your physical therapist can take it off during therapy." She replaced the shell and pulled the straps tight. "You will need to keep it on for your leg to heal properly. If you take care of yourself, full recovery could be in six months. My advice is let someone else clean your gutters next time." And, without so much as a wink, she left my room.

"That woman scares me," Bartholomew whispered after she was gone, "but she's right about the gutters."

"Dr. Akufo is usually right about everything," a booming voice announced from the door. "She's the best damn orthopedic surgeon in Indiana." The jovial orderly filled the doorway smiling. Roger was a bear of a man - a big, friendly bear. Calvin and Hobbes tattoos ran up the length of both arms. He wore a Pacers ballcap backwards. He hoisted me into my wheelchair. "Tasha time! Ready to go?" He pushed me toward the door without waiting for an answer. "This is your first physical therapy session, right? Well, you got the best. If you want to walk again, Tasha's the PT most likely to get you there." He chuckled. "If she doesn't kill you first." I flinched. "Don't worry Jeremy. She hasn't killed a patient yet. Hell, you'll come to love her. And the pain."

He wheeled me out of the room, through the double doors, and down the long maze of hallways to the PT room on the far side of the hospital.

My Unremarkable Life
Funeral

Five days after my father died in the toilet I sat on a hard wooden pew in the front row of the church we attended religiously every Christmas Eve. Mother sat beside me in a short black strapless dress she wore only at funerals and New Year's Eve parties. A heavy black shawl covered her shoulders. Her face was hidden behind a black mesh veil. She sniffed and dabbed a tissue at her eyes. My mom's name was Hazel Druckenmiller Moore but everyone called her Hazy - the implication of which I would not get until I was in high school. She was a small woman with tiny hands. After all these years, I remember her hands more than I remember her face. Short, thin fingers with long bright red nails that she seemed to be buffing constantly. Each finger on her right hand sported a different ring every day. Sometimes they had a Navajo flair with lots of turquoise and silver. Other days they were positively Victorian with large faux jewels ensconced in ornate gold bands. Sometimes they were rustic, simple rings carved from wood or soft stones. She seemed to have an unlimited number of rings - probably to make up for the numbing sameness of her daily life. Her left hand was always bare except for the modest wedding band. At my father's funeral, she wore four bright zircon diamond rings. I wasn't sure if she chose them in pious memory of my father or in honor of some kind of liberation.

I don't think my mother was ever happy when my dad was alive. She craved more excitement from life than marriage to my father offered. I understood that early on. I read adventure books. She read romance novels. I pored over magazines about discovery and danger. She clipped articles about sex and handsome movie stars from Redbook magazine. We were both living our lives through the stories of others. I am sure she was shocked by the sudden demise of her husband but her grief felt reserved, partial, like grief from losing a distant uncle. So I wasn't surprised when six months later she brought home a truck driver five years younger than she was - the first of a long line of men who made Mom happy through the years. Mom and the truck driver spent a lot of time sleeping. He worked odd hours and was often home during the day. Sometimes when I came home from school early, I'd hear them in the bedroom giggling or making odd moaning sounds. One time when I was going through the drawers in mom's nightstand looking for some change to pay the paperboy, I found a feathered mask and a pair of handcuffs. I guess mom found what she was looking for.

In the church she sat beside me crying softly. People quietly entered the church. Mother nodded at each person who came by to give their condolences. "I'm so sorry for your loss," they'd say then try to think of something specific to say about my dad. "He was a good co-worker, He always cleaned the coffee pot when he took the last cup." "He was very polite." "I didn't know him well but he seemed like a nice man." Mother quietly thanked them. She sighed after each exchange. Then the preacher called the congregation to order. He spoke about how my dad was in a better place now, happily adjusting to life in Heaven. He tried to add personal comments about my dad which only proved he had no idea who he was. He asked if anyone wanted to share their thoughts about my dad. No one moved,. People reluctantly (or maybe hopefully) looked around the room to see if anyone would speak. The silence was painful, broken only by a few nervous coughs and a baby cooing in the back of the room. Finally, old Mr. Karnatz, our next door neighbor, stood and looked around. Seeing no one else moving, he shrugged his stooped shoulders and slowly made his way to the front of the church.

Old Mr. Karnatz was a cranky old man who hollered whenever kids stepped on his tiny front yard. He was always called "Old Mr. Karnatz," never just Mr. Karnatz - even by the grown-ups in the neighborhood. The kids were sure he had to be at least a hundred years old. When he stood up, I saw relief on the preacher's face and heard my mother softly sigh once more. At least someone was going to say something about my dad.

Old Mr. Karnatz reached the altar and leaned on it with both hands. "Hinkley Moore was a good man," he mumbled. "He always kept his yard neat. No weeds. I appreciated that." He glanced at mom and me like he was hoping for our approval, then he walked slowly back to his seat.

After another awkward minute when no one else moved, the preacher thanked everyone for coming, said a brief prayer, and reminded everyone there were cookies and punch in the vestry.

That night, after Mom went to her room with a coffee cup full of vodka and a tattered paperback of Lady Chatterley's Lover, I climbed onto the roof to look at the moon. The air was thick with smoke from the paper mill outside town. The crescent moon was yellow - a crooked smile low in the western sky. I wanted to cry. That's what a kid is supposed to do when his father dies. He's supposed to cry. But I couldn't. I was sad, of course. I felt a loss - a hole where something used to be. But I couldn't really identify what was gone. Sure, my dad was gone, but it didn't feel like that big a deal. I guess I was still in shock and my senses were shut down.

My mind drifted to Hillary and Norgay. People like them don't die in the bathroom. Men like them challenge death every day. They stare death in the face and prevail. That's what I wanted to be like. I wanted my life to be an adventure - something so extraordinary that people would want to read about it. I didn't want my father's life. I didn't want to die with my head in a toilet. I wanted my life to be remarkable.

I stood up on the slanting shingles of my roof and imagined myself holding my ice axe aloft at the top of the world, banners flapping in the bitter wind, the entire world stretched out below me. Then I opened my eyes and saw how close I was to the edge of the roof. I quickly sat down and scooted up away from the edge. I stayed there until the dim grin of the moon set behind the house across the street. I crawled through my window, got under the covers of my bed, and quietly, finally, cried myself to sleep.

———

This is what I do a lot now. I relive my life in pastel-tinted memories. Things worked out OK in my life. Not the way I wanted but whose life works out the way they wanted? Our dreams that inspired us as children almost never become the lives that we live as adults. And now that my life is almost over, I'm tempted to look back because looking forward doesn't lead to much. So maybe my life didn't turn out to be a great adventure story. No Clive Cussler best-seller. No action movie starring Harrison Ford. Not even a Hallmark Special with Hal Holbrook. Maybe my life fell short of my dreams. Well, no maybe about it. My life is a long, dull story of an average guy. But it's my life and I can't complain. I sit here in my hospital gown lost in my thoughts. I'm watching a retrospective of my life play out in my head. It's making me sleepy.

Tasha Time

The Mount St. Anne Hospital campus sat on forty acres at the top of Progress Hill, the highest point in town. A former girls' school founded near the turn of the last century, its main building was an imposing edifice of marble and red brick. The girls' school closed during the 1930s and a group of local philanthropists purchased it for the purpose of creating a hospital. In the decades since opening, the Mount St. Anne Hospital grew to become the largest healthcare institution in the three-county region. The original main building looked down Progress Avenue, the wide boulevard to the city below, like a grand old dowager frowning down on her vassals.

The long route to Physical Therapy turned and twisted through different sections of the hospital each added over the years as the facility expanded. Cardiology, Oncology, Neonatal, Diagnostic Imaging, Geriatrics, Gastroenterology, OB-GYN. Serious-looking doctors with their faces bent over clipboards hurried through the halls avoiding eye contact with everyone. Nurses in crisp blue scrubs and soft-soled shoes worked behind tall counters or walked in and out of patient rooms. Orderlies carefully pushed gurneys and wheelchairs through the traffic speaking quiet words of encouragement to their nervous cargo. We passed waiting rooms where family members huddled anxiously awaiting news of loved ones in surgery. A young man handed each of us a chocolate cigar as he danced down the hall. "It's a boy!" he said, "twenty-two inches, seven pounds six ounces!" After a few days in the hospital, I had learned that statistics were an essential part of every new birth announcement. Like the weigh-in at a professional fight.

The energy of the hospital's hallways amazed me. So many sick people. So many people working to make them better.

Bartholomew walked beside me yammering about the part he was auditioning for that afternoon - an old gay ex-professional football player with a much younger boyfriend. "It's a film. A political satire, sort of a cross between Moliere and Mamet. I am reading for the lead." Bartholomew hadn't landed a leading role in decades. He got by (barely) on commercials, some bit parts in TV dramas, and occasional corporate training videos. In the last one, he played a clueless old sexist manager demonstrating what not to say and do in the workplace if you want to keep your ass out of court. His acting career had pretty much peaked just a couple years after college when he landed the part of a red-shirt crew member on Star Trek. Red-shirt crew members never survived the first scene of the program. Bartholomew's character was one of the few red shirts who spoke. "Over there, captain. It's a…" Then he died. He was on screen for only seventeen seconds. But he was the most famous person ever to come from Mount St. Anne, Indiana.

Finally, we entered the PT room, a large brightly lit room with floor-to-ceiling glass along the far wall looking out over a garden. It smelled of BenGay and disinfectant. Therapists worked on patients who responded with moans and grunts. Metal weights clanked in a far corner. Several people puffed nearby as they pedaled stationary bicycles that whirred steadily. Everywhere were padded benches and tables with people being pushed, pulled, and twisted by therapists. Many of the patients looked young and healthy - maybe high school or college athletes recovering from sports injuries. Fit girls with long ponytails wore loose t-shirts and skin-tight leggings.

Brawny boys wore sweatshirts with the sleeves cut off exposing well-toned biceps. All of them working hard to regain their health while sneaking glances at one another.

Other patients looked to be as old as me. Some even older. Unlike the young patients, the older ones seemed oblivious to anyone else in the room. They concentrated on the slow, probably painful movements their therapists were putting them through. Broken hips, knee replacements, compressed disks, frozen shoulders. Old bodies have so many ways to fail. The people in the PT room were trying to undo whatever trauma their bodies had experienced. Young or old, so many people doing painful exercises trying to regain something they had before their injury or operation. Everyone just trying to get back the person they were before. I was amazed at the shared focus of so many different people.

I scanned across the large room until I caught the eye of an intense looking Black woman in PT scrubs scowling at me. She was a large woman - tall and broad-shouldered. Her black hair was pulled back in a tight bun that showed strands of grey. Her dark skin set off her sharp black eyes that bored into me. The room got cold. Roger wheeled me in her direction.

"That's your therapist, my man," he whispered as we moved through the room, "that's Tasha." I gulped.

"I'm out of here, old man," Bartholomew patted my shoulder and hurried out of the room as fast as his ancient legs would carry him. "See you tomorrow," he shouted without looking back, "and good luck."

As we approached Tasha, she slowly cracked her knuckles, like a street fighter loosening up. "You're late," she growled when Roger deposited me before her.

"Morning to you, too, Tasha," he said, "May I say you look particularly lovely today. Doing something different with your hair?"

"Can it, Roger. You're late and I got work to do. You can go back to the playground now but be back in forty-five minutes. Sharp."

"Yes, Master," Roger replied bowing repeatedly and backing away. "Good luck, Jeremy," he chuckled and headed for the door.

Tasha took the clipboard that was hanging from my chair and scanned the documents quickly. Her bright orange fingernails were perfectly manicured. I took a closer look at her face. Her square jawline and high cheekbones gave her an exotic look, like a Nubian warrior. She would have been very attractive if it weren't for the intimidating scowl that etched deep creases into her brow above her broad nose. "Jeremy Moore. Broken femur," she read out loud.

"Yes, that would be me. Jeremy Moore Broken Femur." I smiled. She didn't smile back.

"OK, Mr. Femur…"

"Please, call me Jeremy."

"OK, Jeremy, I'm Tasha, your Physical Therapist. For the next…" She flipped through the pages on the clipboard until she found what she was looking for, "…four to eight weeks, we are going to work together four days a week to make you healthy. It won't be fun. In fact, it's going to hurt like a bitch some of the time - but it will be productive. I can promise you that. Now, Jeremy, what is your goal?"

"My goal?" I thought, do I have a goal? What kind of goal would she expect from a seventy-seven-year-old man? At one time I would have said my goal is to find Bigfoot or meet the Dalai Lama or discover a new land. I might have said my goal is to be an astronaut or mush a dog sled over the North Pole. Or maybe I would have said my goal is to cure cancer. Maybe my goal should be to have a second chance at a life of adventure and excitement, to live a remarkable life.

"I want to be able to walk to the bathroom and take a dump by myself."

Tasha peered at me over her reading glasses. "Lofty goal, indeed. Jeremy. We wouldn't want to shit ourselves for lack of an orderly." I think she may have been mocking me. "We can get you there. In fact, we can do better than get you safely to the crapper. But," she took off her glasses and frowned, "if you really want to walk again, you need to be ready to do the work. Don't waste my time or your Medicare money by thinking this is going to work without your full commitment. If you don't want to work hard and feel a little pain, we will find you a different PT who doesn't give a shit. But I have a perfect track record of getting people to their goal and I am not going to let that record end any time soon. So you see, this is not about you, Jeremy. This is all about me. Are you going to help me out here, or do I trade you in for someone who wants to get better?"

I could feel myself shrink under her hard stare. I wanted more than anything at that moment to let her trade me in. She was not a nice a person and I was afraid. Then she winked. It was fast. So fast I wasn't sure I actually saw it. Her face remained dark. Her eyes continued to bore into me. But I knew she had winked. I smiled. "OK. I'm in. Let's do this."

She smiled back. "I knew you'd see it my way. Now let's get to work. Unlike old retired people with nothing better to do than waste time and make noises with their body, I have a job to do."

Five minutes later I was begging her to stop the pain. My so-called good leg was only a few inches off the bench, and she was pushing it from side to side. I was whimpering like a badly beaten puppy. "Tell me when it hurts," she said manipulating my leg to bend my knee.

"It hurts now!" I said.

"No, that's not pain. That's discomfort. You need to feel discomfort to make progress. Discomfort is good. Pain is bad. Pain means we could be doing more damage. You need to listen to your body and hear it when it says it feels discomfort and when it says it feels pain."

I moaned. Loudly. "This hurts." God, I would be really bad under torture.

"That's good. You're listening to your body. It's telling you it's healing."

"It's telling me I should confess. I killed Jimmy Hoffa! I was the shooter on the grassy knoll! I stole a box of Raisinets from Kroger when I was five."

"Good for you, Mr. Capone. Just a few more minutes and we're done for today."

When she finished making me cry like a baby she handed me a towel to wipe the sweat from my face. I was happy the ordeal was over. "You know, I didn't really kill Hoffa."

"Damn. There goes my reward."

"But I actually did steal those Raisinets. I never told anyone that."

"I'll notify the authorities."

"The guilt was a burden on my life. I'm relieved I finally admitted it to someone. A weight has been lifted. You should be a priest and take people's confessions."

"I hear they got a problem with woman priests. Besides, I don't like little boys."

After wrapping a ridiculously large bag of ice around my knee, Tasha picked up her clipboard. "Your next session is tomorrow morning at 9:30. Don't let that moron Roger be late. I'll show him the difference between discomfort and pain."

Junior
and the P-51 Mustang

I was staring at my stupid toes and wondering what sort of pasty mush the candy-striper would bring me for lunch when my revelry was broken by a soft rap on my open door. A familiar bald head peered around the jamb. "Is it ok if I come in?" Arnold "Junior" Pocketmaster was another one of my oldest and dearest friends—one of the Horsemen of the Acropolis. He was a remarkably successful insurance agent. At seventy-seven he still managed a few individual accounts including mine.

Junior had the natural make-up of an insurance agent. He was the most risk-averse person I ever met. As a kid he was always finding the potential disaster in everything we did. If we wanted to climb a tree, he'd worry that the branches were too weak and someone would probably fall and break their neck. If we wanted to swim in the creek, he'd complain that the undercurrents were too strong and someone would be sucked under and drown. If we wanted to hike up the hills behind our houses, he was sure we'd run into a bear or a rabid raccoon and someone would be attacked. None of us ever broke our neck or got sucked under a river rock or got attacked by a raging raccoon. Much to our disappointment. But that was Junior for you - danger lurked behind every corner but it never seemed to find us.

Fear of the worst ran in his family. Junior grew up a few doors down the street from my house. His parents were the neighborhood weirdos. They were convinced that if the Russians didn't nuke us all first, we'd soon be invaded by Martians or decimated by polio or done in by some yet-to-be-identified existential disaster. They were the only family in the neighborhood with a fallout shelter. They had a giant cache of canned food to last through any calamity until the world was safe again for them to leave the shelter. One time when we were climbing trees in the woods behind Junior's house, we saw his father carry an armload of rifles to the shelter. Junior thought his parents were nuts. Even as a twelve-year-old, Junior was convinced that real security came from proper risk management and responsible financial planning. Yes, he was a born insurance agent.

Junior was a short, chubby kid who grew to be a short, chubby man. Every year his large soft head melted a little more onto his shoulders. His soft double chin of childhood grew into a bulging bag of pasty skin that dropped straight from his round cheeks to his chest and shoulders. His thin blond hair that he kept in a spiky crew cut as a kid quickly receded out of sight when Junior was still in his thirties. Even though he grew up to look like a cross between a fire hydrant and a bubble gum machine, he managed to marry a beautiful woman. Daisy stayed with him for nearly fifty years before dying from lung cancer three years ago. Junior was only recently starting to show signs of recovering from the loss.

"I stopped by your house and got your mail." He held a stack of catalogs, fliers, bills, and assorted junk mail. "I also brought you some candy. Sugarless chocolates from the vegan place in the mall." Junior waited at the door for permission to enter.

"C'mon in, Junior." I waved him toward the chair beside my bed. "Dump the mail on my table. I'll ignore it later. And thanks for the candy. Put it with the rest of the stuff on the dresser over there." I had a sizable stockpile of cards, candy, balloons, and flowers collected over the last few days. Not so much as some of the other patients in the ward but more than I expected. People love to send you little gifts when you're laid up in the hospital. Easier and less icky than visiting.

"How are you feeling?" he asked.

"Like a seventy-seven-year-old man loaded on massive pain pills." Junior frowned. "No," I said, "that's a good thing. These pills are pretty amazing."

"Be careful. You know people get addicted to that stuff and the next thing you know they're selling their homes to buy heroin."

"I'll be careful. Besides, bourbon is still better. You didn't bring any, I suppose?" Junior looked over his shoulder like he was afraid someone would hear.

"No, I didn't bring any bourbon," he hissed, "You know it's against the rules to bring alcohol into the hospital."

"Yeah, I know. They don't like the competition. Can't have patients enjoying a couple of shots if it means they may sell fewer $20 aspirins."

"Speaking of $20 aspirins, are you happy with the new Medicare supplement we have you on? Is it giving you the coverage you need?"

"I have no idea. It's only been a few days. I haven't seen a bill yet and I suppose they'll wait until I'm home before they risk a fatal coronary letting me know how much my injuries cost."

"Well, try not to die too soon after you get the bills. You're my first customer to make a major claim on Armadillo MediGap and I'm interested to see how it goes."

"Don't worry, Junior. You'll be the first person I call."

"Great. But really, how are you? You were acting kind of morose even before your accident. You OK?"

"I'm fine," I snapped, "I'm freakin' great. I got a bunch of broken and cracked bones, tubes sticking in places where tubes shouldn't be, my shoulder hurts like hell, and I think a goddamn squirrel is crawling around in my cast. Could not be freakin' better."

"See, that's what I'm talking about. You've had a bad attitude for months. Lyle and Bartholomew have noticed, too."

I sighed. Junior meant well. I had been feeling blue lately. I was getting tired of the daily regimen of aches and pains associated with just being old. Old age sucked and it was only getting worse. I was looking at a rapidly accelerating slide toward the abyss and feeling like I should have done more with my life. Too little to look back on and nothing to look forward to. Yeah, I guess I had a bad attitude.

"Sorry. I'm just not dealing with this whole mortality thing very well."

"Probably because you're an atheist."

"So are you."

"True, but I don't take it seriously. I even go to church."

"Don't you think about your life? Don't you ever think that maybe you didn't live as fully as you should have? Don't you have regrets about things you didn't do?"

"My only regret is bringing this up. Are you allowed to eat solid food? I'll get you a piece of pie from the cafeteria."

"They took me off strained prunes yesterday. A piece of pie sounds good. Coconut custard if they have it. My daughters are stopping by later with some brownies."

"How are the girls?" The "girls" are my fifty-three-year-old triplet daughters. Junior has the right to call them girls since he was there from the beginning. He was with me when the three nurses brought the tiny creatures to the window of the nursery and gave me my first look at the new focus of my universe. And he has been there all the way since - school, girl scouts, puberty, dating, college, marriages, children of their own, everything. Junior can call them girls. Since he and Daisy never had kids, they're the closest thing he has to children of his own.

"They're fine. Same as usual. Working hard and living the dream." Funny thing about my daughters. Even after fifty years, they still travel as a pack. They coordinate their clothes. They eat the same food, drink the same liquor, read the same books, and, beyond all my expectations, they made a ton of money on one crazy idea after another over the years. And they love Uncle Arnold.

I heard a high-pitched squeal coming down the hallway. Junior and I stopped talking and looked to the door. The squeal grew louder as it rapidly came down the hall. A small girl wearing a yellow jumpsuit and bright green ball cap ran into the room shrieking like a fire alarm, her arms spread wide. She pulled up short, looked at us, and got quiet. She blinked and said, "Oops, wrong room," tilted her arms, did a quick spin, and ran back out renewing her piercing screech. We listened as the little girl disappeared down the hall.

"What the hell was that?" I said staring at the empty door.

"I think it was a P-51 Mustang," Junior said.

"Someone needs to bring that fighter in for a landing, or a spanking."

A woman's face appeared at the door. She was breathing hard, her face flushed. "Sorry about that. My daughter is a little wound up this morning." She shrugged and ran after the girl.

"That woman has her hands full," Junior said.

"Reminds me why I really don't like kids."

"You are such a liar. You love kids."

"Only when they are sedated or leashed."

"Lunch time, Jeremy." Roger stood at the door with a tray. "Today's menu is yellowfin tuna tartare and a nice strawberry arugula salad." He took the plastic cover off the plate. "Damn, they got the order wrong. Hope you're ok with a grilled cheese sandwich, Velveeta, of course, and lime Jell-O."

"Oh, good. My favorite. Junior, don't forget about that pie."

Lyle and Bigfoot

I had been deep in thought about a mild itch under my cast that seemed to be moving up the inside of my thigh. I was trying to decide if it was just a weird nerve thing, or if a spider was working its way toward my scrotum. My contemplation was interrupted by a familiar voice.

"Listen to this. Says here that some experts are starting to think Bigfoot may actually exist." Lyle Strawberry peered at me over his reading glasses. Lyle was another of my childhood friends, the fourth member of the Acropolis Four. His family moved down the street from me a year before my father died. His parents had owned a reasonably successful bookstore in downtown Indianapolis. The family lived close enough to walk to work every day. They moved their store and their home to Mount St. Anne, they said, to allow Lyle, who suffered occasional bouts of asthma, to grow up in clean country air. But Lyle said the real reason they moved was his father was worried too many Negroes were moving into the old neighborhood. There weren't any Negroes in Mount St. Anne in those days.

The family opened a new bookstore on Main Street sharing a building with the U-Wash-'Em Laundromat and Bev's Main Street Diner. Lyle helped out in the store most days after school and Saturdays so about the only time he got to join the rest of us for fun was Sunday. Lyle's parents were good businesspeople and, in a few years when the laundromat closed because everyone had a washing machine and Bev's closed because of the new drive-in burger place on the edge of town, they bought the building and expanded into the new space. Business was good for a while thanks, in part, to adding a coffee nook and expanding the product line to include comic books. With television changing the reading habits of Americans, it became difficult for the bookstore to survive on books alone. By the time we were in high school, it was common knowledge that they had a backroom where you could buy books and magazines that were banned—a quiet concession to the marketplace the Strawberrys had to make to keep revenue flowing in. The world's thirst for pornography was one of the great constants in the universe. Lyle was our regular source for dirty magazines, making him one of the popular kids.

Years later, Lyle took over the bookstore when his parents retired and moved to St. Pete. He was determined to make the store succeed as a traditional, independent bookstore providing the community with the best literature available. He said it was his duty to bring knowledge and enlightenment to the people. He invested in first editions—Fitzgerald, Hemmingway, Woolf, Blixen, and others. He pored over the international book reviews looking for the best new books. He started reading groups to encourage people to explore great literature while drinking 50-cent coffee.

But by the end of the seventies, Mount St. Anne was not interested in great literature. The few who were interested in great literature bought at discount prices from the big box bookstores that had opened outside of town. The only thing that consistently produced profit for Lyle was the backroom with its illicit publications. In further capitulation to the demands of the market, Lyle expanded that part of his business. He added XXX videos. He added magazines aimed at every kind of sexual preference and interest. When customers began asking for them, he added a complete line of "adult toys." Within months of expanding his adult merchandise, the store was producing more profit than ever. Lyle still wanted people to read Proust and Plath. He still had rare and expensive first editions in his window. He still hosted book clubs every night. But it was Mount St. Anne's indefatigable thirst for sexual arousal that paid the bills.

By the end of the century, Lyle had a string of adult novelty stores called Aphrodite's Closet scattered throughout southern Indiana. He still had his bookstore on Main Street. He'd never give that up even though it hadn't made real money in years. Even then, at the age of seventy-seven, Lyle went to work every day committed to bringing joy and happiness to his dozens of loyal literature customers.

Lyle was not generally a happy-looking guy. Over the years, his tall frame had collapsed into itself, his shoulders hunched and his long, thin neck projected straight forward. His bald head and deep-set eyes under a heavy brow gave him the appearance of Ichabod Crane crossed with a cartoon vulture. Today, he brought me the latest Margaret Atwood novel and a Smithsonian magazine.

He turned the magazine toward me and poked the page with his long, gnarly finger. "This isn't some National Enquirer Elvis-landed-in-a-UFO magazine, you know. This is a respected periodical." He turned the magazine back to himself and read, "While researching the impact of climate change on caribou in Nunavut Territory, a team of zoologists from the University of Northern Saskatchewan discovered remains buried in a frozen peat bog that they think may be from a previously unknown sub-species of Homo Sapiens. They have affectionately labeled the nearly six-foot tall fur-covered proto-human Bigfoot."

"That's what we did wrong," I said. Lyle looked up from the magazine, a quizzical look on his face. "We were looking in Shipley's Woods," I explained, "We should have been poking around frozen peat bogs in the Yukon." The light started to come on for Lyle. Shipley's Woods was a tract of forest that stretched behind our backyards when we were kids. We assumed it continued unbroken at least to Canada since, despite our courageous explorations of discovery, we never managed to reach the far side.

"I forgot all about that time in Shipley's Woods. We were hunting for Bigfoot, weren't we?"

"We found that big footprint - or at least something we decided was a footprint. Who knows what it really was, but we were what, twelve, thirteen years old? Junior was there too, wasn't he?"

"You led us so far into the woods we got lost. Remember?"

"We were not lost," I objected, "we just didn't exactly know where we were. I got us out of there, didn't I?"

"Well, technically, it was dumb luck that got us out of there. We must've walked ten miles." Lyle chuckled. "Junior whined most of the time. He was convinced we'd be attacked by Apaches or mauled by a grizzly."

"Seems to me you thought we were going to starve to death and started trying to eat pine cones."

"I was ahead of my time. Euell Gibbons made a lot of money eating pine cones a few years later."

"Never did find another footprint. We decided Bigfoot traveled through the trees like Tarzan. That was the obvious reason for no footprints."

"Then there was Brainfart," Lyle said

"Oh, crap! I forgot about Brainfart. Must have blocked that part out." I hadn't thought about that fiasco in years but it came back to me in sepia colors and muffled sounds. I hope it's a story worth telling.

My Unremarkable Life
The Great Bigfoot Fiasco

igfoot was a big deal at the time. Seemed like there was another Bigfoot sighting in the news every week. Pennsylvania, Montana, Colorado, Tennessee, Florida. They were everywhere. Even more than UFOs. But they were wily, those Bigfoots, Bigfeet, whatever. Even with dozens of sightings, no one could get a decent picture of a Bigfoot. I knew that if I could get a good Bigfoot photo, National Geographic would offer me a lot of money for it. I'd tell them to keep their money and just hire me as their head nature photographer. Send me to Borneo and the Congo and Patagonia to hunt down exotic animals and lost tribes and take their picture. I just needed to get that first great Bigfoot picture and my life of adventure would be guaranteed.

I was sure there had to be a Bigfoot somewhere in the woods behind my house - Shipley's Woods, so named for some ancient fur-trapper who was supposed to be the first white man to die there. Legend had it he was killed by a bear when he was checking beaver traps. Since there were no bears within a hundred miles of Shipley's Woods, we knew he must have really been killed by a Bigfoot. It was obvious that descendants of that Bigfoot still inhabited the woods. I had found all kinds of evidence in my sojourns into the forest. I knew exactly what to look for from watching Daniel Boone on TV. Bigfoot sign was everywhere. Broken branches six feet off the ground where one obviously walked by. Pieces of wiry black fur hanging from tree bark where he must have scratched his back. Matted areas of ground cover where he probably slept recently. And, most frightening, the fetid skeleton of a deer with pieces of hide hanging from the empty ribcage, leg bones scattered among the bushes. I was sure there were Bigfoot bite marks on the bones.

So, one warm summer day, I talked Junior and Lyle into helping me hunt down our local Bigfoot and get The Picture. We grabbed our canvas backpacks and loaded them with the tools and weapons to survive a week in the woods. Fishing poles, Swiss Army knives, a magnifying glass to find clues and to start fires, an old shower curtain to be our tent if it rained, wool blankets, and an extra pair of socks for each of us. We had a bag of apples, a loaf of bread, a jar of peanut butter, and a big summer sausage. Enough food for several days. Then we would live off the land catching fish and rabbits that we'd cook over campfires.

And, of course, I had my trusted Brownie Cresta camera my grandmother gave me for Christmas. It had a built-in flash which was important since it seemed that most Bigfoot sightings occurred after sundown under dim light. My plan was to sneak up real close behind the Bigfoot then yell something to make him turn and look at me. I'd snap the picture and the flash would blind him long enough for us to run away before he could grab one of us and eat him. It was a perfect plan.

We left home right after lunch. My mom made us peanut butter and banana sandwiches, our favorite pre-adventure meal. We started hiking up the steep trail into the woods. I marched off in the lead. Since the Great Bigfoot Hunting Expedition was my idea, that made me the lead guide. Junior and Lyle followed close behind. The sun beat down on us through the canopy. The humid July air was thick with gnats, mosquitos, and probably tsetse flies. Our pace slowed. We were huffing and sweating. Ten minutes into the Great Bigfoot Hunting Expedition we stopped for a rest. Our packs were so heavy the straps were digging into our shoulders and we were sweating like lawn sprinklers. Lyle looked at me with worry etched across his face. "I gotta go to the bathroom," he said shucking off his pack. "I'll be right back." He started jogging back down the path.

"Where you going? Just go over there behind that tree," I yelled to him. Apparently the sandwich had detonated something in his gut.

"Can't! Gotta take a shit! Right now!"

Well, every thirteen-year-old boy knows how to go as much as a week without taking a shit if they put their mind to it which is why we didn't bring any toilet paper - just needless weight. But a case of diarrhea could be an existential disaster. So I couldn't argue with Lyle as he ran home. I'd never seen him cover ground that fast before. "We'll wait here for you!" I yelled after him. He just waved a hand over his shoulder without slowing or looking back.

Junior and I ate apples and waited in the shade. Fifteen minutes later, Lyle came sauntering up the trail eating a chocolate chip cookie and looking happy as a damn poodle. "My Ma gave me some cookies," he said finishing off the last one.

"And you didn't save any for us?" Junior said looking like he might have to get physical.

"Well, don't blame her. She gave me some for you guys but, well, sorry, it was a long hike back, you know. I was hungry." Lyle picked up his pack and tossed it over his shoulders. "What are you guys waiting for? Let's go find Bigfoot." He started up the trail. Junior shrugged. "Damn, his mother's cookies are really good."

"Yeah, let's give that bastard a wedgie when we get close to camp." I didn't actually know what a bastard was but I used the word a lot.

"OK. But let me do it. You always get to have all the fun."

We walked all afternoon stopping every few minutes to inspect a suspicious looking twig or to listen for telltale sounds of large beasts roaming among the trees. We were deeper into the woods than we had ever gone before. We had walked for more than nine hours. Well, we started nine hours ago, but we took a lot of rests and, of course, we had to try to catch some fish when we got to the beaver pond (that was a wasted half hour), then we spent a lot of time arguing over whether we were going in circles. But even with all of the distractions and delays, I figured we had to be twenty miles into the forest, maybe thirty. Probably no white man had been in this area in a hundred years. By the time it started to get dark, we had forgotten Lyle's transgression. We were disappointed not to have found a single sign of Bigfoot. Like Tonto or Daniel Boone, we squinted our eyes and scanned side to side as we walked through the twilight forest. We were highly skilled trackers and Bigfoot didn't stand a chance. Yet somehow he managed to avoid our fine-tuned observation skills.

"We're lost aren't we?" Junior sniffed.

"No, we are not lost," I insisted. "I know exactly where we are."

"Then how come we are walking past that same rock for the third time." Junior pointed to a large, lichen-covered boulder teetering high on the steep hillside above the trail. "We've been walking in circles all day."

"You're nuttier than a squirrel turd. That's not the same rock. There are a lot of big rocks in the woods. Some of them look alike. But we aren't going in circles."

"So does every big rock have 'Corky loves Susie' spray painted on it?" Junior asked.

We stopped in mid-stride and turned to look where Junior was pointing. High up on the edge of the rock white letters clearly stated Corky's feelings for Susie.

"Maybe every big rock does have that on it. Maybe Corky painted every big rock he could find. The guy is clearly nuts for this girl to be this far out in the wilderness just to paint rocks."

Lyle kicked a stone from the path and cleared his throat. "I don't know, Jeremy, this place does look kind of familiar. Junior may be right. I think we are walking in circles. Maybe we should just camp here so we don't get more lost than we are."

"No way!" I was offended to think my friends had so little faith in my navigation skills. "We are getting real close to Bigfoot habitat right now and the best time to find one is right after sundown. In fact, we should have a quick snack so we have the energy we're going to need when we find Bigfoot soon. Let's have an apple. They're in your bag, Lyle." Lyle avoided my eyes. He looked at the ground and pushed a stick around with his toe.

"No, they're not," he said.

"Sure they are. We split up the food this morning and I know we put the apples in your bag."

"They aren't there anymore."

"You ate them?!" I yelled.

"Some of them." Lyle looked at Junior. "Apples are heavy. I ate some of them while we were walking. I might have dropped a few along the way."

"You threw our food away?" I was livid. "Don't you know the first law of living in the wilderness is Never Waste Your Food!"

"I thought you said the first law is wear good shoes."

"That is the first rule. That's different. The first law is Never Waste Your Food. Break the first rule and you get blisters. Break the first law and you STARVE TO DEATH!" I was about to hit him when I saw a faint light flicker through the trees. It was far away down the steep hill.

"Look at that," hissed Junior pointing at the light.

"What do you think it is?" whispered Lyle.

I squinted even harder adopting what I was sure was the proper look of a steely-eyed adventure hero. "This far out in the woods, it's probably Bigfoot's camp. He must have evolved far enough to make fire. They're smart, you know. Living this close to humans for a couple hundred years, they pick up a lot of life skills. Let's go." I started to bushwhack through the ground cover on a straight line toward the light. Lyle and Junior hesitated then began to follow.

"Shhh!" I hissed. "We need to be quiet or we'll scare him away. Walk like an Indian." I didn't really know what it meant to walk like an Indian, but we knew that Indians can walk through the woods without making a sound. We all reflexively started walking on tip toes carefully trying to pick our way over fallen branches, through gnarly rhododendron thickets, and around rocky drop-offs. It was slow, tedious work. But we were finally on the track of Bigfoot. I could see the television people gathering in my driveway to get pictures of the brave young man who finally proved the existence of Bigfoot. I could hear the cheering crowds as we drove through town in an open Cadillac convertible, a blizzard of confetti and ticker tape falling from the windows above. I knew I'd get congratulations mail from all over the world including from Edmund Hilary and probably even from President Eisenhower.

The forest got darker as we slowly worked our way down the steep hillside toward the light below. We could see now that it was a small fire throwing an eerie orange glow just a few feet in each direction. I stopped about a hundred feet away and silently signaled for Junior and Lyle to crouch down behind me. Junior stepped right on my hand. I squealed. Junior stopped and Lyle stumbled into him knocking both of them over top me. The three of us lay in a tangled pile on the ground hissing at each other. "I signaled you guys to crouch down behind me," I said through clenched teeth.

"It's dark. I didn't see any signal," Lyle snapped. "Besides, we don't even have a signal for crouching. I'm not a mind reader, you know."

"Uh oh," Junior said quietly. "I think Bigfoot heard us." We all looked up. It was hard to see anything. The fire had died down to coals that threw little light into the darkness.

"I don't see anything," I whispered.

"Listen," Junior whispered back. We held our breath and listened. I could feel my heart pounding in my chest. I could hear Junior and Lyle's raspy breathing. Everything else was silent. We lay in a pile on the forest floor unmoving, our senses on high alert. This was our moment. We were close now. I carefully pulled my camera from my pocket and aimed it toward the fire. If Bigfoot came close to us, the flash would surely capture him. I was on the verge of the greatest photographic coup of the century. We waited. And we waited. And we waited.

"You boys lost?" The voice boomed out of the darkness just a few feet away. Lyle screamed. Junior jumped up so fast he stomped on my back and fell into the underbrush. I snapped a picture before I realized Bigfoot probably would not have asked if we were lost. The flash blinded all of us.

"Whoa," the deep voice said, "Don't get yourselves all in a panic. You're safe now." I thought I recognized that voice. It was a nightmare in its own right.

"Mr. Branford?" I croaked.

"Jeremy? Jeremy Moore?"

Oh, shit, I thought, it *is* him. It's Brainfart, our gym teacher.

"Jeremy Moore, what are you doing skulking around the woods this time of night? And is that Lyle Strawberry and Junior Pocketmaster with you?" We were busted. Our lives were over. Brainfart was a sadistic physical fitness Nazi gym teacher. On a good day, his class was brutal. When he was having a bad day or just decided he didn't like you, he could make gym class a humiliating, excruciating, painful death march. I was afraid he'd make us run sprints or do sit-ups until we puked or suffer some other unspeakable torture for invading his backyard.

"Hey, is that a Brownie Cresta? I got me one of them cameras, too. C'mon. Let's get you boys down to the house. I'm done burning the trash. My wife just took a pie out of the oven. You all like peach pie?" None of us had said a word. We stared in stunned silence not entirely sure what just happened. Brainfart turned and walked toward the house that we now saw situated just beyond a line of tall arborvitae.

"What are we going to do?" hissed Junior, "That's Brainfart. Do you really think there's a peach pie in the house? Brainfart will probably kill us. No one will ever find our bodies."

"Shhh," I snapped, "Brainfart isn't going to kill us. He'll just make us wish we were dead in our next gym class."

"I think I smell pie," Lyle said and trotted off to follow Brainfart. Junior and I exchanged glances and ran toward the house.

An hour later we were full of peach pie and hot chocolate and sitting in the backseat of Mr. Branford's Nash Rambler. It was a two-mile car ride to my house. Who knew that our feared gym teacher lived just over the ridge from our road? When we got to my house, my mother came out the front door to meet us. The porch-light backlit her showing her legs through the thin night gown she wore under a knit cardigan. "You boys back already? I thought you were going to be in the wilderness for a few days." Brainfart opened his door and stepped out. "Why, Mr. Branford, what a surprise." My mother smiled and pulled her sweater closed which only drew attention to her substantial cleavage peaking over the top.

"Well, hello, Hazy, I didn't realize you were Jeremy's mother." I didn't like the way Brainfart smiled at her. "Haven't seen you at Harley's in a while." He winked.

My mother shot a quick glance at me and blushed. "Come on in the house, boys. Thank you for bringing them home, Wally."

Wally? Mom calls Brainfart Wally? They're friends? That realization conjured up all kinds of disturbing thoughts. On the other hand, maybe Brainfart wouldn't kill us after all.

Tasha's Family

The afternoon after my third PT session with Tasha, they moved me to a new room. As fast as they could move me, I was out of the high-cost hospital accommodations and into the econo-rate long-term disability and rehabilitation center on the other side of the medical campus. My room was smaller than the four-person hospital room, but it was a private room with more space for visitors. The room had a bigger window that looked out at three large dumpsters and a shed where they kept the riding mowers and garden tools. Not very attractive, but it let a lot of sun into the room. The room was comfortable enough. Standard hospital bed, three green vinyl upholstered chairs for visitors, a two-drawer dresser for my stuff, a television attached to the wall in a corner by the ceiling, and a small bathroom with all the handles and supports and hardware an old invalid could ever need—once I could get that far on my own. It was a short commute to the PT center now, just a quick roll across a parking lot and through the little pocket park garden visible from the treadmills and stationary bikes. Dr. Akufo told me I could be there as long as six weeks until I recovered my "independence." She defined that in terms of range of motion, strength, and balance. I defined it as being able to take a crap by myself. As soon as I could do that, I'd be out of there.

I'd just finished my breakfast after an uneventful first night in my new room. A nurse had given me a sponge bath and changed my dressings. She helped me with the bedpan—one of the more profound indignities of a broken body that I was still trying to get used to.

A moment after she left, Roger knocked on my door. "Tasha time, Jeremy!" he said with his ever-present smile. He glanced around the new room. "Nice digs. Complete with the deluxe dumpster view."

"Yeah, like staying at the Ritz Carlton." Roger helped me into the wheelchair and wheeled me to PT. I probably could have wheeled myself the short distance to PT. My dislocated shoulder was feeling better, but the doctors didn't want me to push myself. So to speak. And I was happy to let Roger do the work.

———

"Morning, Jeremy. Ready to go to work?" Tasha cracked her knuckles.

"I think so."

She looked at me over her glasses. "You *think* so? We need to do better than that, Jeremy."

"I mean, yeah, sure. I'm ready to go to work. Got a lunch bucket and shovel around here somewhere."

"Glad to hear it. You won't need that shovel this morning. Or the lunch bucket. This ain't no union job." She started working on my leg pulling and pushing and twisting. It hurt like hell, but I could tell she was already getting more motion in my leg.

"Am I making progress?" I hissed through clenched teeth.

"You are. Good thing, too. You wouldn't want to disappoint me now, would you?"

"No ma'am. I live to make you happy."

"Good. That's the way it should be." She leaned hard on my knee. It hurt but it was discomfort, not pain. I was learning the difference.

"You got a family, Tasha?" I asked trying to distract myself from the increasing discomfort she was putting me through."

"Not really. Had one. The Army. But that didn't work out too well."

"How long were you in the Army?"

"All my life pretty much. My dad was career Army. Retired a Master Sergeant a few years ago. I served nine years myself." She pushed her thumbs deep into my hip. The discomfort was extreme.

"You were in Iraq?"

"Two tours in Iraq; one in Afghanistan."

"Must have been rough."

"I had a job to do. I did it."

"Then you left the Army and came here? Why'd you leave the Army?" The discomfort in my hip went up a couple notches. Tasha's face darkened.

"Long story."

"I have time."

"I don't. Maybe sometime." She relaxed her thumbs. I felt the discomfort swiftly dissipate. Even this old fart was empathetic enough to realize this was a subject Tasha did not wish to discuss. "How about you, mister inquisitor? You got a family?"

"Three daughters. Triplets. They live here in Mount St. Anne."

"Nice to have them so close. Grandchildren?"

"Nine. Most married and all of them gone. They decided life is more interesting in big cities on the coast."

"Can't argue with that. If you're into the interesting thing." Tasha bent my knee and gave it a gentle twist. The pain took my breath for a moment.

"I don't know. My daughters have interesting lives and never left here. They're 53 years old and they own several companies they started together. They work hard and travel the world. Basically, they do whatever they want to. It's a good life. For them."

"No wife?"

"Had one. For about a year. We're still in touch now and then." I felt a small pop in my knee and the pain decreased markedly. Tasha kneaded the spot, a satisfied smile on her lips.

"Never remarried? Good looking man like you?"

"Never found the right woman, I guess."

Tasha frowned.

"Oh, it's great. I'm a confirmed bachelor. I like it that way. I can scratch and make body noises any time I want. It's a good life."

"Hard to argue with that." Tasha patted my leg. "You made some good progress today. Did you feel that scar tissue give near your patella?"

Before I replied a loud metallic bang echoed through the room. Everyone stopped what they were doing and turned toward the noise. We watched a little girl run out the door chasing a large exercise ball. I recognized her as the screaming fighter plane in my room. Behind her was an overturned stack of aluminum cafeteria trays. Her mother was struggling to restack the trays then dropped them and chased the girl down the hallway.

"That little girl is a handful," I said. "Somebody needs to reel her in."

"That's Samantha," Tasha said, "and her poor mother Monica."

"I feel sorry for her. A kid like that must be a royal pain."

Tasha stopped working my leg and frowned at me.

"Did I say something wrong?"

"Samantha is a patient here. Oncology unit."

"Oh, shit. That little girl has cancer?"

"Can't really talk about other patients, you know. But, yeah, something called Stafford Sarcoma. She's a very sick little girl. She just doesn't seem to know it yet."

"Now I really do feel sorry for her mother. That must be scary as hell."

"Samantha and Monica are here three or four times a week. Treatments, checkups, more treatments, more checkups. When Samantha is not knocked down by the treatments, she's a normal little girl. Maybe a little high-energy and definitely a little reckless, but a normal little nine-year-old girl. You'll probably see her around."

"Actually, we met. Well, sort of met. She flew into my room did a quick evasive barrel roll and flew back out again. Her mother apologized and ran after her down the hall. She seems to do that a lot. Apologize for her daughter."

"Monica's a devoted mother. That kid is everything to her. I don't know what she's going to do when…" Tasha stopped talking and picked up the clipboard. She shuffled through the pages. "It's going to be tough for her. For all of us. But especially for her."

"It's that bad?" I asked. "I mean, you think the little girl isn't going -?"

Tasha slammed the clipboard down. "Samantha is a very sick little girl. I can't talk about her. Rules, you know." She picked the clipboard up again and glanced at a page. "See you here tomorrow afternoon. We'll work on that other leg." I was dismissed.

I wheeled myself back to my room, the little girl high on my mind. Tasha said 'when' not 'if.' I had been moping around feeling sorry for myself about a few injuries and the indignities of old age. But I knew I would get better. I knew I would go home someday. And from the look on Tasha's face, I knew Samantha was in a different place. I knew Samantha was going to die.

I spent the rest of the afternoon Googling Stafford Sarcoma.

The Acropolites
Meaning of Life

Degenerative nerve disorder. Mortality rate: 100 percent. Life expectancy after initial diagnosis: four to six months. Stafford attacks the lower spinal cord initially then migrates to the Medula. Recommended treatment: There are no proven treatments, surgical or medical. Chemo and radiation can slow the disease's progress, but treatment has not been generally effective in significantly extending life expectancy beyond six months. Several promising experimental treatments are under development in Europe but are years from any possible FDA approval.

I was devastated. Stafford Sarcoma affected just one in 300,000 children. And it killed them. Why Samantha? Intellectually, I knew it was a stupid question. There is no reason for things like this. No grand design. Just a terrible draw in a lottery from Hell. But emotionally it was so senseless. How could this beautiful little person be so unlucky, so ill? Monica must ask that question every moment of her waking hours. It isn't fair.

For a while I forgot all about my battered body and my aches and pains. I forgot all about any regrets I had about my life. All I could think of was that little girl and her mother. And how helpless I was to do anything to help them.

I was staring at the blank TV in the corner of my room and wallowing in my helplessness when Lyle, Junior, and Bartholomew came in. It was the first full session of the Acropolites since my accident. After meeting regularly for coffee and pastry for years, my accident was a painful disruption to our regimented lifestyle. The guys were happy to be together to gripe and argue even if my sterile room lacked the ambience of Lyle's coffee shop.

"Nice view," Junior said pointing to the dumpsters. "And you know that works better when you turn it on," he added nodding toward the TV.

"I doubt it," said Lyle, "Ever watch daytime TV? I'd rather stare at a blank screen."

"Hey, there's some excellent daytime TV. *Edge of the City* is topnotch drama," Bartholomew said plopping into the seat by the window.

"Bullshit. The only *Edge of the City* episode ever worth watching in its thirty-some years on TV is the one you were on."

"Why thank you, Lyle."

"You were brilliant. I really believed you died. You made me cry."

"Thank you, again, Lyle. That's very nice."

"But everything else about that show sucks and you know it."

"True. *There is nothing either good or bad, but thinking makes it so*," Bartholomew said in his deep Shakespeare voice, "and I think *Edge*, like pretty much everything on daytime TV, sucks."

"What's with you, Dr. Gloom?" Junior said to me. "You look like your catheter is clogged. Are you OK?"

Am I OK? Am I OK? No, I thought, I am most certainly not OK. A little girl is dying, and I don't give a shit about soap operas. Or anything else right now.

"I'm OK. Just a little tired." I forced a smile. "Let's get some pie." Junior wheeled me out the door and the rest of the Acroplites followed.

We got our coffee and pie and grabbed a table near the windows looking at the garden. The sun was shining, and the azaleas were blooming. I watched several butterflies flit around the bushes. I sipped my coffee and poked at my piece of coconut custard pie.

"What's the problem, Jeremy?" Junior tried again. "Something's bothering you."

"Just the normal stuff. You know. Life. Death. Jock itch."

"Clotrimazole will take care of that," Junior said.

"Good to know."

"Well, not the Life and Death stuff. But it's pretty good for jock itch."

I took another sip of coffee. "What are we doing here?"

"Eating pie," said Lyle raising a forkful of coconut custard to his mouth.

"Not what I mean."

"I know it's not what you mean. But it's the only answer to that question you can say for sure." Lyle closed his eyes and savored his cafeteria pie. "And right now, it's good enough for me."

Junior picked up his fork and scrutinized the gelatinous lump of pie. "I like to think there is more to why we're here than immediate gratification. But I'll be damned if I can think of anything."

"There must be more to it than pie. Shouldn't we have a purpose to our lives?" asked Bartholomew forking a piece of pie into his mouth and carefully dabbing the corner of his mouth with a paper napkin.

"I think it's a little late for that," I said, "Maybe we can look back and manufacture some purpose for having been here. Maybe we can discover a purpose only in hindsight." I shook my head. "But what if you were ten years old?"

Lyle sipped his coffee and scowled. "If I were ten years old, I wouldn't drink bad coffee. And I wouldn't worry about the meaning of life. Life is too short for either."

"Isn't that the point, though?" Bartholomew asked adding a fourth sugar packet to his coffee. "I mean, life is short so shouldn't it have meaning? Or are we just bags of chemicals reacting to the world for a little while then we die? That's hard to accept."

"Well, this bag of chemicals decided a long time ago that there is no meaning lying around out there waiting to be discovered. You going to eat that?" Lyle reached over and grabbed a piece of graham cracker crust from the edge of my plate and popped it in his mouth. "You have to create your own meaning."

"But what if you're ten years old? What if you haven't even lived yet and they tell you you're going to die?" My hand began to shake so I put my coffee down. "Or what if you were the mother whose kid was ten-years-old and going to die? How do you explain that?"

Nobody said anything.

"Where is the purpose to that?" I asked looking at each of my friends. "Rhetorical question. There is no purpose. Life sucks and then you die. For some it comes a lot sooner than for others. It doesn't matter if you are a worthless old fart or a beautiful young girl. It's all random."

After more silence, Junior said, "I guess this is not a hypothetical conversation."

I sighed and turned to look out at the butterflies outside the window. "It's not."

"Sometimes life really does suck," Lyle said, "and then you die."

"We are such stuff as dreams are made on; and our little life is rounded with a sleep," Bartholomew said.

"So, I guess we need to make the most of our little life," I offered, "Dream while we can. Then sleep."

"I do most of my dreaming while I'm asleep," Roger the orderly was standing beside me holding a tray with a plate full of gooey looking nachos. "Not sure how you dream before you sleep but I'd be willing to try."

"We're discussing the meaning of life."

"Perfect conversation for pie and coffee," Roger said. He smiled and waved at a pretty nurse across the room. "I'd love to join you and explore the ontological complexities of life, but I see a beautiful woman who needs a conversation partner. See you this afternoon, Jeremy."

"Two-thirty. See you then, Roger."

As Roger walked away, I looked at my empty plate. "Anyone up for seconds?"

The Acropolites
Remember the Circus

A couple days later we had the first relocated Acropolites breakfast in the hospital cafeteria. I was having some difficulty following the conversation. My meds were still working hard, and Samantha was very much on my mind. Junior stabbed his newspaper with his finger. "Did you see this? They want to cancel *Rags to Riches*."

"Oh no!" Lyle gasped in mock horror.

Junior ignored him. "It's a great show. They take poor people with great bodies and give them a chance to make it big. You learn more about human nature from *Rags* than from any college psychology class. Can you believe they want to cancel it."

"They should cancel all those reality shows." Bartholomew said stabbing the air with an unlit cigarette. "Bunch of amateurs taking jobs away from real actors. The producers make a ton of money, and they don't have to pay union rate."

"Still, it's great entertainment. I never miss an episode," Junior said. He poured another artificial creamer in his coffee. "What do you think?"

It took a moment for me to realize Junior's question was directed at me. "Actually, I've never seen it. I don't watch much TV anymore." I frowned at my coffee. "Could they make this stuff any weaker? It's brown water." I dumped my cup into a potted Ficus beside my wheel chair. "I guess it must be a good show. Seems like half the people in PT talk about *Rags* all the time."

"The last episode had people work at a circus for a week, They competed to get to be part of the acts. Most of them ended up picking up elephant shit and hauling bales of hay for the horses and giraffes. One woman - a real bitch I might add - won and got to ride an elephant wearing a bikini in the show."

"I wouldn't pay to see an elephant wearing a bikini."

"She was a bitch alright, but, man, did she have a body."

"Remember when we tried to join the circus?" I wanted to change the subject. Nothing bored me more than a conversation about a TV show I didn't watch.

"One of the legendary moments of our childhood? Of course I remember. Seems to me Bartholomew pissed his pants if I remember right," Lyle said.

"I most certainly did NOT piss my pants," Bartholomew snapped, his cigarette darting at Lyle.

"Well, actually, that was me," I confessed.

Lyle looked over his paper at me. "You sure? I'd have sworn it was Bartholomew."

"Not the kind of thing you remember wrong...."

"Cliff and Goldie were there, too. Remember?" Bartholomew said.

"Cliff and Goldie were at the circus?"

"They sneaked in through the back of the tent."

"I don't remember that."

"Sure you do. They bought hot dogs and Cokes but we couldn't afford any food. We spent all our money on tickets."

"No, that doesn't sound right."

"Sneaking in was Goldie's idea. She talked Cliff into doing it," Lyle added.

"I don't think so."

"Funny you not remembering that. You always remember everything where Goldie was involved."

My Unremarkable Life
The Great Circus Escapade

e were thirteen years old. We were adventurers. We were pirates, soldiers, cowboys, or baseball stars depending on the day and our mood and the last movie we saw. That summer we learned everything we needed to know about the world from the movies. Everything seemed possible.

One Saturday, Lyle, Junior, Bartholomew, and I went to see *The Greatest Show on Earth*. We sat through three consecutive shows including four cartoons and about a hundred commercials for Good & Plenty candy and buttered popcorn. By the time we wandered down main street toward home, we were committed to a life in the circus. I wanted to be Cornel Wilde and fly through the air holding Betty Hutton by her luscious legs. Lyle wanted to be Charlton Heston and be the boss running the whole crazy enterprise. Bartholomew wanted to be Jimmy Stewart's clown and make people laugh and cry at will. Junior wondered how many circus people and animals were injured making the movie.

Two weeks later the Cristiani Brothers Circus came to Mount St. Anne. The four of us spent a week scouring the neighborhood for discarded pop bottles we could redeem for the deposit. It was amazing how people just tossed empty pop bottles out of their cars instead of returning them for two-cents. Their poor judgment meant there was almost always a ready supply of cash for enterprising kids.

We walked to the field just beyond the train depot where the circus had set up its main tent the night before, our pockets full of hard-earned coins. A band was playing Sousa marches. People were yelling and laughing. Unseen animals roared, trumpeted, and squawked from train cars and corrals. Swarms of people walked in every direction buying spun cotton candy, caramel apples, and funnel cakes from the vendors along the midway leading to the big top. We planned to sneak under the tent to get into the circus just like kids did in the movies. But when we neared the back of the tent we ran into some nasty looking men smoking cigarettes and speaking a language that wasn't English. They looked mean. We chickened out and spent nearly all of our money on tickets.

The real circus was better than the movie. No kissing, No boring conversations. Pure action entertainment. The parade of animals. The clowns and their crazy cars, bikes, and stilts. The pretty girls in wild sparkling outfits. The handsome men strutting with all the confidence and bravado in the world. The acts themselves. The trapeze artists scared the hell out of me. How they could swing so high up then just let go and fling themselves through the air to the next swing made my stomach go woozy. The elephants were so much bigger than I imagined. When one sat on a pretty girl's head I closed my eyes, sure her head was going to split like a ripe pumpkin. The seals, horses, chimpanzees, and dog acts were ok but boring—no risk of serious injury or death. But the big cats were incredible. The deep, primeval roar of the lions as they sat on big red pedestals in the cage reverberated through my body. I stared in awe at the lion tamer as he barked orders and snapped his whip and the lions responded. It was amazing. This one man locked in a cage with half a dozen lions and tigers, each of which could kill with a single swipe of a huge, clawed paw, and he was in charge. I wanted to be that guy. I no longer wanted to be a trapeze artist playing with long-legged girls. I wanted to be a lion tamer. I wanted to be brave enough to look a man-eater lion in the eye and bend its raw physical power to my will.

That night I lay in bed most of the night thinking about that lion tamer. I ached to be him. I thought about my father. I thought about all of the grownups I knew. Their world seemed so pale compared to the world I had seen under that big top. By the time I fell asleep, I had decided I would run away with the circus and start a new life.

Late the next night, Bartholomew, Lyle and I sneaked out of our rooms and met at the tracks. No way was Junior going to be part of an adventure with this high risk-reward ratio. The plan, if you can call it a plan, was to walk up the tracks to the train lot where the circus cars were parked and stow away in one of the equipment cars until the circus got to its next town. Once they saw how committed we were to joining the circus, they would certainly give us jobs and our new lives of adventure would commence. When we got to the lot, the circus was already packed up. The last of the ramps were being pulled into the box cars. The engine was warming up spitting out loud hisses of steam. Crew leaders were shouting some final instructions to the few people yet to board. The lights of the lot cast dark shadows behind the train cars. We ran into the shadows looking for a way to get on a car. But up close, the train seemed much bigger. Too big for us to just hop on. We were running alongside the track, me in the lead followed by Junior and Bartholomew when I ran head first smack into a big, angry gorilla. Well, actually it was a roughneck tying down a large crate on a flatbed car. I bounced off him like I had run into a brick wall. The man was so big and strong I was sure I had run into the gorilla they kept caged near the entrance of the circus tent earlier that day.

The big man was startled to have some half-pint runt bounce off him in the dark. He gave out a deep yell in some foreign language confirming my worst fear. I did run into the gorilla. That's when things got a little uncomfortable. That is to say, I pissed myself. By the time I turned to run back down the track, Lyle and

Bartholomew were disappearing into the distant shadows far ahead of me. The gorilla grabbed my collar. He lifted me like I was a bag of dirty laundry and carried me to the circus manager who called my mom to come and get me.

I was relieved when Mom pulled up in her car. She leaned out the window and smiled at the gorilla who captured me. Her dressing gown open slightly exposing more than I was comfortable seeing. "Hello, Bill. Thanks for taking good care of Jeremy. His imagination gets the best of him sometimes."

"My pleasure, Hazy." The gorilla smiled and leaned down toward my mother's window. "Gets some of that imagination from his mother, huh?" She patted his hand and laughed. "See you next time the circus is in town?" she asked.

"You bet. I have your number." He aimed his finger at me like a pistol and pulled the imaginary trigger. "You take good care of your momma, Buddy, she's a special lady." Then he went back to work. Mom sighed. I was speechless. My mom was friends with a gorilla.

Lyle and the Triplets

I was staring out my window contemplating how many bags of urine this place must dispose of each day when a loud rap on the door jamb woke me from my reverie. A tall, thin body with bad posture stood in the doorway, a potted fern in one hand and a book and magazine in the other.

"Up for some intelligent conversation and witty repartee?" Lyle asked as he folded his long frame into the chair by the door.

"What's got you smiling? Someone buy your second edition Dickens?"

"Better. I got a deal that I think you may be interested in." He proceeded to tell me about his visit to an adult novelty manufacturers trade show recently where he met a couple of young female mechanical engineers who had invented a high-tech sex toy that was guaranteed to give any woman an orgasm every time. He said he had seen other products over the years that made the same promise, but his customers were more than willing to tell him when the products fell short of the promise.

"This one is different," he said, "These are women and engineers who invented this thing. It's called the XTC3000. Get it? XTC?"

"Yeah, I get it."

"It's programmable. You can control it with a phone app. It can do things that no man can do. They tested it on hundreds of women of all ages and, well, body types. It worked every time.

Every single woman. Every single time. Do you have any idea what that means?"

"I think I have a pretty good idea."

"I mean commercially. This is going to be huge. Bigger than Candy Crush. Bigger than Fifty Shades of Gray."

"That's pretty big."

Lyle sat back in his chair with a smug look on his face. "And I have the option on exclusive tristate distribution of the XTC3000."

I wasn't sure how to react to this news. Lyle was, by nature, a conservative businessman who did his due diligence before any significant investment. He was not one to show much enthusiasm over anything except century-old first editions. "And why would this interest me?" I asked.

"Because I want you to be a partner. I'm going to need to raise some money fast to be able to exercise the option and get this thing on the market. Once we get the first production run into some key adult stores, the buzz—pun intended—will go viral almost instantly."

If Bartholomew had given me such an offer, I would have joked my way out of it. If Junior had given me such an offer, I would have jumped on it. But with Lyle, I was unsure. "How much?"

"As much as you want. We can talk about this later, after you're not so drugged up."

"I'm not drugged up." Actually, I was. "But that's probably a good idea. Interesting opportunity. We'll talk tomorrow."

"What interesting opportunity, Daddy?" My three beautiful daughters were at the door.

"Nothing that interesting, girls. Lyle is looking to expand his business."

"Hi, Lyle. You expanding the book store or the novelty stores?" The girls knew Lyle and his businesses all their lives. It takes a lot to surprise them. Sometimes I wonder if they've been customers but, of course, that's a question I'd never ask.

My daughters. Binkie, Birdie, and Byrne. Their mother Goldie named them. I wanted to name them Laurie, Carly, and Mona, but Goldie gave the nurse their names while I was still pacing in the waiting room, so the birth certificates were finalized without my paean to the Stooges. Somehow the girls grew up without any visible damage from their names. I think the sheer force of their combined presence intimidated anyone considering making fun of their names. From the time they could talk, they were a trilateral powerhouse that bent the world to their will. Well, at least they bent me to their will. I am sure I spoiled them terribly. The girls were a team - a small army completely devoted to each other and aligned to take on the world. Somehow, we made it through childhood even after Goldie left. And, despite my erratic parenting skills, they grew into well-adjusted, happy, and amazingly successful women.

They stood around my bed looking lovely in their matching yoga clothes. They were fit, perfectly groomed without a hair out of place. Even at fifty-three years old, they still acted like appendages of one another. They coordinated their clothes. They went to the same hairdresser. They drove matching cars. They lived within a couple of miles of each other with their respective husbands. Even the husbands seemed to be color coordinated and styled. I thought of them as simply "the husbands." They made my daughters happy, but they bored the heck out of me. The poor guys were batting way above their league when they married my girls. The husbands all worked boring middle management jobs in small companies in Mount St. Anne, while their brilliant and beautiful wives built their own business empire. Somehow, everything they touched seemed to turn to gold. They lived in large houses that were far more spacious now that the grandchildren were grown and on their own. If I had a hard time keeping track of the husbands, I was hopeless when it came to the grandchildren. I thought of them in terms of their mothers and birth order. So, the nine grandchildren went from BinkieOne, BirdieOne, and ByrneOne, the three oldest, through BinkieThree, BirdieThree and ByrneThree. I didn't even try to keep track of the great-grandchildren which seemed to be popping out at least twice a year.

"You brought me candy!" I said before Lyle could answer their question about the interesting opportunity.

"And cookies, Daddy," Birdie said handing me a box tied with a bright red bow. "They're from the Ethiopian bakery that just opened." My girls are true gourmets as well as fanatic health nuts. I can be sure that everything edible they give me will be good for me and will taste weird. I untied the bow and opened the box. The cookies looked like small cow patties left in the sun to dry out.

I failed to hide my grimace. "Just try one, Daddy. If you don't like it, Lyle will eat them. Lyle reached over and grabbed a cookie from the box. "Ooh, I love these!" he said biting into the mini-dung disc. "You're a lucky man, Jeremy. When my kids bring me food, I'm lucky if it's not a Happy Meal."

I laughed and felt a sharp pain in my back. I sucked in air and waited for the pain to ease.

"Daddy, have you been meditating? It will help with the pain, you know. And with the boredom."

"I kind of got out of the habit recently, I'm afraid." (I hadn't meditated in probably three years.) "My knees hurt when I sit cross-legged on the floor. It's hard to get up. So I let myself get out of the routine. And now…" I gestured to my cast.

"Oh, Daddy, you don't have to sit on the floor like the Maharishi. You can sit in a chair. You can even just lie in bed. The important thing is to be comfortable."

"I'm too old to be comfortable. Even before the accident, new pains pop up and disappear every day. It's part of the excitement of my life—which body part is going to hurt today? It's a lottery."

But I remember back when the girls first convinced me to try meditation. I had just broken up with a professional bowler who moonlighted as an advice columnist for a magazine that catered to middle school girls. That was a fun relationship for a couple of months, but she spent too much time on the road competing in bowling tournaments for us to really ever get serious. And she had a bad habit of giving adolescent advice to anyone in her target range including me. I didn't need to be reminded almost daily not to let anyone tell me that I'm not special just the way I am. When she called me from Enid, Oklahoma, right after winning five-hundred dollars in the Cherokee Invitational Bowling Tournament, she told me she was re-evaluating her life plan and needed some time away from me. She wrote me a letter a few weeks later saying that she used her winnings to run off to a Choctaw spiritual retreat with the director of the tournament— an actual Cherokee shaman who was teaching her the ancient ways. Fortunately, I never heard from her again.

At that time, the girls owned a new-age shop in a renovated garment factory in downtown Mount St. Anne called Crystal Blue Persuasion—a franchise specializing in crystal healing therapies and something called Universe-Centered Happiness. Much to my surprise, the shop made money hand over fist. I suppose I should not have been so surprised. This was the late 80s and neurosis was rampant in small-town America. Hippies had aged out of beads and flowers and berated themselves for living lives of material comfort and spiritual poverty. Many women were entering middle-age struggling to find purpose in the Reaganomics-obsessed post-ERA era. People flocked to Crystal Blue Persuasion. The girls sold more than eighty different kinds of minerals at outrageous mark-ups to lonely doctors' wives, female attorneys bumping up against the glass ceiling, and other wealthy, disillusioned women who couldn't shake the sadness of their successful lives. But the real money was in the UCH classes the girls provided. Each of the girls got "certified" by the National Universe-Centered Happiness Center to lead the full array of copyrighted classes. They began with one class a week at 6:00 a.m. on Mondays and within six months had classes with waitlists running every morning and five evenings a week. Within a year they had opened franchises throughout the tri-state area. People—nearly all of them women—would attend forty-minute sessions where they would sit on thin mats on the floor in a dim-ly-lit room with soft music droning in the background while one of the girls talked them through the day's UCH lesson.

About a year after launching Crystal Blue Persuasion the girls sold the company for a ridiculously huge sum and invested in an organic hog farm. But that's another story.

They tried to get me to attend the UCH classes thinking that either it would help me deal with my "negativity problem" as they diagnosed it, or meet someone new. I politely turned down the invitation. (I believe I said, "No, no, no. No f-ing way. No, no, no!" They chose not to argue.) So they decided I would get private classes in the art of meditation. I agreed reluctantly with the under-standing that if I didn't like it after three sessions, I could quit and they would never mention it again.

The problem is after three sessions, I loved it. Damn if they weren't right. I was happier. I slept better. I drank less. So for a long time afterward, I meditated almost every day.

"You're right, of course. Maybe I'll try meditating tomorrow. Probably a good habit to get back into."

"That would be great, Daddy. It'll be good for you."

"They're right, old man, it would be good for you. Get in touch with your inner self. Find your spiritual G-spot." Lyle took another cookie and headed to the door. "I need to make some calls. I'll drop by later."

The girls got off my bed and kissed me on the forehead. "We need to go, too, Daddy. Yoga starts in ten minutes." Lyle held the door for them. After they walked by, he winked at me. "Girls," he called down the hall, "wait up. I have something I want to discuss with you."

I took a small bite of one of the cookies. It didn't taste like cow shit. It was surprisingly good.

My Unremarkable Life
Free Solo Rock Climbing

few months after the Great Circus Escapade, I joined the Mount St. Anne Junior High Hiking and Climbing Club. I heard they did a lot of wilderness hiking and mountain climbing and thought it would be a good way for me to start my dream of climbing with Hillary someday. Now, if you know anything about Indiana, you know there aren't many mountains there. I probably should have looked into that before I joined. The first time I went on a weekend outing with the club, they said we were going to climb Ayer's Rock. Not the one in Australia. The one in Shipley's Woods. I had never heard of Ayer's Rock but learned from the club newsletter it was the highest rock face in the county and named for a guy who had a moonshine still nearby during the Civil War. Early one chilly Saturday morning five kids followed the club leader up a trail deep into Shipley's Woods. There was me, of course, and two girls from seventh grade plus their little brothers. The Mount St. Anne Junior High Hiking and Climbing Club had a membership problem.

We walked a mile or two into the woods to a familiar rock where Corkie exclaimed his love of Susie in white spray paint. The club leader announced that we had arrived. *This is it? This is Ayer's Rock?* I was devastated. I had never climbed on it, but I certainly knew the rock. It was just a stupid rock. *This is the best we can do? I could climb this thing in two seconds.* The face of the rock was maybe fifteen feet high and nearly vertical. It was striated with several small shelves running diagonally along the rock face. Trees clung tenaciously to the top of the rock, their roots weaving down the full height of the rock creating a pattern of cascading vines.

The group leader was Mr. Borger, the eighth-grade science teacher known to all the kids as the Booger. I knew him but he didn't know me. I wouldn't have his class for two more years. He was an old man—at least forty - with a bushy black mustache and a safari helmet. He carried a gnarly pine walking stick and liked to identify all the wildflowers and trees we walked by. He said he was a trained botanist. After listening to him for an hour on the trail, I knew I did not want to be a trained botanist when I grew up. He was the most boring human being I had ever met. And that included Junior.

The Booger called the group together. "We will climb up the rock face by using these roots—he pointed with his walking stick—"and these small indentations for toeholds." He looked at the five of us. "Anyone want to volunteer to go first?"

I shot my hand up. "Me, I'll go first." I was going to show everyone how a real climber would scramble up that puny cliff and stand atop it like Tenzing on Everest.

"Well, aren't you Mr. Enthusiastic," the Booger said. "Very well, let's see how you do."

I stepped up to the bottom of the rock face and looked up. I don't understand physics or optics or geology or whatever science was at play there, but the rock face suddenly grew from fifteen feet to at least fifty feet. It loomed over me like a huge, dark beast daring its unsuspecting prey to disturb its repose. I looked back at the Booger to see if he realized how the rock had suddenly grown, but he was oblivious. "Grab that root right there with your right hand," he pointed again with his stick, "and step on that ledge with your left foot. After that, the rest will be obvious."

I turned back to the cliff. *Okay, I can do this. Tenzing could do it. Hillary could do it. I can do it. Here goes.* I grabbed the root with my right hand, stepped on the ledge with my left foot and froze. I had no idea what to do next. "Go ahead. Grab that root on your left then step up onto the next ledge on your right," the Booger directed from the safety of flat ground. I slowly reached up toward the root and gripped it in my hand like a vise. Then I stepped up with my right foot and found the next ledge. I was on my way up. *This is going to be OK, Just keep moving one hand or foot at a time. I can do this.* I slowly worked my way up the cliff, hand over hand, one foot then the next. Slowly leaving the safety of flat land far below. Then I took one quick glance down to my feet and saw how high I had climbed. I swooned from the height. My head spun and I was sure I was going to fall to my death. I gripped the roots with both hands and pressed my face into the knotty wood. I didn't want to die. I just wanted to get off that damn cliff.

"You're doing fine, Moore," the Booger said. I didn't move or speak. All my attention was focused on holding onto the roots and staying alive. "Are you OK, Moore?" the Booger asked. "You seem to be shaking." *I am not shaking. I am cogitating. I am concentrating on my next death-defying move up this brutal cliff.*

Then I felt a gentle hand on my waist. I turned to look down wondering who could have climbed up here with me. The Booger was smiling up to me and holding me by the belt. He was standing on flat land. I was maybe four feet off the ground. "Let me help you down, son." He easily lifted me by the belt and lowered me to the ground. "Climbing isn't for everyone," he said and turned to the group. "Who wants to go next?" The two girls and their little brothers all scampered up the roots and ledges and stood atop the rock looking back at me and the Booger.

"That was fun!" the smaller girl yelled. Then they quickly scrambled back down, and we walked back to the van.

That's when I decided climbing cliffs is stupid. I'd look for better ways to have a life of adventure.

Meditation Redux

The pain was irritating. Nothing so bad that I couldn't function. Nothing that would make me beg for more drugs. But bad enough. It was an unwelcome visitor who wouldn't leave. The pain, the cast, the indignities of being a hospital patient, and the general malaise of old age were all testing my normally sunny disposition. I thought about the girls' admonition about meditation. It had been years, but I was pretty sure I could do it. It was worth a try, anyway. So, after everyone left, I tried to get comfortable in my bed. I closed my eyes and searched my dusty memory banks for anything I could remember about meditation. I let my body relax and I began a conversation in my head. I could hear my daughters' voices—soft, ethereal, like whispers from inside my head.

Breathe.

Inhale. Imagine you are bringing air in through every pore of your body, absorbing air through your skin.

Exhale slowly through your nose letting the toxins wash from your body.

Inhale.

Exhale.

With every breath, you become more relaxed. With every breath, your body becomes more cleansed.

Inhale.

Exhale.

You can feel yourself melt into the floor, melt into the earth. Inhale. Exhale.

With every breath let it go.

Let fear go.

Let anxiety go.

Let anger go.

Let hate go.

Inhale. Exhale.

With each breath let it go.

Let worry go.

Let sarcasm, insult, and demeaning thoughts all go.

Imagine you are in a bubble. A powerful force field surrounds you holding out all of the fear, anxiety, and anger.

What do you feel when fear is gone? What is left when anger is gone?

"Nothing."

Nothing?

"Well, maybe not nothing. Maybe something. Something nice."

What is left when anger and fear are gone? What do you feel?

"I feel...I feel good. Content. I feel joy."

The force field is strong. It's keeping out all the toxins, all the negatives, all the pain. What else do you feel?

"I feel...I feel...happy. I feel love. I feel real love. Is this God?"

Call it what you want. When we strip away all of the negative feelings that make us unhappy, the weaknesses of character that make us fearful, angry, spiteful, when we push away all the external feelings that poison our mind and spirit, there is joy. There is love. An infinite ocean that surrounds us all the time, but the fog of everyday living hides it. Take time to relax, breathe, and concentrate. You can find this ocean that is universal and there for everyone.

Be grateful for life. Be grateful for love.

"Foot cramp! Foot cramp!"

Thus ended my first meditation in a long time.

My Unremarkable Life
Stan Musial

My sophomore year in high school I thought I wanted to be a professional baseball player. My idol at the time was Stan Musial. The guy was an amazing ballplayer, maybe the best all-around hitter in the game. He was a monster on the ball field and a tall, handsome, charismatic icon off the field. Stan the Man. I wanted to be like him. So I tried out for the JV baseball team. It didn't last long.

My first time at bat during an intra-team practice game, I stepped into the batter's box, knocked the dust off my cleats with my bat just like Stan, and turned my steely eyes to the pitcher 60 feet 6 inches away. I was sure my fierce stare and demeanor of invincibility would intimidate the pitcher, leaving him a shaking mound of doubt and uncertainty. Unfortunately, the pitcher was Cliff Masterfield. I hated Cliff Masterfield. He was tall, broad-shouldered, and could grow a beard since eighth grade. As a sophomore he was the school's starting quarterback, starting point guard, and starting pitcher. He also held the school record in the mile, high jump, and javelin. Every girl wanted to be his steady. Every boy wanted to be him. I hated him. He spit on the pitcher's mound, patted his glove, and smiled at me. His eyes twinkled, He chuckled. That son of a bitch chuckled. I hated him. I was going to crush his first pitch so far over the left field fence they'd be talking about it for the rest of the season. I was going to wipe that damn smirk off his face with one fierce swing of my mighty bat.

Cliff nodded to the catcher, stepped back into his wind-up, and threw. The ball was coming straight at my head, He was trying to kill me. But my lightning reflexes were too much, and I quickly dove backwards landing hard on my butt. The umpire called "Strike one!" I stared at him in disbelief. "Get up, kid," I heard my coach call, "Stand in there and swing."

I got up, dusted my butt and stepped into the batter's box. The catcher hissed, "Nice dive, Moore. Maybe you should try out for the swim team." He was an asshole.

Cliff took the sign from the catcher, wound up, and threw another pitch. This one was coming straight at my ribcage, He fooled me with the first pitch but this one was aimed directly at me. My reflexes took over and I flew backward to the ground, the ball whistling by inches from my body.

"Strike two!" the umpire called. I was outraged, No way that was a strike. It was so far inside I could count the stitches as it whizzed by. "C'mon, kid," the umpire said shaking his head, "Get back in the box."

I heard my coach yell from behind the backstop. "Moore, this isn't dodgeball. You're supposed to hit the ball with the bat." The catcher snickered. "Dodgeball. That's a good one."

I dusted myself off again and stepped back into the batter's box. I'm gonna crush this next pitch. Bring it on Cliffy-boy, I thought. Show me what you got!

Cliff took a long look at the catcher and then smiled. I was going to wipe that damn grin off his face with one swing of my bat. I tried to smile back to show him I wasn't intimidated, but my lips stuck to my teeth. I realized I couldn't spit if I wanted to. Cliff wound up and fired the ball. I closed my eyes and took a mighty swing with everything I had. The ball hit me square in the gonads. I mean square in the goddamn, uncupped gonads. I fell to the ground like a sack of peanuts and rolled up into a ball like a pill bug. I wanted to scream from the pain but I couldn't inhale. The only noise I could muster was a sucking whimper sound while I gasped for breath. Coach was at my side trying to roll me over and telling me to breathe slow. "Well, you sure stood in there that time, Moore," he said. I could hear the mocking behind his words even as the world was starting to go dark. I felt a hand on my shoulder and heard Cliff's voice. "Sorry, buddy, I assumed you were going to take another dive. I never expected you to hang in there like that."

I threw up on his shoes.

A week later my scrotum still looked like an eggplant. Yeah, a small, tiny eggplant, I know. But still. I never played baseball again.

Samantha and Monica
Paper Airplane

My hip ached as Roger wheeled me across the garden toward my room. I wondered if I should rest a while before doing my Tasha-prescribed exercises. A nap sounded like a good idea. I was looking forward to some quiet time in my bed when a paper airplane zipped past my chair and landed lightly in an azalea beside me. I reached for it. "That's mine!" a high-pitched voice behind me yelled. An elf wearing a familiar green ball cap ran past me and grabbed the plane. She smiled at me and held her plane out. "I made this," she said proudly. "Mom only helped a little." Roger pivoted my chair so we could better watch this little creature. Thin blonde hair curled out from under her baseball cap. Her bright blue eyes shone with infectious joie de vivre. It was hard to reconcile the knowledge that she was terribly sick with the happy young girl in front of me. I asked Roger to give me a few minutes before we went to my room. He was happy to have some time to sneak out and grab a quick smoke.

Samantha pouted her lips in concentration as she studied her paper plane. Then she wound up her skinny little arm and threw the plane into the air. It did a quick loop de loop and crashed into another bush.

"Darn!" she said stamping a foot. "I can't get it to go right."

"It's OK honey. Keep trying. You'll get it." The young mother was sitting on one of the benches watching the little girl. She waved at me. "Please excuse Samantha. One of the orderlies showed her how to make paper airplanes. She's been trying to get one to fly. Not very successfully, as you see."

"Hi, Samantha. Maybe try not to throw so hard. Just give the plane a little push." I mimicked a quick dart throw.

Samantha pulled her plane from the bush and studied it intently for a moment. It looked like she was assessing its aerodynamic worth. She held the plane over her head and started to wind up like a javelin thrower.

"Easy," I said, "Throw it easy and it'll go farther." Mimicking the dart throw again.

She glanced at me with a look of doubt on her face, then pulled the plane down to her shoulder and replicated my arm movement. The plane drifted up several feet then started into a gentle dive. Just before crashing into another azalea, the plane rose again and roller-coasted its way up and down across the garden until landing softly on the mulch pathway. I was shocked. Even on my best day I could never have made a paper plane fly like that.

"Good throw, Samantha," her mother said clapping excitedly. The little girl squealed and ran to retrieve her toy.

"Thank you," she said to me. "That was pretty amazing."

"Well, your daughter did all the work. That really was pretty amazing."

"I'm Monica Bradshaw," she held out a small hand. Her nails chewed to the quick. "And that," she said pointing to the little girl gyrating through the garden with her plane in her hand and making motor noises with her lips, "is my daughter, Samantha."

"She is a lively little girl."

Monica's smile faded. She dropped her eyes to her lap. "Yes, she is."

The happy moment in the garden had passed. A darkness fell over Monica. "Yes, she is a very lively little girl." Then she put a hand to her cheek and wiped a tear.

Not sure what to say, but feeling a need to say something, I asked, "Is there anything I can do?"

"No. No. I'm sorry. It's just…" Samantha ran between us chasing her plane. Monica gave me a sad smile. "You're right. She is a lively little girl." She got up and composed herself. "Maybe we'll see you here again. Samantha likes the garden. It's her favorite part of the hospital."

"Mine, too," I said. "I'm Jeremy. It was nice to meet you, Monica. And Samantha."

"Come on, Samantha. We have to see Dr. Sanjeewa in five minutes.'

Samantha started to leave the garden then ran back to me. She held out her tiny hand. "I'm Samantha Bradshaw. Thanks for showing me how to do it right." I shook her hand.

"My pleasure, Samantha. I'm Jeremy. I'm happy to meet you."

She pulled her hand free and ran back to Monica who tried to smile. I saw sadness in her eyes and wondered how anything could be so wrong with that delightful little girl.

As Roger wheeled me back to my room, I thought about the two conversations I'd had. Tasha and Monica, two very different women, both wrestling with something dark. Everyone has something lurking in the dark recesses of their head, some demon to be wrestled with. Maybe it's regret over something done or not done, maybe it's guilt, or anger, or fear, or hate. A big part of living for so many of us is just getting through the day without letting the demons run free. Keeping them hidden, buried while we go through our day.

When I think about it, I think the most destructive demons come from war and from family. Both affect people at their deepest core. Both require sacrifice and both expect sacrifice from others. Both are built on a foundation of common values and trust that, when broken, leave us building lives on shifting sand. Over time, most people learn to contain the demons and maintain normal— whatever that means—lives. But for others whose foundations have been more deeply shattered, the demons have a constant gravitational pull. They create the ebb and flow of emotions like the tides. For some, the tides are Bay of Fundy—huge and treacherous. The currents rip deep through the water like a powerful, unpredictable river that changes direction several times a day. Even worse, are people whose demons have such a powerful gravitational pull that they become not their moon but their sun. Their demons don't just pull at the edges of their being, they are the center of their being. Their lives orbit around the burning star of their demon.

I suspect Monica's world is captured in an orbit of fear and anger. Fear of what will happen to her daughter. Anger at the unfairness of it happening at all. It is only her love of Samantha that holds her together right now. I can't even imagine what will happen to her when Samantha is gone. Fear will turn into deep sorrow. Anger could turn into hatred directed at the world and the god that created it.

Who could blame her?

My Unremarkable Life
Our Town

I thought I found my avenue to an adventurous life while eating popcorn at the Odeon and watching The Domino Kid starring Rory Calhoun. I had already seen Rory as a gangster, a soldier, and a mercenary just that year alone. That's the way to do it, I thought to myself. I didn't have to choose between being a cowboy or a soldier or mountain climber or a jungle explorer. I could be all of them. I could be a movie star. Why hadn't I thought of that before? I mean look at Bogie, and Alan Ladd, and Audie Murphy. They could be a fighter pilot shooting down enemy bombers in one movie, a pirate terrorizing the seas in the next movie, and a gunfighter out-drawing bad guys in the Old West the next. That's the way to do it, I decided. Become a bigtime movie star and become anybody I want to be. I had a plan. I was going to be a star.

So, I tried out for the high school play. No pirates. No fighter pilots. Not even one gunfight. But it was a chance to show the world my incredible acting talent. We were doing Our Town.

I read the play. Well, I read the first ten pages of the play. It was kind of boring. I am sure it would be riveting when I was on stage delivering my lines and commanding the spotlight. On paper it was not exactly Zane Grey or Jack London. I knew I wanted to be George Gibbs. His role wasn't as interesting as the Stage Manager, but George got to kiss Emily Webb right on the stage. And I knew that Goldie Eaton was sure to get the role of Emily. Goldie was the prettiest girl in school. It was weird that I had known her from a distance since she moved into Mount St. Anne in third grade, but I never really thought much about her before. Then when we came back to school for seventh grade after the summer, something about her was different. She had curves and bumps in places where she didn't used to. No other girl in our class looked like that. I couldn't help but stare. I didn't even understand why I stared. But, man, I couldn't take my eyes off her newly obtained chest. I was in love. Of course, I didn't tell her that. Five years later, I still obsessed over Goldie Eaton's tits even though by then most of the girls in the class had sprouted all kinds of interesting bumps and curves.

Goldie was the most beautiful and popular girl in Mount St. Anne's High's senior class. Cheerleader. First chair clarinet in the band. Featured alto in the chorus. Class vice president. (It was 1960 so no one expected a girl, even one like Goldie Eaton, to be class president.) She was also that jerk Cliff Masterfield's girlfriend. It was obvious that Goldie would get the role of Emily and it was just as obvious (at least to me) that I was the perfect George. We would probably have to rehearse the kissing scene many times to get it right. I was ready to work hard to attain perfection.

Unfortunately, the stupid English teacher, fat old Miss Whitcomb, who was the play's director was too dense to recognize the raw talent I demonstrated in my audition. She gave my part to Cliff Masterfield. Damn! Why did it have to be Cliff? Sure, he was tall and strong and looked like he was twenty-five instead of sixteen. And, yeah, I will admit he could deliver lines well. And he moved around the stage without bumping into the furniture. (They could have told me about the damn coffee table before I tripped over it.) And he was probably good-looking if you like the big-jawed, misunderstood-puppy-dog James Dean kind of look.

The only good thing that came from the play was my friend Bartholomew got the role of the Stage Manager. He was amazing. When he started to say his lines, he became someone I didn't know.

He stopped being Bartholomew and became the Stage Manager. I was speechless. Of course, he got the role. He was great. I didn't even get a minor role. So, I joined the stage crew.

The play was eminently forgettable except for the final night when someone accidentally tripped the main power switch just as George kissed Emily and the entire stage went dark. Those stage crew guys, what a bunch of jokers. When the lights came back on a short while later, George and Emily were still kissing. From behind the light panel above the stage, it was obvious this was not a stage kiss. It looked like they were trying to choke each other with their tongues. It took them a while to realize the lights were on and a couple hundred parents were watching. Even though it broke my heart to see that kiss, I thought it was pretty funny. Cliff looked like he thought it was fun. Goldie looked like she thought it was fun. Fat old Miss Whitcomb did not look like she thought it was fun.

I spent three weeks in detention.

The Acropolites
Nostalgia

"You're being sentimental. It was never that wonderful. You're deluding yourself." The Four Horsemen of the Acropolis were gathered in my room doing what we did with increasing frequency lately, romanticizing the past. Junior was having none of it.

"Nostalgia used to be considered a mental illness, you know." Junior, always the voice of reason, the no-nonsense killjoy who couldn't find the bright side in a basket of puppies.

"*Mal du pays*," Lyle said, scowling at his coffee. "Homesickness. They used to think nostalgia was a potentially debilitating or even fatal illness."

"Exactly," Junior said. "A potentially fatal illness."

I pondered that thought for a moment. "What's your point?"

"On whaling ships that went to sea for years at a time, they would keelhaul someone just for singing a sad song of home if it made the men morose. They knew nostalgia could lead to madness, mutiny, even suicide, and it was contagious. Can't have that on a ship 10,000 miles from home. Better to keep the crew sedated with rum."

"I'll drink to that." I toasted with my Styrofoam cup of coffee. "But those drunk sailors usually got home eventually. The past is a lot further away than the opposite side of the world."

"Exactly my point. We can't go back. It's not just a long, slow boat ride away. The past is gone. It doesn't exist. We waste our time talking about the past like it was the Garden of Eden or something. It wasn't Eden, I can tell you that." Junior sipped his coffee and frowned at his Styrofoam cup.

"It was more fun than the Garden of Eden," I said.

"Well, it was better than now anyway," Junior conceded.

"It was a better time. Wasn't it?" Bartholomew spoke up. "Baseball was better. Picnics were better. Comic books were better. Everything was better."

"Beer wasn't. It was pretty bad," Lyle said. "Yellow water."

"True. Coffee, too. It's a lot better now," Junior looked at his cup. "Except this stuff. Kind of reminds me of the old days. Seems like everyone drank instant. Nasty stuff, instant coffee. Weak and bitter."

"Sounds like my ex-wife," I grunted.

"Goldie wasn't weak," Junior said.

"Maybe. But the beer was. One of the best innovations of the last seventy years has to be microbreweries. You can get some very good lagers and porters even in Mount St. Anne, the Bud Light Capital of Indiana."

"Very true," Bartholomew said, "Beer and coffee are definitely better today."

"So is cheese," I added, "Remember Velveeta? No one ever heard of brie or camembert back then. Cheese is a lot better today."

"And porn! Remember the black and white magazines of nudists playing volleyball Lyle used to get for us? That was porn back then. Porn is a lot better today. With the Internet, porn is like Alice's Restaurant."

We all stared at Junior.

"You know. 'You can get anything you want…?'"

We continued to stare. He dropped his eyes and his face flushed. "Well, it's true isn't it?"

"Yeah, porn is better now," we all said at once.

I raised my cup. "To beer, coffee, cheese, and porn! Forget the past. Life is good."

We sat in silence for a moment reflecting on our perspicacity. But the good cheer slowly gave way to a quiet malaise. Each of us drifted into our own memories. The only sound was the occasional quiet sip of bad coffee and the shuffle of soft-soled shoes hurrying past my door.

"What's the date today?" I asked suddenly aroused from my thoughts.

"April 1," Junior said, "Why? You have an appointment?"

"It's my mother's birthday. She'd have been 101 today."

"Happy birthday, Hazy," Lyle said lifting his empty cup. "I imagine she's up there shaking things up in heaven."

"I always liked your mom," Junior said. "I remember she took us to Biloxi that time. That was nice."

"Biloxi! The Great Mudflats Adventure," Lyle said. "That was a good time, wasn't it?"

Junior cringed. "It was a memorable time, that's for sure."

My Unremarkable Life
The Mudflats Joyride

A couple months after the play, I got my driver's license. It took me three tries to pass the test. I had a hard time parallel parking my mother's big Oldsmobile. I didn't know why she wanted such a big car. It barely fit in our garage and the wide bench seats were very uncool. Later I figured it out. One cold morning I started up the car and the defroster came on. It blew air across the windshield and foggy patterns briefly appeared on the glass before they evaporated. It took me a moment to realize that the patterns were footprints. Small feet with perfect little circular toe prints. Mom's. It kind of grossed me out at first, but then I thought *good for you, Mom. But next time you should wipe the windows.* Then I thought, *I wonder what Goldie's footprints would look like on that windshield?*

A week after I got my license, it was Spring Break at the high school. Lyle and Junior joined me and my mom for a trip to Biloxi where my grandfather lived. He owned a gas station with an outside lift so he could do minor auto repairs when the weather was good. One day I borrowed my grandfather's pickup truck to go up to March Point County Park on the Gulf with Lyle and Junior. We were going to swim for a while then catch the sunset at the beach and build a bonfire after it got dark. We loaded the back of the truck with beach chairs and a cooler full of soft drinks and sandwiches and headed to the beach. We stopped to get ice. Lyle took a few extra minutes in the little general store while Junior and I dumped the ice in the cooler. When he returned to the truck, he showed us a small brown paper bag. "Mad Dog, boys," he announced pulling the neck of a bottle out of the bag just far enough to see the label. "Mogen David 20/20. The guy didn't even ask for an ID."

Junior gasped, "Alcohol? You got alcohol? We could be arrested for having that stuff, you know."

"It's OK. This is Mississippi. The drinking age is eighteen. We look old enough. No one is going to care." Junior looked unconvinced. "Don't worry, we won't break it out until it gets dark." Lyle was having fun already.

March Point was a long spit of low land at the end of a barrier island. A road ran the length of the island ending in a small cul de sac. On the gulf side was a beautiful white sand beach. On the bay side were miles of shallow flats. When we got to the beach, it was nearly empty - just a couple of families hanging out on blankets near the water, small children digging in the sand, inattentive parents reading paperbacks or lying back trying to catch the last tanning rays of the day. The road we were on was on a bluff about five feet above the beach. We drove down the bluff and out onto the sandy beach. I headed to a spot at the end of the island I knew from previous visits to my grandfather's. During low tide, the mudflats would extend for hundreds of yards out from the sandy beach. I had seen locals drive out on the flats in their trucks to look for big shells when low tide happened at night. I wanted to do that tonight.

The late afternoon and evening passed quietly. We threw a football around a little, waded in the shallow waters feeling for sand dollars with our feet, and enjoyed the sandwiches my mother packed for us. As the sun set and the tide was well on its way out, we built a fire and opened Lyle's bottle of Mad Dog.

"This is the life," Lyle said sipping from the bottle then passing it to Junior. Junior stared at the bottle. "C'mon, just a sip and see how you like it. Don't be such a baby." Junior snatched the bottle from Lyle's hand and took a long swig. He wiped his mouth with the back of his hand.

"That's pretty good," he coughed, "Just like wine at Christmas dinner." He took another deep swig. Lyle grabbed the bottle away from him.

"Easy, boy. It's not *exactly* like the wine at Christmas dinner. This stuff is jet fuel."

Lyle handed me the bottle. I drank lustily. I was thirsty. "I've tasted better cough syrup," I said holding the bottle in front of me considering the label. "They should tell you how many spoonfuls you need for a sore throat."

Lyle took the bottle from me. "My professional advice is to consume copious quantities as a prophylactic for illnesses of all sorts."

"It's a rubber?" Junior asked reaching for the bottle. "I thought a prophylactic was a rubber." He took a long swig adjusting easily to the sin of underage drinking.

"Yep, it's a rubber. Lubricated and ribbed for extra enjoyment."

We finished the bottle and stared at the dying embers of our fire as stars began to populate the dark sky over the calm ocean. The tide was starting to come in. We could see long ribbons of white foam rippling closer across the dark expanse of mudflats. When the last embers winked out, and feeling exceptionally mellow, we decided it was time to head back to my grandfather's place before the tide got any closer. We loaded up the back of the pickup and jumped in the cab. I started the engine, put the truck in gear, and pressed the gas pedal. The truck slid slightly side-ways and the rear end seemed to drop a foot. The rear wheels spun but the truck went nowhere. We were axle-deep in the muddy sand.

We hopped out of the truck and studied our situation. "No problem," I announced. "You two push and I'll drive. We'll get her out of here."

Junior and Lyle took their positions behind the truck, hands firmly placed on the tailgate as if they had been ordered to "assume the position" by the local sheriff. "Ready?" I yelled out the window.

"Ready," they yelled back. I hit the gas, they pushed their weight into the back of the truck. And nothing moved. The drive wheel spun wildly spraying damp, gritty sand across Lyle's bare legs.

"Shit! That hurts!" he said backing quickly away from the truck. "We aren't going to move it this way. It's just gonna take all the skin off my legs."

I got out and rummaged through the stuff my grandfather kept in the back of the truck. Under a box full of hubcaps and various auto parts, I found a couple of one-by-ten boards about three feet long. I looked behind the seat in the cab and found an empty coffee can I assume he used for worms when he went catfishing in the river.

"Here," I said handing the can to Junior, "You dig a trench in front of the rear wheels. Lyle and I will wedge these boards under the tires and we'll drive right up the ramps and out of here. Junior kneeled beside the truck digging with the can like a tiny dragline in one of the strip mines near home. He dragged wet sand up along the slant and tossed it to the side. In a few minutes he had dug a ditch about five feet long leading up from the bottom of the tire. Lyle and I leveraged the end of one of the boards in under the tire while Junior dug the other ditch. A few minutes later were ready to roll.

"You two get in back and push. Don't stand directly behind the wheels."

"Excellent advice," Lyle said. "Once you get out, don't stop. You'll get stuck again. Just keep going back to the road and we'll walk."

Junior looked back across the mudflats toward the road which was invisible in the dark a quarter mile away. He looked unhappy at the thought of walking that far in the dark. Before he had a chance to voice his concerns, I started up the engine and yelled "Push!"

The wheels spun a bit then began to catch some traction before sliding back down the ramp. "Rock it!" Lyle yelled. I pressed the gas pedal again and the truck started up the ramps. When it slowed and began sliding back, I pushed in the clutch and let gravity pull the truck back. When I felt the wheels lift slightly in the sand behind the boards, I let the clutch out and the truck rolled forward a little higher than the first time. When I felt the truck start to slide back again, I pushed in the clutch. The guys stepped back and the truck again rocked back up the sand.

"This is it!" I yelled, "Push!"

Junior and Lyle leaned everything they had into the tailgate. I let the clutch out and hit the gas. The truck jumped forward and began to inch up the ramps, the drive wheel spinning on the rough wood. "Keep going." Lyle yelled from the back. "It's almost out." I feathered the gas pedal a bit, felt the tire catch a little traction, and then hit the gas hard. The truck leaped up onto the surface and fishtailed wildly. I wrestled with the steering wheel to bring the truck under control then shifted into a higher gear and took off across the mudflat quickly gaining speed.

Now, you might think that mudflats are flat. I mean given the name and all. And in most respects, they are flat, even two hundred yards from the high tide mark they may be only a foot deep. But what is not always obvious, is how bumpy the flats can be—a combination of corduroy highway and irregular bumps that are only obvious when you are driving across them at forty mile an hour. I held tight onto the steering wheel fighting for control whenever the truck fishtailed as it bounced across the expanse. I thought I was heading for the road when the headlights caught a long white horizon coming at me. At the last minute I realized I was looking at an oncoming ripple from the ocean. I was going in exactly the wrong direction. I didn't want to brake and risk getting stuck again, so I gunned the accelerator and cranked the steering wheel hard to the left. The truck went into a hard spin and, much to my amazement, ended up pointing directly away from the water. I kept the pedal down and sped across the bumpy mudflats until I saw the bluff ahead with the road at top. I was momentarily distracted by the sound of a siren somewhere in the distance. *Sheriff,* I thought for a moment. Then ignored the noise figuring even if it was the sheriff, he was probably chasing a speeder on the mainland.

When I approached the bluff, I floored the accelerator to make sure I had enough momentum to make it over the sandy rise and onto the road. The truck hit the bottom of the bluff and leaped up the steep slope. I overestimated the height of the bluff and the truck went airborne before landing roughly on the pavement. I slammed on the brakes screeching the truck to a stop in the middle of the road. I breathed for the first time. I could still hear the siren, closer now. And oddly familiar.

I hopped out of the truck and the siren became a wail. "ARE YOU NUTS? DID YOU JUST TRY TO KILL ME? DIDN'T YOU HEAR ME?"

Junior was standing on the rear bumper, his hands in a death grip on the tail gate. His face was a combination of unadulterated hatred and mind-boggling fear. His eyes bugged out. His face was bright red—made even more-so by the truck's taillights. Spit was flying from his mouth as he cussed and yelled until he suddenly stopped, stepped off the tail gate and sat on the ground crying like a baby. I handed him a warm Fresca. "Wow, man, I didn't know you were back here. That must have been one hell of a ride. How was it?"

Junior took along swig of the soft drink and blinked his eyes. "How was it? How the hell was it? You want to know HOW WAS IT?" He was panting. I thought he was hyperventilating. "I'll tell you how it was you fucking asshole. It was coolest thing I ever did. That's how it was. It was far fucking out amazing." He took another long drink from the can. "And if you ever do anything like that to me again, I will run you down with a lawnmower and feed the chopped-up pieces to the seagulls."

"I can buy that," I said as he handed me the half-empty Fresca. I drained the can, burped loudly, and offered my hand to help him up. Lyle showed up about then panting and wheezing from his long run across the flats. "That was amazing!" he coughed, hands on his knees. "You should sell tickets for a ride like that!" We drove back with Junior reliving his roller coaster ride in increasingly vivid detail the entire time.

Faith, Samantha's Wheelchair Skills,
Monica Meets Tasha

"So, here's the thing," Lyle looked at me over his half-lens reading glasses. Junior was meeting with one of his ancient clients and Bartholomew was filming a commercial for dental implants, so it was just Lyle and me. "In the beginning God created everything—the entire universe—simply by saying it is so. He created a trillion stars in billions of galaxies across a universe that is billions of lightyears across. Yet he had to use his hands to mold clay to make the first human and he actually made clothes for him and Eve. This tiny planet less than a single grain of sand on the beach of the universe that God created simply through his word, he then got dirt under his fingernails creating Adam from clay, planted a garden, took a walk in the cool of evening, and even made clothes for his humans. That is weird. Why didn't he just say the word to create humans and get it right the first time?"

I shrugged. "Beats me. Maybe we're special. Maybe in all the universe we are the only sentient beings, the only creatures made in His image."

"I know you don't believe that."

"I don't, but lots of people do."

"True. And I don't get it. How can anyone believe that with everything we know today? How can they reject everything we know about the physical universe and believe the Bible is the literal word of God?"

"Maybe faith is not about rejecting evidence. Maybe real faith is accepting everything we understand about the universe yet still believing in the omnipresence of an all-powerful God who actually cares about us anyway."

"Man, that is a stretch."

"I think that's what faith is supposed to be."

Roger appeared at my door. "Ready for your photo shoot?" I didn't believe in God, but I did believe in Medicare. If the hospital wanted another few hundred dollars for their budget, I was OK with yet another fully covered procedure.

Roger returned me to my room after the session with the Imaging Department. They took some x-rays to check on the hardware in my hip. As with nearly every process in healthcare, it was painful and undignified. An hour later I was bored staring out the window at the dumpsters. I decided to wheel myself to the cafeteria for a cup of coffee and a piece of pie. The hospital people didn't want me to leave the hallway outside my room without an orderly. But everyone was busy so when I got to the end of the hall, I pushed the button to open the doors and wheeled myself out. My shoulder hurt like hell, but it was exhilarating. It was the first time since my injury that I was outside without someone in scrubs controlling my every move. I crossed the garden area and entered the main building. The cafeteria was across the way from the Physical Therapy Rehab room. The space between smelled of Bengay and stale coffee. I wheeled over to the coffee urn and was just able to reach the foam cup dispenser and pour myself a cup of tepid brown water. I dropped a dollar by the unmanned cash register and headed toward the garden.

I was admiring my improving skill with the wheelchair when another wheelchair blew out of a side hallway and careened straight at me. Samantha was on her knees on the seat and pushing her hands hard against the wheels. She was so intent on going fast she didn't see me until we nearly collided. I tried to move to the side but only succeeded in pivoting my chair completely around like a subway turnstile spilling coffee on my lap. At the last second, the little girl saw me and grabbed one wheel of her chair. It immediately turned ninety degrees and she shot by me. I was about to shout at her about her reckless driving when her mother ran from the side hallway. "Samantha! Stop! You'll hurt somebody!" she yelled chasing past me after the little girl. "Sorry," she panted running by. "Samantha! Stop this second!"

Samantha stopped. She was smiling ear to ear. "It works! I can go a lot faster on my knees." She was so damn cute kneeling in the big chair and beaming with pure joy, I wanted to hug her. After I spanked her. Of course, I did neither.

"Samantha," her mother sighed, "I'm glad you figured out how to go fast all on your own. That was really smart. But you can't race in the hospital. You could hurt someone."

The smile fell from Samantha's lips, but her eyes continued to shine with delight. "Sorry, Mom. I won't do that again."

"That's good sweetie. We have to be careful in the hospital."

"I know, Mom. Next time I'll race in the parking lot." The little girl let her mother take the handles of her chair and start back toward where she had appeared a minute before. "Hi, Jeremy," she said as they approached me, "Sorry I almost ran into you. I'm practicing using a wheelchair in case I need one for later."

Monica patted her daughter's shoulder. "Sometimes Samantha's legs get tired. The doctor suggested she may want to learn how to use a wheelchair." She forced a smile. "She likes her wheelchair."

"Wheelchairs are fun. Sorry I almost ran into you, Jeremy. Want me to show you how to move your chair out of the way better? I'm very good with wheelchairs."

"Maybe another time you can give me some wheelchair pointers. Right now, I need to get another cup of coffee."

She turned in her seat to look at her mother. "Mom, can we get something to eat? I'm hungry for a piece of pie."

"I guess a small piece won't ruin your dinner."

"Want to join me?" I asked after we got our food. Samantha had a piece of pumpkin pie and a glass of milk. Her mother settled for a cup of decaf.

"Thank you. That would be nice. I think we could use some company." She pulled two chairs away from a table to make room for her daughter and me to roll our chairs up. Samantha easily parked her chair under the table. I bumped a table leg causing our drinks to slosh on the table. Samantha laughed. Monica grabbed a handful of paper napkins and cleaned up the mess.

"I'm not very good with my wheelchair, am I?" I asked Samantha.

"I'm good with mine. I almost never hit anything. I can teach you." Samantha reached over and patted my hand. "You just have to focus on where the chair is going."

"Excellent advice," I said reveling in the touch of her little hand.

Tasha walked by our table carrying a tray in one hand and a paperback in the other. She nodded at us and headed toward a table near the window.

"You're the doctor from the gym," Samantha called to Tasha. "You make people exercise to get better."

Tasha came back to our table. "I'm not a doctor, honey, but I try to help people get better. Like your friend Mr. Moore here. How are you doing today, Jeremy? Keeping up with your stretches?"

"Twice a day. Just like you said." Tasha nodded and started to leave.

"Sit with us," Samantha said, "We're having a snack."

"I don't want to interrupt your conversation."

Monica indicated the chair beside her. "Please, we'd love to have you join us. I mean if you want to. Maybe you'd rather be alone on your break."

"No, I'm alone enough. Thanks." Tasha put her tray on the table and sat down between Monica and Samantha. "And how are you today, little girl?"

"Good. I'm getting very good at my wheelchair."

"That's not an easy skill. You must be very strong."

Samantha flexed her skinny little arm and patted the tiny bump of her bicep. "I am strong. Mom says I'm very strong."

Monica reached out her hand. "I'm Monica and this is Samantha."

Tasha shook her hand. "I've heard about you, Samantha. You certainly get around this hospital. Nice to officially meet you both."

We talked for a while enjoying our snacks and avoiding the giant elephant of Samantha's prognosis. Tasha watched Monica's face. Monica caught her eye once and quickly looked away. Samantha chatted on about wheelchairs and paper airplanes.

"Mom, can I get some more milk?" she asked.

"I'll get it for you sweetie," Monica said starting to stand.

"I can do it myself, Mom." Samantha's lower lip stuck out. "I'm not a baby."

"No, you're right. You're not a baby. Here." Monica gave Samantha a dollar bill. "You can get your own milk."

We watched Samantha wheel herself to the end of the short line at the counter. "Your daughter is pretty amazing," Tasha said.

"Yes, she is. She amazes me every day." Monica watched her daughter chat with the other people in line. "She makes friends so easily. She is so comfortable in the world. I envy her for that."

Tasha patted Monica's hand. "I know about Samantha's illness. I can't imagine how hard it is for you. If there's anything I can do…"

Monica interrupted her. "No. That's kind but, no. There isn't anything you can do."

Tasha squeezed her hand. "I can pray for you. For both of you."

"I don't believe in prayer anymore. But thank you. If science can't heal her, maybe a miracle can." Her eyes watered but she kept the tears from falling. Tasha's eyes also shimmered with tears. Mine probably did, too.

"It must be nice working in this hospital," Monica said changing the subject. "Everyone here seems so nice. And very professional."

"Well, not everyone is so nice I can tell you, but it is a good place to work. I get to work with people like Jeremy." Tasha smiled at me. I felt like a kid getting an approving look from his teacher. Samantha returned to the table with a small carton of milk and a large chocolate chip cookie.

"Honey, how did you get a cookie?" Monica asked. "I only gave you money for milk."

"The lunch lady gave it to me," Samantha said breaking off a piece and popping it in her mouth. "She said I was cute. Want some?"

"Thanks, honey, but I'm not hungry. Maybe Mr. Moore and Tasha would like some."

Samantha broke of generous pieces for me and Tasha.

"Thank you, Samantha," Tasha said accepting her piece. "Very tasty!"

"I love these cookies dipped in coffee," I said. A chunk of the soggy cookie broke off in my cup.

"Do you have kids?" Samantha asked Tasha. "If you have kids, you should bring them here for pie and cookies. They're very good here."

"No, I don't have any kids. I don't even have a cat. I'm too busy taking care of my patients to have a family."

"You should get a cat. They are very independent."

"I'll have to think about that. Thank you for the recommendation."

"You're welcome." Samantha turned her attention to her milk carton and the remainder of her cookie.

"I hope you'll excuse Samantha," Monica said, "She doesn't really have any filters sometimes."

"She's a delightful little girl. Nothing to excuse."

Another awkward silence as we considered the delightful little girl at the table. Tasha reached across the table and patted Monica's hand, her dark skin and bright orange nails a stark contrast with Monica's pale skin and badly chewed nails. "I have to go back to work. Please, if there is anything I can do, just ask. I know the hospital can be kind of impersonal so if you need help getting something, anything, let me know." She picked up her book and tray. "And you behave, little girl. I hear you have been racing that wheelchair of yours." She gave Samantha a frown which quickly melted into a warm smile. "I hear you're very good with it." She winked and walked out the door.

"I like Tasha," Samantha said watching her leave.

"Yeah, I do too," I said, "More and more every day."

Lyle's Edibles

"What's that?" I asked watching Lyle take a piece of soft candy from a plastic vial and cut it in half with the plastic fork that came with my lunch.

"It's my prescription. Edible cannabis." He carefully cut the two pieces in half again. "When my back acts up, this stuff is great."

"I didn't know you were into that. I thought you gave up drugs when Nancy Reagan told you to just say no."

"I did. But now THC is considered medicine in Ohio. It's worth the drive. My doctor helped me get a prescription."

"Why are you cutting it up?"

"This stuff is strong. It's a lot stronger than the stems and seeds we used to smoke in college. I like a little buzz but I don't like being toasted. At least not at lunch time." He popped a piece of the chewable candy into his mouth. "Want to try some?"

I was tempted. I hadn't been stoned in decades. I wasn't concerned about the legality of it. But I just wasn't really into the pot high anymore. "I think I'll stick with my Vicodin for now."

"Walking on the wild side, Jeremy. That stuff is a lot stronger than this candy. And it's addictive."

"I'll take my chances. But thanks for offering. Maybe when I'm out of here I'll take you up on it."

A half hour later the candy kicked in. Lyle closed his eyes and sighed contentedly. He laughed. "I do like this stuff. Always did. You remember that time on the Rio Grande.?"

"That isn't exactly something one could forget, is it?"

My Unremarkable Life
The Rio Grande

Lyle and I were taking the long way back to Indiana after a disastrous trip to San Francisco. It was the summer after we graduated high school. Lyle's parents closed the bookstore for the summer to do some major renovations, so he was free for a couple of months. With college looming before me, we decided to do something adventurous while we could. Road trip to California.

Bartholomew had a summer internship at a small theater company in Indianapolis and Junior wanted to spend the summer studying for his property and casualty insurance license. Besides, he was sure he'd be carsick the entire trip. So Lyle and I headed out to the Golden Gate in the '56 Chevy Bel Air my grandfather in Biloxi sold me for $200. Smoking joints that Lyle rolled and listening to AM radio, we drove across the country with Kerouac dreams and Woody Guthrie songs playing in our hearts. We had lined up summer jobs in San Fransisco through one of Lyle's cousins, the assistant supervisor of a road repair crew for the city public works department. But when we got to the Golden State after four hard days on the road, we found Lyle's cousin was in jail. Something about pissing on a cop's leg when the officer surprised him relieving himself on a parking meter on Van Nuys Avenue.

San Francisco was the biggest city we had ever been in except one crazy night when we got lost and ended up in Chicago. We were quickly overwhelmed by the people, the cars, the noise, and the lack of parking spaces. Not to mention the high rent and lack of jobs. So after a couple of frustrating days in a youth hostel not far from some rundown neighborhood called Haight-Ashbury, we decided to turn around and head home via back roads and interesting looking paces.

A week into our eastward sojourn we were hiking along the Rio Grande River through a steep canyon in Big Bend National Park. It was hot as hell under the mid-July sun. I was wearing an oversized straw cowboy hat I bought from a roadside vendor at the entrance to the park. Lyle had opted for a Houston Colt 45s baseball cap. We carried a pint of tequila and an orange. The trail was a ribbon of sand and flat rock edged between sheer cliffs on one side and a ten-foot drop off to the muddy river on the other. It was a different planet from anything in Mount St. Anne. Almost no vegetation. Just some tenacious scrub trees twisting out of cracks in the cliffside and an occasional grassy weed. Stark. Empty. Beautiful.

The trail led us out of the narrow canyon. The tumbling river immediately relaxed broadening out into a wide, shallow waterway. The flat Mexican desert shimmered in the hot sun across the river. To the north, dry Texas hills rolled into the distance. We sat on a flat rock at the riverside and enjoyed a few swigs of the tequila and ate the orange. Everything seemed the color of stone—gray, brown, tan, faded colors without a hint of primary color. Except a single bright red spot in the middle of the river. A man wearing a red shirt rode a bony, dappled horse slowly across the river. He wore a dusty gray cowboy hat pulled low over his eyes. From his slumped posture, I thought he may be asleep in the saddle. The horse looked like it was nearly asleep too as it slowly moved one hoof at time through the shallow water. Large burlap sacks hung along either of the horse's flanks bulging like long cushions from an old sofa. The rider must have seen us although I never saw him look up from under his hat. The horse slowly turned toward us. We watched with a mixture of curiosity and alarm. No one was anywhere within miles of us. We were in the middle of the desert on our own and a guy who looked like a character straight out of a John Ford film was coming toward us. Our alarm became acute when we noticed the rifle hanging beside one of the burlap bags. But the rider's slouching posture and the slow, deliberate pace of the horse was almost comical. Like something from a Yosemite Sam cartoon.

We were in no position to avoid the rider so, as he got close, we acknowledged him with a quick wave. The horse stepped out of the river onto the trail in front of us. The rider looked up. His face was cracked leather. Deep lines forked from the corners of his squinting eyes. He stared unsmiling at us.

"Hola," I said nervously calling on the little high school Spanish I could remember.

"Hola," he replied. His voice hard, deep. He sat motionless. We were checking him out. He was checking us out.

Lyle tapped my shoulder and whispered. "I think those bags are full of marijuana." I gasped. This guy is drug smuggler? Shit. We're dead. He's going to shoot us and leave our bodies to the vultures. No one will ever know. I focused hard to keep from pissing my pants.

Lyle calmly pointed at the bags. "Es eso marijuana?" he asked. His bad Indiana-accented Spanish must have been good enough. The rider smiled.

Lyle turned to me. "Give me your hat."

"Are you insane? That guy's going to kill us."

"No he's not. Just give me your hat. It's bigger than mine. I'll give it back." Reluctantly I gave Lyle my hat. I hung back as Lyle approached the rider. He smiled and held my hat upside down by the brim. He reached into his pants pocket drawing a fierce frown from the rider. I stopped breathing. Then Lyle pulled out a ten-dollar bill and waved it toward the bags on the horse. I felt cold sweat roll down my back. The rider looked at Lyle for a moment.

Unmoving. Assessing his offer. Then he turned in his saddle and opened one of the sacks. He grabbed a large handful of marijuana and held it toward us. Lyle motioned for him to put it in the hat. When the rider dropped the pot in the hat, Lyle gestured at the hat again. The man put another handful of pot in it and reached for the money. "Mas," Lyle said pulling the money back and pointing at the hat. The rider stared again. His face was hard. He could just kill us right here and take the money. No one would know for days, weeks maybe. The sweat on my back reached my shorts. Lyle kept smiling and gesturing with the hat. The rider slowly grabbed another handful of marijuana and dropped it into the hat. The hat was now nearly full. He reached for the money.

"Mas," Lyle said again. I almost threw up. *We are dead, dead, dead.*

"No mas," the man replied with a deep growl.

Lyle shook the hat and waved the money. "Un poco mas," he said.

I whispered, "For the love of God, give him the money. He's got a gun and we got nothing."

"Un poco mas," Lyle repeated. I sucked in air hoping to avoid an embarrassing and potentially fatal projectile vomit event.

The rider shook his head and reached back toward the sack. His hand stopped over the rifle. My heart stopped. Lyle froze. Then the rider's hand continued to the sack where he grabbed another handful of marijuana. He held it over the hat but did not put it in. "No mas," he said. It was nonnegotiable. Lyle nodded. The man dropped the weed into the hat and Lyle handed him the money.

"Gracias," I croaked, truly grateful to be alive. I knew he got the better of us. But we had just scored at least a pound of Mexican weed for ten bucks. We watched the rider continue his ride north into Texas. His red shirt the only bright color for miles around.

"We better get back to the car and stash this stuff someplace safe," Lyle said pushing my hat under his shirt. "Texas is not a place we want to get caught with this much pot."

I slapped him hard on the shoulder. "You are nuts, man. That guy could've killed us without a thought."

"But that is a lot of pot for ten bucks!" Lyle laughed. "You have to admit is was worth it."

The Acropolites
Courage

The Acropolites were gathered in the cafeteria drinking coffee and solving the great problems of the world when Monica came into the room pushing Samantha in her wheelchair. Monica looked drained, her shoulders stooped and a dark shadow on her face. Samantha sat quietly in the chair holding a brown teddy bear in her lap. Her green ball cap was pulled low over her face. She looked tired. Monica saw us across the room. She forced a smile and waved. She stopped at the counter to get a coffee for herself and a milk and cookie for Samantha. She whispered something to Samantha who looked up to see us. She gave a tired wave and said something to Monica. Monica waved again and pushed Samantha to a table at the far end of the room where she could look out at the garden. And be away from us.

Monica situated Samantha's chair at the table and came over to our table. "Hi Jeremy," she said acknowledging the other guys with a nod. She hadn't slept. Dark circles under her eyes and a tired frown made her look older. "Samantha had a tough couple of nights after her treatment two days ago. They increased the potency." She hesitated. I knew what that meant. The treatments weren't working as well anymore. Before her last treatment, I noticed that Samantha was having increased difficulty walking. She shuffled down the hall like someone my age. The disease was progressing. "They decided to keep her in the hospital for a few days. She finally was able to eat something this morning."

Monica glanced over to see if Samantha was OK. She was looking out the window, her milk and cookie untouched. "She misses her own room at home and wanted to get out of her hospital room. She just wants to be with Bear, her teddy. He comforts her when she's down. I'm sorry, but she doesn't want to deal with people just now."

"Don't apologize. I'm glad Bear is there for her. She is a tough little girl and I'm sure she'll be back in form in no time."

"She is a trooper. She'll bounce back tomorrow, I'm sure." Monica went back and sat with Samantha, two beautiful people fighting hard for each other.

"We think we can solve the world's great problems over coffee and pie, but we can't do a damned thing for that little girl or her mother," Lyle said.

We silently sipped our coffee and contemplated our impotence.

"I admire their courage," Junior said.

I nodded. "Monica's courage is extraordinary. She sees the abyss and manages to smile anyway. That little girl has amazing courage, too."

"Does she?" Lyle asked, "I mean she is fearless. But does she understand enough to be courageous?"

"Doesn't matter to me, I admire them. Courage has never been a big part of my existence. It took me a while to realize I am the least courageous person I know. Most of my adult life has been spent avoiding situations where courage would be needed."

"You mean you never swam with sharks or climbed frozen waterfalls," Lyle said.

"That's just thrill-seeking. It's not courage. It's recklessness. It's self-indulgent. It ignores life in search of thrills."

"I think you just described your ex-wife's partner."

"Cliff was fearless," I said, "That's not the same as having courage. Being without fear means having no need for courage."

Junior nodded. "I agree. Courage is recognizing peril, seeing danger, knowing fear—but acting anyway. It is the opposite of self-indulgent. It is selfless."

Lyle sipped his coffee. "If you are in a house on fire and your only way to survive is to run through a wall of flames, it doesn't take courage to run through the inferno. But if you are outside and realize someone is in the burning house, and you run through that same wall of flames to help them escape, that's courage."

"Cliff is fearless. Was fearless. He was an adrenaline junkie. Maybe he did have courage, but that wasn't what allowed him to climb mountains, sky-dive, or wrestle with crocodiles.

"Courage requires you to look into the abyss and act anyway," I said. "The abyss isn't impending death somewhere off in the distance. It is real death, nonexistence. It is the ultimate epilog to every life. But knowing that epilog is coming offers you a choice. You can ignore it and pretend you're immortal. Or you can choose to acknowledge your mortality and devote yourself to finding purpose in your life."

"Finding purpose or creating purpose, it doesn't matter. The two most important days of your life are the day you are born and the day you learn why," I said.

"Been reading Existentialism again, haven't you?" Bartholomew said, "You always get a little weird when you do that. It's why I stick to Patterson and King. Sartre and Tillich mess with my mind."

"Actually, that was Twain."

"Listen to us," Junior said, "talking about courage like we actually know what we are talking about."

"Since when did we start worrying whether we know what we are talking about? That would seriously curtail our most interesting conversations."

My Unremarkable Life
The Strange Trip

Coll^ollege was four years of irresponsible fun punctuated by moments of intense cramming. Between all-night beer parties and all-night study sessions we managed to get passing, if truly mediocre, grades. It was our final semester at Ball State. Bartholomew, Junior, and I decided not to go anywhere for Spring Break opting instead to stay at the college. Each of us had at least one or two courses that were at risk of keeping us from graduating. The plan was to use the break to catch up on term papers and reading assignments hoping we could at least pull gentlemen Cs in our courses. But when Bartholomew's sister Angelica invited us to a party at her college in Terre Haute, we forgot our plans and headed off expecting an evening with a bunch of friendly coeds. Another plan that didn't exactly go as expected.

Bartholomew didn't tell us Angelica wasn't a student at the college. She was an employee, a secretary in the Civil Engineering department at Rose Polytechnical Institute. He also failed to tell us RPI was an all-male college. It changed its name to Rose-Hulman Institute of Technology a few years later and two decades after that finally allowed women to attend. But in 1965 RPI was a bastion of male exclusivity. Angelica was dating one of the students and had become an unofficial member of an odd assortment of characters sharing a house just off campus.

The house had earned a reputation among the more avant-garde RPI community for wandering outside the lines of traditional college life. Located on the aptly named Highline Avenue, the place was known around campus as Highline House. Rejecting the bourgeois confines of official Greek fraternity life, the denizens were all smart GDI students—God Damn Independents—with nonconforming approaches to life in general and to academia, in particular. They were regularly threatened with suspension or expulsion by the dean of students, but their grades were so good he never pulled that trigger.

After a three-hour drive across central Indiana, we picked up Angelica at her apartment and she navigated the way to Highline House. It was a cool evening in early April and the windows of Highline House were open. We could hear music a block away, muffled bass throbbing across the neighborhood. I thought the place must be really hopping inside. But when we walked through the open front door, the large foyer of the three-floor house was empty. Angelica knocked on the door at the far end of the foyer then opened it without waiting for a response. The Zombies blasted on the HiFi, the volume approaching DC-10 levels. We walked in.

The room was dark except for a dozen or more brilliantly colored posters that glowed on nearly every square foot of wall space. I had never seen black light before. It was otherworldly. A weird purplish light showed a room full of people, some sitting cross-legged on the floor, others sitting on both levels of three bunk beds, their backs against the wall and feet projecting over the edge. Wine bottles, mostly Lambrusco and Lancers, were scattered around the room. Incense burned in a small ashtray, its thin smoke snaking into the air where it mixed with thick pot smoke. It wasn't like any party I had been to. No one was dancing. They weren't even talking. Everyone was lost in the music. No one paid us any attention except a tiny monkey sitting on one of the upper bunks eyeing us warily.

Angelica pointed to a guy on one of the beds. "That's my boy-friend. They call him Red Ralph." She had to yell into my left ear to be heard over the music. The guy's eyes were closed, and he swayed slightly to the music, a happy smile on his lips. She pointed at some other guys around the room. "That's Dingle. That's K-moko. That's Pops. The guy smoking the waterpipe over there is Sergeant Trips." She pointed at the monkey. "That's Bogart. He's a squirrel monkey. Don't try to pet him. He bites." As if on cue, the monkey bared its teeth and scooted to the far end of the bunk.

"Want to join the trip?" a voice yelled into my other ear. A guy wearing coke bottle glasses and an old leather football helmet was holding a tiny half-filled paper cup out to me. I wasn't sure what he meant but accepted the cup. Angelica put her hand on my arm. The guy handed cups to Junior and Bartholomew.

"Do you know what that is?" she asked.

"No idea."

"It's called LSD. You may want to avoid that. I mean, unless you really do want to try it. It isn't like anything else you've ever heard of."

"How so?"

"You really never heard about this stuff?" Angelica asked. "It's the biggest thing. It's all over California. Unlike marijuana, it's legal." I wasn't going to admit that I was so square that I'd never heard of LSD, although I hadn't. Besides, if it's legal, what could a little drink like this do?

"Oh, yeah, I've heard of LSD," I lied, "Sounds like fun."

I drained the cup. Bartholomew did the same. Junior hesitated, then shrugged and drank his. Six hours later we staggered out of Highline House. I'm not sure I ever looked at the world quite the same again.

———

I shared my reminiscence of that night so long ago with Bartholomew when he stopped by to drop off my mail. "That was a weird party, for sure," he said, "Those guys were really out there. But the music was incredible. I mean, it's the only time I ever saw music. Literally. I remember seeing colors and swirls and flashes that were the sounds of the music."

"Yeah, and remember the traces? Everything that moved left traces behind. I think I moved a lit cigarette in front of my eyes half the party." I shook my head. "I'm glad I did that once. And I'm just as glad I never did it again."

"I wonder whatever happened to those guys," Bartholomew said, "They seemed so out of it. I wonder if they even finished college."

"You know Angelica married one of them, right? Not the same guy she was seeing back then. One of the other guys. She told me that the Highline House guys all did well. One became a heart surgeon. Another was a Green Beret. One was a nuclear researcher at Princeton. One started his own engineering company building bridges and roads. Another became a renowned physics professor. One even became an opera singer."

"I feel like an underachiever. Maybe I should have tried more of that stuff."

"I don't think that's why they did well."

Flowers from Goldie

Roger came into my room carrying a small vase with a few red roses and a card. "More flowers, Jeremy," he announced placing the vase on the table and handing me the card.

"They're from Goldie," I said, "I haven't heard from her in a while."

"One of the few good things about getting laid up in a hospital is you tend to hear from old friends."

I smiled. "Goldie's not a friend." I looked at the card again. I recognized her young-girl handwriting with loopy letters and circles instead of dots. Could've been written by a ten-year-old girl if they still taught script in school. "She's my wife." Roger looked surprised. "My ex-wife."

"I got a couple of them, myself," Roger said, "Neither one would send me flowers if I had a broken neck and was lying on my death bed. I stepped out on both of them a few too many times." Roger smiled. "But man could those women cook. I miss that."

"Goldie couldn't cook. She…"

Bartholomew poked his head through the door.

"You decent?" he asked.

"Come on in, Bartholomew. Roger was just getting ready to change my catheter. You can help."

"I'll come back later," and the head disappeared.

"I'm kidding!" I yelled. "Roger doesn't do catheters. Do you, Roger?" I asked just in case.

"Nope. I just deliver flowers and push wheelchairs around. Touching sick people gives me the creeps."

"You're both nuts." Bartholomew sat down and picked up the card. "*Heard you fell off the roof. Get well soon. And stay off the roof! Find a safer hobby. Goldie.* Isn't that nice of her. Sending a card."

"And flowers, too." Roger pointed to the vase.

"That woman always was a hopeless romantic." Bartholomew's smile faded. "Maybe she wants to get back together. I hear she's been kind of drifting since Cliff died."

"Oh, yeah, I'm sure that's it. We haven't been together in fifty years and when we were together, we weren't together. We need each other now about as bad as Sonny needs Cher."

"Sonny is dead."

"That just confirms my point."

"Still, it's nice she thought of you and sent a card. Must mean something, don't you think?"

"I'm not sure what to think. To be honest, I really don't think about Goldie much."

"Liar."

"No, it's true. I used to think about her. How could I not? It's like when I quit smoking. I thought about cigarettes every time I had a cup of coffee or a beer. I thought about cigarettes when I was in the car. For years after I quit, I would walk past a smoker and the smell would make me crave a butt. Hell, I dreamed about smoking for decades after I quit. But eventually the craving evaporated. I could go days or weeks without wishing I had a smoke. After a while, walking past smokers didn't just fail to attract me, it actually made me nauseous. I don't think I've had a smoking dream in years. That's the way it is with Goldie. She's a habit I broke long ago. It took a while but I never think about her anymore. And when I do, it's not pleasant."

"Me thinks you doth protest too much."

"Maybe. But right now, I'd rather have a cigarette than see my ex-wife."

"If you say so."

"Still, it was nice of her to send me flowers." I drifted into a memory from a million years ago—the greatest two minutes in my life.

My Unremarkable Life
Summer After College

It was the Labor Day weekend of 1965. My mother was somewhere in Europe honeymooning with her third or fourth husband, owner of several new restaurants around town where you could get a ten-cent hamburger and twenty-cent milkshake in less than a minute. Even people in sleepy southern Indiana were looking for the fast, cheap lifestyle. The bigger world was a spasmodic mass of noise, confusion, and youthful naiveté. We were all home having just graduated college - me, Bartholomew, Junior, Cliff, and most of the rest of our old high school class. Lyle skipped college and went straight to work in his parents' bookstore. He was taking business courses from a correspondence school in Sarasota, Florida. Goldie didn't go to college, either. Instead, she enrolled in a modelling school hoping to use her good looks to make her mark in the world. She was doing well with local advertising agencies who used her in magazine and TV ads for everything from garbage disposals to fake diamond rings.

Over the next days and weeks, many of the kids would reach escape velocity and break away from the fierce gravitational pull of Mount St. Anne. My own unformed plans involved buying a motorcycle with some money I got for graduation and riding out to British Columbia where some guys had organized a group to find Bigfoot. I also considered riding my motorcycle down to Patagonia like Che Guevara. I was unclear whether roads even went that far but such was my life plan.

But for a few more days, we were still kids from the neighborhood and it was time to party. Junior reserved a picnic shelter at the city park and we put the word out that the William Henry Harrison High School class of '61 was having a reunion picnic. The park officials were fascists about beer and alcohol, but they were also clueless about electric Kool-Aid, hashish brownies, and diet pills. So serious inebriation was not going to be a problem.

The shelter had electricity so Lyle, the only one in the group with steady income, brought a brand new stereo and a crate of records. By midafternoon everyone was high as Sputnik and dancing to Jay and the Americans. Cliff stood to the side watching the party but not participating. In a week he was heading to Fort Dix to begin training for deployment to Vietnam. Goldie draped over him like kudzu on an oak tree. "C'mon, Cliff, I wanna dance," she slurred.

"Then dance," he said smiling, "you don't need a partner. Just look at them."

He was right, of course. A mass of people wiggled, shimmied, and twisted to the music, each person lost in their own hazy world. No one paying attention to anyone else.

"But I wanna dance with you, Cliffy," Goldie poked him in the chest and stuck out her lower lip.

"I'm not into that stuff, Goldie. It's stupid. I mean, look at them. They look epileptic. I'm going to take a ride. Want to come?"

Goldie hated Cliff's Harley. He rode it too fast cutting close around slow cars and taking curves so fast she thought her knee would scrape the road. "No, I want to dance."

"Fine. See you later." Cliff walked toward the parking lot.

"Maybe," Goldie yelled after him, but he didn't hear her over the loud music.

Goldie watched him go. She sighed and turned to the dancers. The acid she took earlier was really kicking in. The music and the dancers seemed to become a single organism moving in orgiastic pleasure. She slowly moved her body, letting the music flow through her. She felt the deep thrum of the bass guitar, the steady pounding of the drums. She forgot about Cliff and waded into the dancing creature and soon forgot herself.

Hours later, I was cleaning up the paper cups, cigarette butts, and other detritus from the party. I was still pretty high. I avoided the Kool-Aid but had my share of brownies and the lingering euphoria still fogged my head. I carried a bag of trash to a dumpster and heard someone singing softly nearby. I walked behind the dumpster and almost stepped on Goldie. She was sitting cross-legged on the ground with her back against the dumpster. Her eyes were closed and she was singing - terribly off key—one of the songs that we played earlier. I coughed a little to let her know I was there.

"Oh, hi, Jeremy," she smiled at me and I felt my stomach drop like a roller coaster just fell out from under me. She was so beautiful, even with her bloodshot eyes peering through slitted lids. I realized she had never smiled at me before. I was a real sucker for a smile from a pretty girl.

"Hi, Goldie. What's happening?" Not the coolest line, I know, but I was happy any words came out at all.

"Not much. Sit down." She patted the ground beside her.

"Where's Cliff," I asked looking around. I didn't want to get into anything with him.

"Don't worry about Cliff. He's gone."

I sat down.

"Some party, huh?" I said trying not to stare at her long legs as she stretched them out in front of her and ran her hands up and down her thighs.

"It was OK. Look, can you give me a ride home? It's a long walk and I'm not sure I can walk real well. I'm still kind of high, you know?"

"Sure. I have my mom's car." I stood up and felt the blood rush from my head. I nearly fainted. I was still pretty high, too. Goldie started to stand and collapsed back on her butt. She held out a hand without looking at me. I pulled her up. She leaned on my shoulder and tried to walk on her own. She teetered and reached out to me with both hands to keep from falling. I swayed a little but kept my balance. Her hands grabbed my shoulders. She pulled herself tight against me.

"Guess I need a little help." She stared into my eyes and smiled. My knees almost buckled. "You're kinda cute, How come I never noticed that before? Maybe college was good for you." She kept looking into my eyes. I couldn't talk. I couldn't even breathe. What happened next is still a blur. I remember a frantic tongue in my mouth. I remember being pulled to the ground. I remember fumbling with buttons and zippers. I remember Goldie climbing on top of me and grabbing me with her hand. I remember thinking, "Oh, God, it's going to happen!"

Then I remember lying there thinking "what the hell happened?" It was over too fast. I think it was great - at least for me - but it is a fog. Goldie lay on top of me, her hot breath on my neck. I thought she was a sleep. Then she sniffed.

"That was weird," she said, "Did we just fuck?"

"Yeah, we did." I was afraid to move, I didn't want the moment to end.

"I thought so." She pushed herself up to her knees still straddling me. She opened her eyes and flinched. I think she was surprised to see me. I stared at her tits, still in shock at what just happened. Without another word, Goldie got up. dressed, and started toward the car. "Well, you going to give me that ride home or not?"

I jumped up, pulled up my jeans, and ran barefoot, carrying my shoes to the car.

Two months later two words changed my life.

Tasha's Father

"**I** don't know, Jeremy, it looks like you've lost a little movement in your right hip this morning." Tasha leaned against my bent knee while holding my other leg flat to the mat. "We were getting at least a couple degrees more motion last session. Does this hurt?" and she twisted my leg outward. It hurt like hell.

"A little," I grunted through clenched teeth.

"Have you been doing your stretches?" Tasha had given me a printout of several stretching exercises I was supposed to do twice a day when I didn't have PT. At first, I was religious about doing them, but lately I was finding excuses to skip them. They were tedious and I didn't see any progress coming from them.

"Most of them. Most of the time."

"You need to do all of them all of the time. If you want to walk out of here someday, you need to do some of the work, Jeremy. I can't do it by myself. You need to help and that means doing your stretches. All of them."

She leaned on my leg one more time, frowned, and let up. "That's it for today. You're doing well with most of your movements. But you need to work on that lateral hip extension." She said something else as she turned around to make some notes on her computer. But I didn't hear her. A sharp pain pierced through my chest causing me to suck in air and grimace. It hurt like hell then disappeared as fast as it came.

"Something wrong, Jeremy?" Tasha asked when she saw my flushed face.

"Just a little muscle twinge. I'm OK."

"OK, so I'll see you next session. And do your exercises. I got a lot riding on you."

"I'll try not to let you down." I wrestled myself off the table and into my chair. My breath was still shallow from the pain, but I was quickly getting back to normal. Whatever that was, it came and went so fast it was easy to dismiss as a spasm or maybe gas. I didn't give it another thought.

At this point my dislocated shoulder had healed enough to allow me to wheel myself to and from PT. Pushing myself down the hall felt like a big step toward independence. On the way back to my room after my session with Tasha, I detoured around the facility to explore and enjoy my newfound freedom. I wheeled across the complex to the main lobby where the floor to ceiling windows gave an expansive view of Mount St. Anne at the bottom of the hill. Progress Avenue that led from the hospital to town looked like a long ski jump ramp. It was relaxing to sit by the windows watching cars go up and down the long hill.

On my way to my room, I decided to stop in the cafeteria for coffee. Even bad coffee was a minor celebration of freedom. I happily nursed my coffee for a half hour then started for the exit. Tasha sat at a table on the far side of the cafeteria reading a paperback. She looked like one of my schoolteachers from a century ago with her tortoise shell reading glasses perched low on her nose and a thin glasses chain hanging loosely around her neck. I grabbed another coffee and wheeled myself over to her table. "Mind if I join you?" I asked.

Tasha peered at me over her glasses. I suddenly felt stupid. I was interrupting one of the few opportunities she would have to relax all day. It was inconsiderate. I felt like an idiot. Then she smiled. It transformed her face into something radiant with life. The deep lines that normally gave her a permanent frown stretched into a beautiful smile accented by deep dimples and lively lines at the corners of her eyes. She actually looked happy. Then just as quickly, her smile disappeared and dour Tasha was back. I thought she was going to dismiss me with some sharp comment.

"Hi Jeremy," she said. "Please. Join me." She pushed a chair away so I could wheel my chair up to the table.

"How's the book?" I noticed she was reading Albert Camus' *The Plague.*

"It isn't an easy read. Lots of people dying. But it is a good book."

"I read it in college. I didn't really get it then. I reread it a few years ago when I was going through a phase and revisiting classic novels. Camus made more sense when I was in my seventies. Especially his concept of absurdity."

"Exactly. I don't buy into his premise that the Universe is utterly indifferent to our search for meaning and happiness. I can't accept that there is no purpose to life except what we choose to make our purpose. I don't think God made the Universe that way." Tasha took a sip of coffee. "But maybe He did. My father recommended Camus and a lot of other Existentialist writers to me after I left the Army. He was an avid reader and believed good literature was the door to understanding. Even more than the Bible"

"Sounds like a wise man."

"Yeah, he was a good guy, too. You know, you remind me of him. You actually look a little like him—wrong color, of course, but your eyes and your smile are a lot like his were. You're grumpy like he was." I started to respond but Tasha cut me off. "No, it's a good kind of grumpy. And you seem to be a good guy. Not enough of those around anymore."

"So, your father was a handsome, intelligent mensch. Just like me."

"Well, he was handsome and intelligent. Maybe a little like you." She put her book down and sipped her coffee. "I miss him."

"Is your mother still alive?"

She grimaced. "Ugh, this coffee is cold." I thought she was purposely changing the subject but then she said, "Last I heard from her, my mother was living in El Paso with a retired border guard. We don't communicate much. Mostly just when she needs some money."

"I'm sorry to hear that. Must be tough."

"I haven't seen a lot of my mother since I was twelve. She kept bringing different men home and some of them were a little too interested in me. When I told her about it, she blamed me for trying to steal her boyfriends. So, I left and went to live with my dad who was stationed at Fort Benning. I became an Army brat."

"That must've been an interesting life."

"I loved it. The discipline. The sense of purpose everyone shared. We weren't at war with anyone, so I was able to stay with my dad at his various postings. Got to see a good bit of the country. Even spent a year in Germany." She absently took a sip of coffee and winced again. "God, that really is bad." She looked at her watch. "Gotta get back to work. I hope you're doing your job, too. Keep doing your exercises and we will get you back on your feet in no time."

I watched Tasha drop her coffee cup in the recycle bin on her way out the door. I realized I was smiling. I reminded her of her father. Huh, imagine that. He must have been a pretty damn good guy, even if he was a bit grumpy.

My Unremarkable Life
Two Words

"**I**'m pregnant."

Life had already done a brutal job pounding my dreams of adventure into a bloody mess. Like a badly overmatched boxer, my dreams slumped on the stool in the corner of the ring, blood, sweat, and snot draining down their face. But they weren't ready to throw in the towel. They took a deep breath, stepped back into the ring, and were permanently knocked flat by two words.

"I'm pregnant."

Two words. Two little words. Ten letters. One apostrophe. It wasn't just a knockout punch from Joe Frazier. It was an avalanche. A million tons of boulders, trees, rocks, large animals, a few abandoned trucks all fell from the sky landing squarely on me.

My first response? Stupid. "Pregnant? You mean you're going to have a baby?"

She stared at me, mouth agape and eyes blazing.

My second response? Stupider. "How did that happen?"

More staring. More blazing.

My third response? Stupidest. "Oh, right. I know how it happened. I mean who is the father?"

More staring. This time mouth closed tight, eyes burning holes through my face with ion death rays. I started to get a bad feeling about this.

"Me? Are you saying it's me? I'm the father?" I was panicking. "What about Cliff? Maybe it's Cliff."

Through clenched teeth Goldie hissed, "It's yours, asshole. It was the only time."

I was speechless. The *only time*? Come on. Goldie and Cliff did it all the time. Everyone knew that. Cliff was king of the hill. The lead dog on the sled team. Goldie was the top female in the pack. Head bitch (although I never would have said that out loud). Every guy in town wanted to have Goldie. Cliff had her. So of course they were doing it. Often.

"You are the only one," she hissed again, the fire starting to go out. "*You*…are the only one," her jaw slackened. "Just…*you*." Her eyes fell to the ground. Her shoulders sagged. She sighed. "You."

Oh shit. She's telling me she and Cliff never did it. She never did it with anyone except me. After the party. Behind the dumpster. Me. My reaction to this information was probably not the most mature. I am the only guy who's had sex with the most desired girl in town. Me. Plain old Jeremy Moore. I had sex with Cliff Masterfield's girl. Who's the alpha dog now, huh? Who's the cool kid now, huh? I felt my chest puffing out. I was starting to preen. I was going full rooster. Good thing I didn't have a damn comb, or it would have flared out like a bright red baseball mitt sticking straight out of my head. Wait until the guys hear about this!

"Hey, moron, are you listening to me?" Goldie yanked me back from my reverie. I nodded. "Good. Now, let's get some things straight." I nodded again. She held up one finger. "First, don't plan to go around bragging that you screwed Cliff Masterfield's girl."

I nodded. "Of course. Of course. I wouldn't think of it."

"I am not a prize in some sort of testosterone competition. And I'm not Cliff's girl. I'm nobody's girl. Okay?"

I nodded.

She held up a second finger. "We're going to keep this our little secret until I can tell my parents and until I talk with Cliff.

He'll probably kill you when he finds out, good thing he's at boot camp."

Where he's learning twenty ways to kill a man with a spoon and a hairbrush. I nodded.

She held up a third finger. "We will get married in a few weeks and give this baby a nice, comfortable, happy home. Understood?"

I nodded. But I most certainly did *not* understand. Did Goldie Eaton just propose to me? Was I going to marry the most beautiful girl in Mount St. Anne, Indiana, all because we had sex when I was stoned and she was tripping? Behind a dumpster? I didn't even know this woman. She was so far out of my league I never even imagined we'd have coffee together let alone get married. She must be crazy. She's probably got all kinds of mental issues. She'll probably make my life hell bitching and moaning about how she "settled" for a bum like me. I could see a life of torment and pain with this unhinged woman. But then I looked at those big, beautiful eyes, those perky breasts pushing against the tight t-shirt, those long, tanned legs with the perfect calves and delicate ankles, those perky breasts. I brought my eyes back to her face. She was staring directly into my eyes.

"Understood?"

"Understood." My bike trip to Patagonia was postponed indefinitely.

Monica's Story

I rolled myself into the cafeteria to grab an afternoon coffee and piece of pie. It was becoming a daily ritual. The coffee was poor-to-adequate in the hospital cafeteria, but the coconut custard pie was outstanding. Now that I was allowed to eat whatever I wanted, I found there weren't that many options on the hospital menu that appealed to me. Coconut custard pie was a delightful exception. As I headed to a table on the small patio to enjoy the afternoon sun with my guilty pleasure, I saw Monica sitting on a bench. Samantha sat in a wheelchair nearby trying to work a yoyo. Bear was on her lap. Monica invited me over with a wave.

"Samantha looks like she's recovered from her treatment," I said as I wheeled up.

Monica gave me a tired smile. "Samantha is doing much better today. She wanted to get outside and enjoy the sunshine before she goes in for her regular weekly check-up." She kept her eyes on her daughter as she wound the string around the yoyo and flipped the toy toward the ground. "She's losing feeling in her legs." Monica spoke quietly. I almost didn't hear her. The yoyo stopped at the bottom but didn't come back up.

"She is so intent on learning how to use that yoyo. She's been at it for twenty minutes and still can't quite get the hang of it."

I was reeling. Samantha was losing feeling in her legs? For the first time, her disease became real to me. *This is really happening.* Samantha looked at us, frustration on her face. "It won't come up," she said winding the yoyo.

"Give the string a little tug just when the yoyo gets to the bottom," I offered. Samantha studied the yoyo and tried again.

"She'll figure it out. When she sets her mind to something, it's amazing what she can do." Monica sighed. "She could be anything she wants to be." I understood that, for Monica, it was more than mastering a toy. Everything Samantha did and every moment she was intent on learning something new were grand events in this precious little life. Every challenge and every success amplified by her frightening prognosis. Looking at the little girl with her tongue sticking out of the corner of her mouth focused on winding the yoyo string just right, I could almost see the future rocket scientist or brain surgeon that Monica imagined dwelt in her energetic daughter.

"I wish Danny could see her now." Monica sighed again.

"Danny is Samantha's father?" I asked tentatively.

"Yes. My husband. Danny died when Samantha was two."

"I'm sorry," I said, "That must have been very difficult."

"Look, Mom," Samantha called, "I'm doing it!" The yoyo went up and down one more time then came up short. "Rats! I was doing it." She started rewinding the string again.

"It was hard. This is harder. Not having Danny to help us get through this. Danny always took care of us. I'm supposed to be Samantha's support but she's the one who keeps me together."

"She is an amazing little girl."

"Danny died in an industrial accident. A cylinder of high-pressure chlorine ruptured. It exploded while he was checking the valve. Samantha doesn't really remember him. She has pictures of him, and she knows he loved her, but he's like a character in a book to her. A hero she knows only through stories and pictures."

I had no idea what to say to that.

"Thank heaven the settlement with the company included health insurance for Samantha until she's twenty-one. I don't know what we would do without that. The settlement didn't include a lot of money. They decided Danny was partly to blame for the accident since he didn't follow proper protocol." She practically spit out the last two words. "My job at the diner keeps us in our apartment and food on the table. But that's about it."

Samantha threw the yoyo down and snapped it back up into her hand and smiled at us.

"Good one honey!" Monica inhaled quickly and looked up at the sky. "It's just so hard," Her body shook as she fought back tears. "I'm sorry. You don't need to hear our troubles. Everyone here has a story. I don't mean to unload all my troubles on you."

"Don't apologize. Sometimes it's good to share with a stranger."

We watched Samantha work the yoyo.

"You aren't exactly a stranger anymore, Mr. Moore. But thank you. You are easy to talk to. I guess I need that right now."

Roger the orderly entered the garden and kneeled beside Samantha. "OK, big girl, time for your check-up. Ah, you have Bear with you. He's my favorite teddy bear." He waved at Monica. "I'll take good care of her and Bear, Mrs. Bradshaw. They'll be back in her room in an hour."

"Thanks, Roger. Samantha, you be good and we'll have ice cream later."

Samantha sat back in her wheelchair like an Indian princess ready to be carried on her palanquin. "Look what I can do, Roger." She leaned to the side and flipped her yoyo deftly and snapped it back up into her hand.

"You have to show me how to do that, Samantha," Roger said as he pushed the wheelchair out of the garden. I could hear Samantha explaining the technical details of effective yoyo management as they wheeled away.

"Samantha has an amazing attitude about all of this. I wish I could be as upbeat about my own treatment."

Monica hesitated. "I think she keeps up her spirits for me. I hate that she has to go through this. She has treatments once a week. She'll be sick for a couple of days after. The next day she won't be able to keep food down. She'll be so weak it breaks my heart. But she bounces back. She's a trooper. Three days after she's wheeling up and down the hallways showing off her yoyo or throwing airplanes or who knows what."

"She is a brave little girl. How long will the treatments last?"

"Until she's…" Monica's pulled a tissue from her pocket and dabbed at her eyes. Her hands shook. "I'm sorry I'm such a mess."

"Please! Don't apologize. I'm sorry. I ask too many questions."

"It's OK. I really do need someone to talk to." She blew her nose into the tissue making a loud honking noise. She laughed through teary eyes. "Well, that wasn't very ladylike."

I laughed with her. "You're a remarkable woman, Monica. Samantha knows that. I hope you know it, too."

"Jeremy, can I ask you a personal question?"

"I'm seventy-seven years old. At this point in my life, nothing is that personal anymore."

"Do you believe in God?"

I wasn't sure how I should answer that. A young mother with a dead husband and very sick daughter needs hope. Monica misinterpreted my hesitation.

"I'm sorry. That wasn't an appropriate question to ask. I'm just not real good at social norms right now" her eyes on her hands in her lap, "You don't need to answer that."

"No, Monica, I don't believe in God." She raised her eyes to me. "Maybe that's not what I should say, but I won't make up stories. I don't believe in God. Haven't for many, many years."

"I don't think I believe in God, either." Her eyes went up to the sky. "I just don't think God is up there. It's easier to believe there's no God than to think He's up there letting my little girl die." A tear rolled down her cheek.

"I don't know if this will make sense. I don't believe in God, but I do believe in the power of prayer." She looked at me quizzically. "I don't mean prayer can affect the weather or who wins the Super Bowl. And all the prayer in the world won't help someone else. But prayer can allow us to tap into amazing power that is already within us."

I reached out and took Monica's hand. "I believe that if someone prays for strength, they will find it. Strength to forgive. Strength to endure. Strength to overcome anything life throws at you."

Monica squeezed my hand. "My mother was a very devout Christian. She believed everything that happens is caused by God. Everything. He makes the sun come. He makes each leaf fall from the tree. He decides who will live and who will die." She shook her head sadly. "She believed that she could change God's mind by praying to him. None of her prayers ever really came true but she never lost faith."

"I don't believe prayer can ever change anything outside ourselves. But you have incredible strength, Monica. You have more strength than you can imagine. Maybe prayer isn't the right word, but whatever it is, look inside. You will find it. I know it."

"After Danny died, I went to church regularly for a year looking for answers and strength. But the words were hollow. Religion felt like a lie. But I did find some comfort in prayer. By myself. Not the hyped-up prayer of the church. Just me alone in my bed praying. Then I realized that I wasn't actually praying. I wasn't addressing myself to God. I was just letting my mind clear, letting my emotions calm, so I could understand. Maybe that's what you mean."

"That's why I meditate. My daughters got me to do it years ago. It helps me in a lot of ways but, to be honest, my life has been remarkably lucky. I've had almost no tragedy in my life. So, my experience is probably not helpful. But it is what works for me."

Monica put both her hands over mine. "Thank you, Jeremy. I just needed to know that I'm not a terrible person if I don't believe in God." She got up and took a deep breath. "I need to get to Samantha's room before they bring her back. She'll be groggy and a little disoriented for a while. I need to be there."

I watched her walk out of the garden. I thought about how the Holy Spirit, or whatever it is, burns deep in the heart of a parent. I thought about death and tragedy. I thought about my father's funeral. The innocence of a child losing a parent is sad, but it is the order of things. The pain of a parent losing a child is an unfathomable tragedy. It is not how the world is supposed to work. I wheeled myself out of the garden and back to my room where I sat for a long time contemplating, looking for answers. It didn't help.

My Unremarkable Life
Wedding

We were married in a simple ceremony with just the two immediate families and friends. No one was especially excited about the wedding. So why make a big deal out of it? My mother was surprised I had actually found a beautiful girl who would marry me. By then everyone knew why we were getting married and I think my mother was even more surprised that I got someone pregnant. She was convinced I'd be a virgin until I died. Goldie's mother hated me. I am sure she thought I seduced her perfect daughter and ruined her life. Her father seemed happy to get Goldie out of his house. Whenever he saw me, he would shake his head and mutter "better you than me" or "I was stuck with her for twenty-two years. She's all yours now. Good luck, buddy," or other gentle words of encouragement.

As the wedding day approached, my mother told me more than once that I was making a mistake. Actually, she told me Goldie was making a mistake. She read Betty Friedan and had been attending "consciousness raising classes." Marriage was an anachronistic institution that had outlived its usefulness, she told me one day after a dinner and a bottle of Chianti. She said marriage was all weighted for the man—a way for him to get free sex whenever he wanted it with a maid and cook thrown into the deal. It was a prison sentence for the woman. With the pill and modern feminism, why would any woman want to get married? She can just have sex with whoever she wants to without all the strings of marriage attached. "Mom, we're having a baby. The free sex and fun train left the station already," I tried to explain, "A baby deserves a mother and a father. Goldie deserves a husband to help raise it."

"So? Do you love her?" That question caught me flatfooted. My mother never talked about love. She never used the word. It wasn't part of our little family lexicon. Did I love Goldie? I hadn't really thought about it. Mom was looking at me with a half-smile on her lips like she had just pulled an inside straight to my pair of sixes.

"I think so."

"Close enough." She took a luxurious drag on her cigarette. "You have my blessing."

That was a month ago. Now she was sitting in the front row in Goldie's family's church. I swear she was wearing the same black dress she wore to my father's funeral only without the shawl and veil. And she shortened the hem to well above her knees. *She'll be trawling for men at the reception*, I thought. From the subtle blush on her face I could tell she had already been into the wine. I was jealous.

Goldie's family was sitting in the front row across the aisle from my mother. None of them was smiling, They looked like they were waiting for a murder trial to start. Cliff was a surprise attendee. He was home rehabilitating from an injury he sustained a week after getting to Nam. Apparently, he took a bullet through the shoulder while carrying a wounded Marine to the evac helicopter. Only a week in the war and he was already a local hero. He sat in the back row wearing his dress uniform—his arm in a sling under his jacket. He was joking with some guys from the old football team. They were sneaking sips from a flask and laughing at some joke that I am sure was at my expense.

Junior, Bartholomew, and Lyle were sitting behind my mom. Like my mother, they had been drinking or maybe smoking or maybe both. For them this was entertainment. Some kind of theatre de l'absurde with me, their buddy, the farcical hero facing the gallows for defiling a poor, chaste damsel. I was jealous of them, too. If I could have gotten away with being stoned, I would have been totally hammered myself. But it bugged me to see my friends giggling and fussing without me. It was the first hint that being a married guy meant I was going to miss out on a lot of the fun the guys had. *Oh hell, what am I getting into?* I thought standing by the preacher. *I should run. I should just tell the preacher I gotta pee and run out of here as fast as I can. Hop a train or something and go to the Yukon until this all blows over.* The Escape Plan was starting to come together in my mind when Goldie appeared at the far end of the aisle on her father's arm. She looked about as happy to be there as I was, but she had a determined look on her face that said this was going to happen or she would hunt me down like a dog and shoot me. Her father had a similar look. It was too late to run.

Ten minutes later I heard the preacher say you may kiss the bride. Goldie leaned in and pecked at me quickly brushing the corner of my mouth. It was over. I blinked and looked around the room. *What happened? Did I just miss my own wedding?*

As we walked down the aisle toward the church doors, Goldie looked straight ahead. "I was at the doctor's this morning," she whispered.

"Everything ok?" I whispered back trying to smile at the people in the pews as we walked by.

"Depends on how you define OK."

"How do you define it?"

"Not like this. The doctor said he heard more than one heartbeat."

"Of course he heard more than one heartbeat—yours and the baby's."

"Not mine. More than one baby."

The world swirled under me like a rowboat in a hurricane. "Twins? You're having twins?"

"WE are having twins. At least twins," she hissed.

"AT LEAST TWINS?" I shouted stopping dead in the aisle. The words echoed around the church. Everyone stared at me, mouths agape and eyes bulging.

Goldie hit me with the bouquet of flowers. "Nice going, Sherlock. Now everyone knows."

"AT LEAST TWINS?" I hollered again hoping for a different answer this time.

"Shut up. Just shut up." She squeezed her sharp nails into my arm and pulled me toward the door. I shut up. Hell, I couldn't breathe. More than one baby. *OHGOD-OHGOD-OHGOD-OHGOD*.

As we walked by the last row, Goldie shot Cliff a quick sideways glance. He winked.

The reception went surprisingly well considering. Probably because everyone got roaring drunk. My mother was too busy chatting up the preacher to process the idea that she was going to be the grandmother of AT LEAST TWO BABIES. Goldie's parents huddled in a corner most of the evening. I wasn't sure if they were calculating the giant bar bill being racked up or plotting how to murder their new son-in-law. The guys and our other friends just drank and danced and sneaked out for an occasional doobie—like any other Saturday night in their untethered lives. Goldie sat at the head table and drank. She was always a quiet drunk anyway. She was especially quiet now. The only thing she said to me the whole party was "fuck off" when I suggested that drinking a whole bottle of champagne may not be the best thing for the babies. In the spirit of self-preservation, I fucked off.

Somehow we got through it all and Goldie and I started our life together in a two-room apartment above the bookstore Lyle's parents owned. Goldie's father pulled some strings and got me a job as a "Collections Advisor" which meant I called people who were behind on their rent or electric bill or car payments and asked them to pay up. It wasn't pleasant work, but it paid our bills, and I could do it on the phone from the apartment.

One night four months later Goldie woke me up with a hard jab to the ribs. "We need to go to the hospital. Now!"

Acropolites
Bourbon and Mayflies

"**I** got a call back!" Bartholomew announced walking uninvited into my room. Lyle and Junior followed behind. "The director wants me to come back for another reading."

"Congratulations," I said genuinely surprised. I couldn't remember Bartholomew getting a call back on a major part in years. Decades, maybe.

"It's not a guaranteed thing, of course, but I really think they are going to take me. I saw the other actors trying for the part. It's obvious to anyone who's read the screenplay that I am the perfect match. I feel really good about this."

Knowing Bartholomew's endless optimism and his past record with major parts, I faked a smile. "I'll keep my fingers crossed."

Lyle pulled a fifth of Maker's Mark bourbon from a folded issue of Nature magazine. "We came to celebrate Bartholomew's pending stardom." He opened the bottle and took a swig. "To the next Best Actor Oscar winner." We passed the bottle around while Bartholomew rambled on about the part and his understanding of the character's inner conflicts. No one listened but no one interrupted, either.

Feeling mellow and insightful, Lyle passed the bottle to me.

"Remember that time we were camping in Shipley's Woods in the winter? It was damn cold that night and Bartholomew was so drunk he ended up with his sleeping bag in the fire."

"In fairness, that sleeping bag was way too thin for winter camping. I got a little too close to the fire, but you have to admit it was freezing cold."

"A little too close? Your sleeping bag caught fire. You could have ended up like a Hot Pocket burrito if Jeremy hadn't woken up from the smell of burning polyester."

"Did I ever thank you for saving my life?" Bartholomew asked me, taking another swig.

"No. But hand me the bottle and we'll call it even." I took a deep drink. "I better stop. The problem with these damn medications is they make alcohol hit me like I was fourteen again."

"Lucky you. Pass me the bottle." I handed the bottle to Junior who was already feeling mellow. We sat in silence basking in nostalgia. The guys quietly passed the bottle until it was nearly empty. It reminded me of many nights long ago when the four of us sat around campfires drinking Southern Comfort or Jim Beam and pondered the great mysteries of the universe. Today in my hospital room, it was much better bourbon and there was no fire. We were not underaged outlaws hunkered down in the woods feeling like the Hole in the Wall Gang. But drinking straight from the forbidden bottle had the familiar outlaw romance. It felt good. Lyle must have been feeling the same.

Lyle broke the reverie. "Life is strange," he observed, a hint of slur in his speech.

"You just figured that out?" Junior asked.

"I mean, look at us. We are four old men sitting in a hospital room drinking good bourbon and pretending to be philosophical. Not much has changed in the last sixty-five years, has it?"

"Well, the venue has," I said, "Not exactly like sitting around a campfire or hanging out at the lake."

"True, but who would have thought all those years ago that this would be our life?" Lyle frowned. "Somehow I expected more."

"Doesn't everyone?" I asked glancing at the clock hoping it was getting to be time for dinner. It wasn't. "I mean, doesn't everyone wish they had a better life?"

"Maybe. But it could be worse, you know. We could've been mayflies."

"What are you talking about?"

"Just that we got it pretty good compared to mayflies."

Silence.

Lyle sighed. "Look at this article here." He waved the Nature magazine at us. "Mayflies live for about two years. For that entire time, they are ugly, nasty-looking bugs that live under rocks at the bottom of rivers. I mean, look at this picture. This is a very ugly little beast living a very ugly little beasty life. Then finally, after scumming around the bottom of a river for two years gripping onto the bottom of a rock with their nasty little pincers trying not to be eaten by fish or crawdads, they let go of their rock and kick their tiny little scrubby feet and twist their ugly little segmented bodies in a mad dash to the surface before they are eaten. If they are lucky enough to reach the surface, their bodies crack open and this skinny-ass wet fly tugs itself out of the shell all the while hoping a fish won't suck it down as it struggles out of its skin like a fat woman taking off a wetsuit. It sits there floating along like a chocolate on Lucy's conveyor hoping a fish doesn't eat it before its wings dry enough to fly. After all this effort and risk, not to mention the two years living under some slimy rock, the mayfly finally breaks free of the water and flies into the air. It is this beautiful insect. See? Beautiful delicate wings. Perfectly tapered little body arcing upward with two perfect little gossamer thread tails. Some are emerald green with translucent green wings like Irish angels. Some are saffron yellow with touches of tangerine. They come in all kinds of amazing colors. They are some of the most beautiful animals on the planet. They fly back upstream, skitter around with a bunch of other mayflies until they manage to mate with one or more. And you know what happens then? Then they drop their eggs in the water and die. One stinking day. That's how long they live. One stinking day of beauty, grace, flying, sex, and sheer unbridled living. Then they die."

"I think you're drunk, Lyle," I said.

He ignored me. "How is that fair? I mean, shit, the poor mayfly spends two years as an ugly monster-like beast living in the dark under a cold rock. Then it lets go of its rock and risks a hundred different deaths to emerge like the swan in the *Ugly Duckling*. And it gets one stinking day to enjoy the payoff? That is just plain cruel."

I rose to the bait. "Oh, I don't know. Sounds pretty good to me. Do you suppose that ugly little beast under the rock knows it's a mayfly? Do you think it is bitching and moaning for two years about the nasty life it is condemned to live just so it can fly and fuck for one day? I doubt it. I have a feeling that the poor creature is perfectly happy under its rock. It has its routines worked out. It's probably got a nice collection of friends sharing the underside of that rock. Life seems perfectly fine then one day this weird urge comes out of nowhere and he lets go of the rock and swims free in the water. It's a miracle, he thinks, why didn't I ever do this before? I am swimming free. The universe is mine to explore. Then just like that, his feels a crack in his armor shell. He floats to the surface and kicks off his shell and what does he discover? He has wings. He is a freaking angel. Better than swimming, the lucky son of a bitch can fly! He is beautiful, and he can fly! Who cares if it's only for a few hours? Who cares if it ends in a quick fuck that uses up the last of his energy and he dies? For one shining moment that bastard was perfect. Don't you think it's a pretty good deal? Wouldn't you be happy to let go of your rock to end your life as fucking angel?"

"And you think *I'm* drunk. You are weird, Jeremy. You know that? You go another bubble off plumb every year."

"I'm just saying maybe we are pretty much ugly bugs living under rocks. And that's all we are. I'm kind of jealous of the mayfly. I'd be happy if it all ended with me sprouting wings, flying through the air, finding love and adventure for a single day. That would be a good day to die." I lifted the bottle to my lips before remembering I wasn't going to drink any more. "Maybe I am a little drunk. So what?"

My Unremarkable Life
Babies

The babies were coming four weeks early. The doctor said this was likely to happen. He warned that multiple births often are premature, so we weren't surprised when the contractions started. We were, however, scared shitless. I ran around in circles in the small room bumping into furniture and hopping on one foot trying to pull my pants on. My brain was flash-fried. I couldn't remember what to do. Where are my keys? Where are my shoes? What are we supposed to take? What are we supposed to do? Why hadn't we prepared an overnight bag like the books all recommended? Why are the babies coming now? Where are my shoes, dammit?

Goldie just sat on the edge of the bed breathing hard and staring at the wall. She was not helpful. "OK, OK, OK. I got this," I said as much to myself as to her." I handed Goldie her heavy coat, pulled her feet up and put her slippers on, and dragged her to her feet. "OK, so far so good. Let's go." I took her hand and slowly led her out the door, down the stairs, and to the car parked behind the building. Well, to where the car was supposed to be parked behind the building. It was gone. Nothing there but an empty space beside the dumpster. In my panic I looked around like maybe the car was just playing hide-and-seek. I looked behind the dumpster. Goldie moaned. "OK, OK, OK, I got this," I said. "You wait here." I ran up to our room and called 911.

A minute later I was back. Goldie had slipped to the ground where she was sitting with her back against the dumpster, her long legs splayed out in front of her. She looked exhausted. And things were just getting started. A moment later we heard a siren keening its way toward us. I pulled Goldie to her feet and walked her down the dark alley to the sidewalk. A couple of cats hissed at us from an overflowing trash can. The street was empty and dark except for the dim streetlights and a few neon signs in some of the store windows. Flashing ambulance headlights come around the corner, siren wailing. The van blew right by us. My heart fell. Goldie moaned. The brake lights came on and the ambulance screeched to a stop a half block away. We ran toward it. Well, we tried to run. I took two steps, tripped over my untied shoelaces, and fell on my face. Goldie nearly fell on top of me but managed to grab a lamp post. She held the lamp post like a wino trying to stay upright. As I got to my knees the ambulance attendants reached us with a gurney. They started to pick me up but I shook them off. "Her, you idiots! Take her! She's having babies!"

The ambulance guys looked at each other. Babies? Quickly, they got Goldie positioned on the gurney and hurried back to the ambulance. I jumped in as one was putting an oxygen mask on Goldie and the other hopped in the driver's seat and tore down the street toward the Mount St. Anne Hospital.

With its lights flashing and siren wailing, the ambulance raced up the long hill to the hospital main entrance. Broad steps rose to large glass doors and the marble-walled lobby inside. Concrete lions sat guard on pedestals on either side of the steps. The impressive edifice was scarred by a long, twisting ramp that was added so gurneys and wheelchairs could access the facility. The ambulance pulled into the circular driveway at the foot of the ramp. An orderly was waiting for us. He helped the ambulance guys pull Goldie's gurney out of the van and pushed it quickly up to the front doors. I jogged after them trying to hold Goldie's hand. She hissed, "fuck off," through gritted teeth and swatted my hand away. I was pretty sure she was having another contraction.

They raced Goldie down the hall and turned abruptly into another hall that led straight to the delivery room. They crashed the gurney through a pair of swinging doors. Another orderly grabbed my arm as I started to follow. "Sorry, sir, patients only beyond the doors. You can wait here." He gestured toward a small waiting room with a half dozen faded plastic chairs and two coffee tables stained with coffee cup rings—reminders of countless fathers-to-be caffeinating themselves into a froth waiting for their child to make its grand entrance into the world. "Coffee machine is around the corner. Cafeteria opens at seven. When the baby is born, you will be able to see it in the nursery though that window across the hall. A nurse will let you know when the baby is here." The orderly turned to leave.

"Babies," I said, "when the babies are born."

"Well, twins! Congratulations, sir. We don't get too many twins here."

"At least twins," I said staring at the double doors where Goldie disappeared a minute before.

"Oh," was all the orderly said before turning and walking back to the main lobby. I heard him mutter as he left. "At least twins? Oh brother."

Three hours later I had just finished my fourth cup of terrible machine coffee and added a couple of rings to the table pattern when a nurse came in. "She's at seven centimeters, Mr. Moore. She's doing fine. It'll probably be a few more hours."

"Seven centimeters?" I didn't understand what that meant.

"Yes, sir. Her cervix has expanded to seven centimeters. When she gets to ten centimeters, we can expect the baby to come soon after."

Ten centimeters? How much is a centimeter? Is that, like, an inch? Maybe I should have paid attention in math class when we did metrics. It sounded painful. I was instantly thankful that men could not have babies. Then I felt guilty about thinking that. Goldie must be pretty tough to go through this. She's a real trooper, I told myself. Then I went to find a pay phone to make some calls.

—

The first call didn't go well.

"Yes, Mom, the babies are coming now. Goldie went into labor an hour ago....I don't know how long it will take....No, I don't know how many babies, none yet....Sorry, I didn't know you had company....I said sorry. I thought you would want to know right away....OK, I'll call as soon as the first baby is born. Go back to sleep, Mom. I got this."

The second call didn't go well.

"I understand, Mrs. Eaton (Goldie's mother never wanted me to call her anything but Mrs. Eaton.) Yes, it is early. Nearly four weeks....Oh, yes, that too, Seven AM. I thought you and Mr. Eaton may be up. I mean, it's a work day and all.....Yes, of course, I didn't mean you need to work. I just thought if Mr. Eaton was up to go to work, you would be up to make his breakfast or something.....No, Ma'am, Goldie doesn't make breakfast for me. Actually, she doesn't make lunch or dinner for me, either. We mostly eat take-out.....Yes, I know it's early in the morning to call to chat about our dining habits.....I thought you may want to know....Ok, I will call as soon as the baby is born.....Yes, Ma'am.....I am sorry I woke you."

The third call went fine.

"Junior, I am at the hospital. Goldie is having babies and I need food." Twenty minutes later I was sharing a large sausage pizza and a Pepsi with Junior in the waiting room.

Four hours after that, I was ushered into a bright hallway where I looked through a large window into a room full of cribs. Three nurses each rolled a crib to the window and lifted out a baby for me to see through the thick glass. They held them up for my inspection like pieces of China at an auction. Three babies. Three girls judging from the pink blankets. Three baby girls. All mine. I wanted to turn and run as fast as I could for the door and not stop until I got to Guatemala. I felt Junior come up and look over my shoulder.

"My God, Jeremy, you are the luckiest man in the world."

"My life is over."

"Your life is just starting, Jeremy. Look at those beautiful babies."

"Maybe they aren't mine. We only have Goldie's word about that. Maybe their Cliff's. Or somebody's."

"They're yours, alright. Look at those little mouths. The same pouty frown you have when you're in a mood."

"What are you talking about? I don't have a pouty frown when I'm in a mood. That's what Cliff looks like when he's ready to spit."

"Jeremy, take a breath. They are not Cliff's babies. They are yours."

I stared at the little creatures. It felt like they were staring at me, looking at me worried that maybe they had gotten the wrong father. We studied each other for a long moment. Then something happened that I can't explain even fifty-four years later. I fell in love. Madly, desperately, totally, ridiculously in love. I was a father. I had three daughters. I had three amazing, beautiful baby daughters. Thank heavens Junior was with me. If he hadn't caught me when I fainted, I'd have hit the floor like a sack of ripe tomatoes.

Tasha Meets the Girls

The girls stopped by to visit on their way to one of their many appointments. I long ago became used to the idea that, whether I was home or in my hospital room, I was almost always just a roadside stop for them on their way to some other more pressing destination. It was a warm afternoon, so they decided to wheel me around the hospital campus—a more comfortable way to visit than sitting in my small room looking at the garbage dumpsters. With the warm sun on my face and my entourage of beautiful women, I felt like a minor pharaoh inspecting his gardens in the company of three magnificent demigoddesses.

"Isn't that your physical therapist?" Binkie asked as we slowly ambled along the sidewalk between the parking lot and the trees. Tasha was leaning on a post in the smoking kiosk, enjoying a cigarillo and looking out over the town. She heard us coming.

"Hi, Jeremy. I assume these are the legendary daughters I've heard so much about." She waved us into the kiosk.

"Girls, this is Tasha. She's the taskmaster responsible for fixing my broken body."

"I suppose that's one way to put it," Tasha shook hands with each of the girls.

"We have heard a lot about you, too," one of them said, "Daddy says you're making him do things he didn't know he could do."

"I'm helping him discover what he is capable of doing with a little work."

"And a lot of pain," I added.

"No pain, no gain, Daddy."

"Speaking of no gain," Byrne said, "we have twenty minutes to get to the bank. We are refitting an old shirt factory into a daycare center and thrift store. We need to open a line of credit."

"Didn't you just open a daycare center?" I asked.

"We did. This new one is in part of town that really needs it. We have a plan to use proceeds from the thrift store to underwrite some of the cost of the daycare so more people can afford it."

"That's a terrific plan," Tasha said, "A lot of the aides and other workers here at the hospital have kids. Affordable daycare is a huge issue for many of them."

"It's a big problem and we think this project will help. We need to go. Can't leave the bankers waiting. They get grumpy, no matter how worthwhile a project may be."

The girls shook Tasha's hand and kissed me, then headed for their car.

"Your girls are amazing. They're successful, beautiful, and really good people. How did you do that?"

"How did I do what?"

"How did you raise such amazing human beings all by yourself?"

I'd often wondered that myself. I wasn't anything special as a father. I didn't obsess over them, but I never neglected them, either. I attended most of their soccer games, swim meets, and field hockey games in school. I never missed a band concert or play they were in. Somehow, they taught themselves to cook, houseclean, and take care of me. But I never let them think that was their role in life. I encouraged them in everything they did but tried not to be one of those tiger mothers who drove their kids to exhaustion. It was a constant source of amazement to me how they turned out. But what did I do to make that happen?

"I never gave them a reason to despise me."

"That's the secret to being a good parent? Not giving your kids a reason to despise you?"

"Not really a secret."

"Seems like a low bar."

"You never had kids."

"True."

"Not such a low bar."

My Unremarkable Life
Divorce

Six months later, Goldie and I were sitting in our very tiny living room feeding three hungry babies. My mother gave us the down-payment for the house as a delayed wedding gift. She had recently divorced her third or fourth husband and was feeling generous. The large settlement she got from the Chevy dealership owner made her momentarily charitable. So, we bought a small Cape Cod house at the end of a quiet lane that dead-ended at a double set of railroad tracks. Other than the rumble of passing trains several times an hour, the house was a comfortable little nest.

Goldie held Binkie in her arms while the baby lustily sucked on the bottle of formula. The girls were strong enough to hold their own bottles so I could easily hold the other two babies in my arms while they enjoyed their dinner. It was a beautiful, almost serene picture of pure domestic bliss. Of course, it was a very misleading picture.

"You know, we've been married for almost ten months. The babies were born six months ago," I said without taking my eyes off the little faces in my lap. "Do you think it's time…"

"Don't, Jeremy!" Goldie snapped. All three babies stopped eating and turned their eyes to her.

"Don't what?" I said knowing full well what.

"You know full well what. We have an understanding."

We did have an understanding. Well, she may have understood but I didn't. Or maybe I did but refused to accept it. We were man and wife and parents to three lovely children. We had a small but comfortable house, food in the fridge, and a color TV. We had all the appearances of a happy family on its way to the American Dream.

What we didn't have was sex. I was OK with that when Goldie said she was too uncomfortable for sex when she was pregnant. I was OK with it when she said she was still recovering from birthing three healthy babies. I was even OK with it when she said she was too tired from taking care of the babies all day while I worked in my dank basement office—even though I did most of the baby caring when I wasn't working. But the babies were sleeping through the night now. Goldie's color was back. She had shed the extra weight from her pregnancy and was back to her slim, athletic self, even jogging several miles every morning.

"But we are married," I whined. I hated it when I whined but it just came out that way. "We are married and it's what married people do. It's sort of the whole purpose of marriage."

"Marriage is an outdated institution of the patriarchy," she said as if she were reading it from a bumper sticker. I was shocked. First by her flat rejection of the solemnity of marriage, and second by the thought that she knew the word patriarchy. I raised an eyebrow.

"I read, you know," she said defensively, "I'm not an idiot."

"No, no, I know you're not an idiot. I just didn't realize you held these, um, unique opinions. I find it very sexy."

"See, that's just what I mean. Women are subjugated by marriage. Everything they say and do is interpreted in terms of male satisfaction. Married women are indentured servants and sexual playthings."

"Wait a minute. Have you been talking to my mom? You are not an indentured servant. I do more cooking, shopping, and cleaning than you do. I've encouraged you to think about getting a job or finding a hobby that you would enjoy. I've tried hard to make your life comfortable and safe. You're not being fair if you think you're an indentured servant." She looked like she was going to argue the point but instead distracted herself by shifting the baby to the other arm.

"And as for being a sexual plaything, we haven't had sex since the graduation party. I've been patient. I know things were tough for a while. But, come on, Goldie, isn't it time to get on with our marriage?"

"Well, that's something I've been wanting to discuss with you."

Uh, oh.

"You know I married you only because my dad would have disowned me if we didn't. Well, that and because he would have killed you if we didn't." Mr. Eaton was president of the local bank. He was also a former offensive tackle at Purdue and a very large man with a very hot temper. While I don't think he was a murderer, I appreciated Goldie's concern for my life. I would not want to test Mr. Eaton's capabilities.

"So, that means we are married but will never have sex?"

"Yes, that's what it means." I should not have been surprised that this was Goldie's idea of an understanding. It was, indeed, the way we had been living all along. I was about to ask a key follow-up question when Goldie continued.

"Look, I know sex is important for men. And I am sure you're getting tired of masturbating in the bathroom." *Oh, Lord, she knows?* "So, you should feel free to find yourself a mistress. It's 1968, forgodsake. Monogamy is on its way out. People are free to make love to anyone they want. You should get a girlfriend. Or girlfriends. Or, hell, boyfriends for all I care. But we are not going to have sex. I don't like sex. Understand?"

I totally understood. My fantasies were rapidly withering away. I had dreamed of us taking showers together, rubbing soapy hands over each other's body under the warm spray of the showerhead;

sitting naked in a hot tub drinking wine and playing footsies; making passionate love on a blanket between sand dunes at the shore, bright stars twinkling overhead. Now it was clear I wasn't even going to experience basic missionary sex in my own bed. She would never love me. I was Ok with that. It was an obvious if unspoken truth. But, damn, now it was official. No sex. Sure, she gave me permission to find a girlfriend (what was that bit about a boyfriend? Sheesh.), but it's hard enough to find a girlfriend when you're single. Finding one when you're already married AND you have triplet babies sounded like an impossibility. Besides, I still hoped there would be a chance to have a normal relationship with my wife. She was still the most beautiful woman in town, and I still got a hard-on just watching her paint her toenails.

"I got a letter from Cliff today."

Uh, oh.

"He's coming home next month. His hitch with the Marines is ending and he's not going to reenlist. Instead, he's going to build his own sailboat and sail it across the Atlantic. He wants me to come with him."

"You want to sail in a homemade boat across the Atlantic?"

"With Cliff. Yes. He wants me to help him build the boat, too."

"Goldie, you can't hammer a nail straight. And you want to sail across the Atlantic in a boat you helped to build?"

"With Cliff. Yes." I was starting to see the common denominator here.

"What about the babies?"

"You're a better mother than I am. They love you more. You will be fine." She was right, of course. I was a better mother than her. I did most of the diaper changing. I fed two of them when she fed one. I washed the dirty diapers. I prepared the formula. I was the one who got up at night when one of them cried. I kept hoping Goldie would wake up one day and take over. That her hidden motherly instincts would break out from whatever burden she buried them under, and she would become the loving caring mother the girls deserved. Not to mention the loving caring wife I deserved.

"You could get an opera to help with the babies." She was still talking.

"An opera? What does opera have to do with it?"

"You know, an opera, one of those pretty Danish or French girls who live with you and take care of the kids."

"You mean an au pair?"

"Whatever. Someone like Mary Poppins."

"A nanny? You want me to hire Mary Poppins?"

"Look, Jeremy, there are plenty of young, pretty women who would be happy to take care of the girls. You'll be fine."

"I won't be fine. I don't need a girlfriend. I don't need Mary Poppins. I have a wife."

"This isn't about you, Jeremy. Stop being so selfish. Can't you think about me for a minute?"

"I am thinking about you." I was thinking, who is this person talking to me? Who is this strange alien being that wants to run away from our family? Why is she doing this to me? OK, so I was thinking about me. But I think it was justified given the direction the conversation had taken.

"I don't need a girlfriend," I repeated, "I have a wife."

"Well, let's talk about that. Maybe you shouldn't have a wife."

"What does that mean?"

"I just think that if we are not going to have sex, and if I am going to spend the next year with Cliff, that maybe it would be better if I wasn't your wife." I wanted to correct her grammar. Would she ever learn the subjunctive verbs? I decided grammar was probably not the top priority at the moment.

"So, what you are telling me is you want a divorce."

"Since I don't recognize marriage as a legitimate institution, I don't consider us ever married." That little piece of truth stung.

"But if you want a divorce, I am sure you can get one easily. I am obviously a terrible mother and worse wife—at least as far as the male-centric establishment is concerned."

And so it was. The next day I watched Goldie drag a suitcase through the front door toward her father's car. She didn't even stop to say good-bye to the babies. I hoped it was because she was too emotional, but who knows? Her father came down the steps from our bedroom with a large footlocker on his shoulder. I held the front door for him. After he deftly dropped the footlocker into the trunk, he came back to the porch. "Here, call this guy. He'll take care of everything for you." I looked at the card he handed me. *Fabiano Guiduicci, Divorce Lawyer.* "You can trust him. I told him she gets nothing. She walks away from the marriage. You get the kids. It's over. You good with that?"

My head was pounding from the bottle of Jose Cuervo I drank the night before. I was sick about Goldie leaving. I was sick that my world was falling apart. "Yeah, sure. I'm good with that."

He looked at me sympathetically. "Sorry it didn't work out between you two. You're a decent guy. She's a...well, she's my daughter and I know her pretty well. Believe me, you're better off without her." He patted my shoulder with his bear paw. "You're going to need to fix up the house for the girls. They'll need more space when they get bigger. And you're going to need some help." He glanced over his shoulder to see Goldie close the passenger door. The back of her head visible through the rear window. She didn't look back. "Don't tell her about this." He handed me an envelope and walked away.

After they left, I opened the envelope. A check for $10,000. A note said, "This isn't a payoff. It's child support. Use part of it on the house. Use the rest for babysitters until you find someone else. Good luck." I almost tore the check up, but then realized the girls needed it. I needed it. Mr. Eaton was right. I should fix up the house. Maybe put an extension on for a playroom. Even after that investment, the check would still pay for a lot of babysitting.

Maybe even an au pair. I folded the check and put it in my pocket. Every year for the next eighteen years, Mr. Eaton sent me a check for $10,000. After the first one, the rest went straight into a savings account for the girls' college tuition.

Eight months after she left, I got the signed papers in the mail from Goldie finalizing the dissolution of our ersatz marriage. The envelope was postmarked from Marrakesh.

Lyle and the Story of Lot

I found a Bible in one of the drawers in my room. I guess I shouldn't have been surprised. It was the Mount *Saint* Anne Hospital after all. I read bits and pieces of it whenever I got bored. I hadn't read the Bible in years. It was eye opening. One morning I was reading Genesis when Lyle came to my room.

"Did you ever read the Bible?" I asked him.

"Of course I've read the Bible. I went to Sunday school."

"Sunday school Bible doesn't count. It's a bunch of white-washed stories for children. Nothing that would freak out a young and gullible mind."

"Oh, I don't know. Daniel was scary. And the snake. He was scary. They freaked me out."

"Only the way a Grimm's fairy tale would freak you out. Have you read the real Bible? As an adult?"

"Well, sure. I mean, yeah, I've read the Bible. I guess. Parts of it. A long time ago. Well, never actually. I've never actually read the Bible."

"If you ever want to get freaked out, read the Bible like a hard-core fundamentalist reads it—every word is literal truth. No metaphors. No allegories. Nothing but absolute rock-hard, capital-T Truth."

Lyle laughed. "Yeah, so the earth is like six thousand years old, and the entire population of the planet came from Noah's kids and

Jesus is coming back some day on a burning chariot. I can see where reading the Bible like that would weird you out."

"How about the story of Lot? You know that story?"

"He's the guy whose wife turned to salt when she looked back at Sodom, right?"

"Lot was a sick puppy. The whole story is sick. Lot had a wife who apparently had no name and two daughters who also were nameless and who were virgins despite the fact they were married (another one of the recurring weird ideas from the Bible). A couple of angels disguised as men were sent by God to Sodom to see if they could find ten righteous men in the town so God would have a reason not to kill every man, woman, child, dog, chicken and pig in the town. Another sick idea if you think about it. That night, all the men of Sodom came to Lot's house and demanded he hand over the two strangers so they could gang rape them. Now think about that for a second; all the men of this town decided they wanted to gang rape a couple of outsiders who they never met. How does that make any sense?"

"I guess it was like an initiation. I was in the band in high school. We had some, um, extreme hazing parties."

"You're kidding, right? I mean you weren't gang raping pledges, were you?"

"Oh, no, of course not. I mean, I just could see how things could get a little out of control. A bunch of guys, a few bottles of wine, you know. Things could happen."

"OK. Let me get back to Lot. So, these guys are pounding on his door demanding these two men and what does the righteous Lot do? He offers the mob his two virgin daughters instead. 'No, you can't have my guests who I just met, but you can gang rape my two daughters.' Are you fucking kidding me? That's righteousness? That is fucking sick, that's what it is. Fortunately for the two daughters, the men of Sodom aren't interested in women.

"Then things get even sicker. The next day the angels transport Lot and his wife and daughters out of the city so they won't be killed when God rains down fire and brimstone on the city. The sons-in-law are left behind. I had a mother-in-law once who would have gladly left me to fry in hell but that's another story. Well, you know what happens to Lot's wife, right?"

"She looks back at the city and is turned into a pillar of salt?"

"Right. Think about that. An entire city is being bombarded with fire from the sky killing every living thing in the city. And you're not allowed to look? It's like God was so ashamed of what he was doing he didn't want anyone to see."

"Been there."

"But this is where this sick story goes completely off the sickness scale into a whole new universe of perviness."

"I don't think perviness is a word."

"Well, it should be. Lot decides he doesn't like the new town they moved to, so he and his daughters go up in the hills and hide in a cave. The older daughter somehow concludes that no man will ever impregnate her or her sister, but she wants to preserve her father's "seed." So she tells her sister she is going to get the old man drunk and have sex with him and she tells her sister to do it, too. And they do it! I mean, think about this. How drunk do you have to be to not realize you are fucking your daughter? And if he is really so shitfaced that he doesn't know what he's doing, then his daughters technically raped him."

"I think I see a theme here."

"If this is mythology, OK, let's talk about what we can learn from this tale. But think about the people who believe deep in their heart of hearts that this whole fiasco actually happened somewhere in the sainted land of Jordan. That Lot actually existed. That everything happened in the world word for word as described in the Bible. And they consider Lot a hero?"

"Well, he was flawed. Made a bad choice here and there. Considered women property, not even needing names. But he apparently opposed men raping men. Something to be said for that, I suppose."

"Do you think God opposes men raping men but is agnostic about men raping women and women raping men?"

"I don't believe in God."

"Pretend! Pretend you are a fundamentalist believer. What do you conclude from this story about God's big plan?"

"Well, chances are, if I am a fundamentalist, I already oppose gay sex and especially gay marriage. So maybe this story is how God explains his opposition to homosexuality."

"Do you think there is a difference between sex and rape?"

"Of course. Rape is a crime no matter who it's done to."

"So, being opposed to homosexual rape is not the same as being opposed to homosexual love?"

"Now you are being rational. You said I had to pretend to be a fundamentalist."

Wheel Chair Races
First Look at the Moon

amantha was spending the night in the hospital. She was scheduled to undergo a procedure first thing in the morning to try to relieve the pressure on her spinal cord that caused her left leg to lose feeling. The doctors warned Samantha and Monica that she may lose use of her legs as her disease progressed, but this was hard news to accept—at least for Monica and for me. Samantha took it in stride as she did everything life threw at her. "That's why I've been practicing using a wheelchair," she said when she told Monica she couldn't feel her leg.

Monica was finally convinced to go home and get some sleep and come back in the morning to be there when Samantha would be taken to the OR. I was rolling myself through the main hospital lobby on my way to the gift store to look for something to give Samantha after her operation. It was late in the day. The normal high energy movement of people moving around the hospital had slowed to a quiet murmur. I was about to roll myself into the gift shop when I heard my name yelled across the lobby.

"Hello, Samantha," I said turning my chair to see her. She wheeled toward me. "I keep meaning to tell you, I like your ball cap. It is very striking."

"Thank you. It's my lucky hat so I wear it a lot. Mom likes me to wear it so she can find me in a crowd, but I just like to wear it for good luck." Samantha turned he chair away. "Come here. I want to show you something."

I followed her into the lobby. "Shouldn't you be in bed?"

"I'm not tired. Look, there's nobody out here." She pointed to the long hallway that extended from the lobby to the children's ward where she was supposed to be resting in bed. "We can race!"

"I don't think that's a very good idea..." before I finished Samantha laughed and slapped my arm.

"Of course, it's a good idea. First one to the water fountain way down there wins. Ready-set-go!" and she was off pumping her skinny little arms and racing down the hall. I wanted to yell at her. She was breaking her promise not to race inside. She was being a brat.

"C'mon, slowpoke," she laughed, her voice like a beautiful bell ringing down the long hallway.

Aw, what the hell.

"I'll show you who's a slowpoke," and I took off after her. I pushed hard on my wheels and got up a pretty good head of steam. I was closing on her. She was leaning hard into her wheels, but the chair was too big for her. I was going to pass her easily.

"I'm winning, slowpoke!" she laughed when I pulled beside her. I let up and she pulled back ahead. "Come on! Try harder!" she scolded me.

"I'm trying as hard as I can," I puffed. Samantha rolled past the water fountain and slowed to a stop. I rolled up after her. "Good race, Samantha. You really are very fast with your chair."

"I am, aren't I?" she smiled. "But you let me win."

"No, I didn't. I got tired. You won fair and square."

"If you say so. Oh, look!" She pointed out the large windows. A yellow gibbous moon hung in a darkening sky above the town. "Let's go look at the moon."

"Aren't you supposed to be in bed?"

"The nurse will make me go to bed when she finds me. But I want to look at the moon. Come with me. Please?"

I looked around to see if any nurses or orderlies were around to stop us. We were alone. "OK, But just for a few minutes. I don't want you to get in trouble."

"I won't!" Samantha turned her chair and headed for the door. "Come on!"

We wheeled to the driveway at the edge of the hill with its unobstructed view to the horizon. Progress Avenue fell away toward the city below. The pale moon was beautiful, hanging in the eastern sky just above the town. We sat in silence enjoying the cool breeze and the beautiful view. After a few minutes I was about to suggest we go back in when Samantha spoke.

"I like it out here." Samantha stared across the city below, the low light of the sun setting behind us cast the town and hills in a warm glow.

"It is pretty, isn't it?" I focused on Samantha's profile, her perfect button nose and deep-set eyes like a China doll.

"Can I ask you a question, Jeremy?"

"You can ask me anything."

"Will you promise to tell me the truth?"

"Of course, why wouldn't I?"

"I don't think Mom sometimes tells me the truth."

"What makes you say that? Your mother loves you. She wouldn't lie to you."

"I think sometimes it makes her sad. Mom loves me too much to tell me the truth."

I reached out and touched her skinny arm. "I don't want your mother to be sad. She is a very strong woman, you know."

Samantha was quiet for a moment. She took a deep breath. "Jeremy, do you believe in miracles?"

Do I believe in miracles? I'm a rational, reality-based person. If a miracle seems to happen, it's just some logical, explainable phenomenon that manages to beat the odds. From our limited perspective, miracles are like magic tricks—they appear to defy the laws of physics but behind the scenes they are totally explainable. I don't believe in magic. I don't believe in miracles.

"I think miracles happen every day."

"I hope so," Samantha said staring at the moon. "I heard Mom tell a friend that we need a miracle. She didn't know I was just outside the kitchen window. I heard her talking on the phone. She was crying. She said we need a miracle, or I wouldn't be around much longer."

I reached for Samantha's hand. "Miracles happen in this hospital all the time."

"Maybe. Mom said there are some doctors in Germany who may be able to cure me. It costs a lot of money."

I didn't know how to respond. Maybe there was some experimental treatment somewhere. Maybe there was a way to pay for it. Maybe it could all happen before it was too late. Maybe, but it would take a miracle.

It was getting late. Streetlights were coming on as darkness slowly descended on the town. Samantha pointed at the sky over the town. "Wow! Did you see that?

"What? See what?"

"The shooting star. It went right over the hill."

"Damn. I mean, darn, I missed it. I was looking in the wrong direction." I was looking at Samantha and wondering at the young girl's wisdom. A young child with an old soul.

"I think it's an oh-man."

"Oh man?"

"Yeah, you know. Like 'oh, man, it's an oh-man!' Roger told me about oh-mans when a butterfly flew into my room. It's a sign that everything is going to be OK."

"Ah, yes, a good oh-man. Just for you. Now, we better get back. We don't want to get into trouble."

"We can go in soon. But can we look at the moon for a few more minutes? It makes me happy."

"Of course. It makes me happy, too."

Twenty minutes later a nurse found us both asleep in our chairs.

Junior and Church

I was pondering on miracles and the likelihood one would save Samantha when Junior came into my room dressed in his Sunday-go-to-meeting clothes and carrying a brown paper bag. "Leftover donuts from the church," he announced opening the bag and placing its contents on the tray by my bed. "I got one jelly and one custard. Your choice."

"I'll take the custard," I said reaching for the sweet treat. "I don't suppose you brought any coffee. I could use some decent coffee."

"I'll bring coffee next Sunday." Junior bit into the jelly donut. "They always have a ton of leftovers. Not as many people coming to the church as there used to be, but the church ladies keep putting out the same amount of food for fellowship afterward."

"How long have you been going to that church? Seems like a long time."

"About six years. We started going there when Daisy got her prognosis. It helped, you know."

"I imagine it was good to have other people help get through that time. Why do you still go? You never were a believer."

"I guess I believe now. I saw what faith did for Daisy. She was so brave. I know accepting Jesus made all the difference for her."

"I'm glad it worked for her."

"Don't you ever think about it? I mean, at our age, you can't help knowing our time is coming. I'm not sure I could really think about that without believing God is out there and he'll make sure I see Daisy again."

"I respect that. But it's not me. We've had the conversation a hundred times. I am an atheist, a proud atheist." We did have that conversation a hundred times. Well, maybe a couple dozen times since Junior found religion. I admired his faith but felt it was based on fear and loneliness—especially *fear*. In my mind, Junior and all believers believe God exists simply because they desperately *want* God to exist. They can't imagine how a world without God could have any value, any purpose. They have to believe.

"You know, Christians think you will spend eternity in hell if you don't let Jesus save you. It's their moral obligation to try to get you to accept Jesus."

"Which is the main reason I don't usually get into these conversations with Christians. Better to stick to discussing the Colts and the weather."

Junior finished his donut, a blot of red jelly on his bulbous chin. "I bet when you are on your deathbed looking at the end you'll think differently. A lot of people find God at the end."

"Maybe. But if someone convinces me God exists and, even less likely, gets me to accept Jesus on my deathbed, it's only because my mental capacity will have deteriorated to that of a Cocker Spaniel. So it shouldn't count. It would be like statutory rape—the victim is fundamentally incapable of giving informed consent."

Junior smiled. "So, do you think the Colts can get past the Chiefs next year?"

"They have to make the playoffs first and that won't be easy. They don't have a first round pick in the draft next week. And if they do make the playoffs, that kid throwing for KC is just going to get better. It'll be tough."

"Amen to that," Junior said wiping his chin with the back of his hand.

My Unremarkable Life
Mr. Mom and Frieda

The next few years after Goldie left were challenging but some of the best years of my life. I quit my job as a head-hunter for an employment agency and started my own placement firm. I could still work from home, but now I was helping people find a good job instead of pushing them to take anything so the guy who employed me would make money. Much better karma. Living off contract work was tough early on, but after a few months I was placing enough engineers and accountants to pay the bills and put a little aside.

The girls were growing into delightful little humans. It was like watching a miracle unfold every day as they discovered more and more of their world. Junior, Lyle, and Bartholomew were regular visitors to the house. They loved the girls and the girls loved them. Junior and Daisy lived a few houses down from us. He would walk over every morning and help feed the babies before I started work. He even volunteered to change diapers when I needed the help. He also baby-proofed the house. He put covers on all the electrical outlets, put child locks on the cabinets with the cleaning supplies and insect killer products, moved all the potentially lethal weapons like pencils, scissors, and anything breakable to higher shelves. He bought and installed gates to keep the girls from crawling onto the stairs. Lyle came over most afternoons after working his shift at the bookstore. He brought stacks of children's books which ended up strewn all over the house. Lyle enjoyed reading to the girls. We all did. Even before they understood the words, the girls giggled and cooed whenever one of us read to them. Bartholomew was their favorite, though. He acted out the stories using weird voices and over-the-top facial expressions that made the girls squeal.

The girls had three uncles and a father. But I felt they needed a woman in their lives. So, I put an ad in the paper for a baby-sitter/nanny—someone to come to the house every day and take care of the girls while I was in my office. Someone to show them what a grown-up woman acted like. The first several interviews were disasters. The first was a retired librarian who shushed the girls during our interview. The girls were lying in the large playpen cooing at each other. The next was a college girl who cracked her chewing gum and said she was qualified for the job because she had a dog and a parakeet at home. Then there was the very large woman with a denim jacket and heavy black boots who said she'd take the job only if she can have her boyfriend over whenever he got out of prison. There was the little old lady who could barely walk up to the front door. She stood at the door with a hand on the jamb panting like she'd just run a 5K. I almost called an ambulance. Finally, a young woman from the next block came for an interview. When I greeted her at the door, I almost made an excuse to avoid inviting her in. She was chubby. Well, to be honest, she was fat. Her face looked like it was pumped full of air and would pop like a balloon if you poked it. Her round cheeks were scarred from years of acne. Her hair was a mass of greasy curls that hung over her chubby ears and oily forehead. She was a most unattractive young woman. Then she smiled. Her eyes twinkled. Really, they twinkled. I didn't know eyes could actually do that. I invited her in.

She introduced herself as Frieda. *Sheesh, even her name is ugly.* "I graduated high school last year and live with my parents. I haven't been able to find a job." She smiled bashfully. "I know it's probably because of my looks. I'm not one of the pretty girls that the shops and offices like to hire." I started to object but she cut me off. "It's OK. I know I'm not pretty. But I am a hard worker. And I am good with babies and young children. I have four younger siblings. My mom works long hours, so I practically raised them. I can cook. I know how to give babies baths. I change diapers. I'm strong enough to push your three little girls in a stroller to the park and back. I think I would be a good nanny for your children."

I had to agree. I liked her. A lot. Not just because of her itemized skills, but because of her quiet self-confidence. I hoped my girls would grow up to be as beautiful as their mother, but I wanted them to grow up confident in themselves regardless of how others may perceive them. Frieda may be the person I am looking for.

"Let's try it out for a few days," I said, "see how the girls like you and how you like the girls. If everything works out, we have a deal." Frieda smiled and held out her hand.

"Thank you, Mr. Moore. I know this will be great."

"Call me Jeremy." I shook her chubby hand. It was warm and strong. "I think it will be, too."

Frieda was the girls' nanny and surrogate mother for the next five years. She was true to her word about being a good cook. Soon her job description was expanded to include cooking my dinner, too. The girls loved Frieda. She played with them, read to them, and held them when they needed strong arms to sleep in. When they were older, she taught them to sing dozens of songs and some simple ethnic dances her grandmother had taught her. She drew pictures with them. Took them to the park when the weather was good. Showed them how to make snow angels when it snowed.

Then one day she knocked on the door of my office. "Jeremy, I need to tell you something." She looked at the floor, avoiding my eyes. "The girls will start school in a month. They know how to dress themselves. They make their own breakfast. They even know how to make sandwiches and pack a lunch. They won't need me anymore."

"Sure they will," I said. "They will still need you. Don't worry about that. We can shift your hours so you are here before school and when they come home, but they still need you."

"Well, Jeremy," she still couldn't meet my eyes, "Here's the thing." She took a deep breath. "I'm getting married."

I was momentarily stunned. I didn't even know she dated. She had never mentioned men. I had to admit that in the five years she was part of our lives, she had become more attractive. She lost weight. Her skin cleared. Her hair relaxed its curl and fell in gentle waves. Her face thinned showing high cheek bones and endearing dimples. She would never be pretty, but I could suddenly see what another man could see. She was a remarkable young woman.

"Congratulations, Frieda!" I said with sincere enthusiasm. "That's wonderful!"

She looked at me for the first time and smiled. "It is, isn't it? It is wonderful."

Frieda was married a month later. Junior, Lyle, Bartholomew, and I sat on the bride's side of the church. Frieda had the three cutest flower girls in the history of weddings.

The Triplets Want Jeremy to
Come Home With Them

Binkie, Birdie, and Byrne stopped by my room on their way to yoga.

"We brought your mail and some books. Hope you haven't read them already."

"I don't read so much anymore."

"Why, Daddy? You have always been such a voracious reader."

"I still read some. Some novels that Lyle brings me though I don't really like fiction anymore. I prefer nonfiction. Books about science or travel or food—something educational and not too personal."

"But you love novels. You always said non-fiction gave you facts and fiction gave you truth."

"I guess I'm tired of the truth. The truth is when I read novels I am constantly reminded of the insignificance of my own life."

"Oh, Daddy, now you're just being maudlin."

"I don't think so. I'm being honest. Any of these books about vegan cooking?"

"Of course. Two of them are. We're so happy that you are interested in veganism finally."

"I figure if my life has no significant impact anyway, I may as well go whole hog and try to eliminate as much of my presence on the planet as I can."

"I know you're being fatalistic, but it's actually very commend-able, Daddy. We are proud of you."

The girls exchanged furtive glances. I recognize a conspiracy when I see it. I'd been on the receiving end of their machinations their entire lives. They began plotting together before they could talk. The surreptitious winks and wry smiles were dead giveaways of sibling collusion and, once again, I was caught in the crosshairs.

"Out with it. What are you three up to?"

"Well, Daddy, we are worried about you," Binkie said.

"You aren't getting any younger, you know," Birdie added.

"Your house is a lot to take care of. Mowing grass. Shoveling snow," Byrne said.

"Cleaning gutters," Binkie said waving her hand across the room as if the point had to be made.

"You're there all alone. What if something happens and no one is there to help you?"

"You mean like if I fall and I can't get up?" I tried to sound snarky.

"Exactly! Or what if you forget to turn the stove off and the house catches fire?"

"Or what if you forget to turn the bath off and the house floods?"

"I've made it through seventy-seven years without those things happening. I don't think I've lost it that bad yet."

"Oh, we know, Daddy. You're still sharp as a tack." *I hate that phrase.* "But as we age, we do tend to lose a bit of our, um…"

"Marbles?" I offered.

"Acuity. It is natural. It's nothing to be ashamed of."

"I am not ashamed of my mental capacity. I have nothing to be ashamed of. I'm sharp as a tack."

"Of course you are, Daddy. We just think you should consider moving in with one of us when you leave the hospital."

"We all have houses that are way too big now that the kids are all gone. You can have your own space."

"You won't have to mow the lawn or pull weeds or shovel snow."

"Or clean the gutters."

"We can do your grocery shopping."

"We can cook your meals."

"We can drive you to your little coffee klatches with the Acropolites."

Little coffee klatches?

"We all have first floor rooms that can be converted into a nice bedroom for you, complete with private bath with all the fixtures older people need."

"Like a walk-in bathtub and comfort height senior toilet." No walk-in bathtub for me! But I may have to think about getting a comfort height senior toilet for my house. I can see the benefit to that.

"You won't need to climb stairs anymore. You can wheel anywhere you need to in the house."

I held up both hands. "Whoa, whoa, whoa. Slow down. First of all, I'm not an invalid. I am going to be out of this wheelchair soon. I will be able to walk and climb stairs. And second of all, I'm not ready to give up my home and become a guest at one of your houses. I've lived in that house since you were in diapers. It fits me."

"You would not be a guest, Daddy. You're family. Families are allowed to live together, you know."

"But I don't want to be a burden. I am fine on my own."

"You would not be a burden. You would be a help. You could water the plants."

"You could be company for the dogs when we are at work."

I don't really like their dogs. Each of them has two little hyperactive yappers that clearly do not like old men.

"You would be a lot of help around the house."

"That's not true and you know it. But I appreciate the offer. We can talk about this when I'm ready to get out of here." I did appreciate their offer. It was true that each of them had a monster house that was way too large for two people. They had large, land-scaped yards with swimming pools, manicured gardens, and stone patios larger than my backyard. I'm not even sure how many cars their garages held. It would be a quantum leap up in luxury to move in with any of them but moving in with one of my daughters felt like the old-man version of moving back into your parents' basement. I valued my independence. It would be an admission of failure to move out of my home. I wasn't ready for that yet. It felt like starting a long slow slide toward death. Of course, I was still relying on the nurses to help me take a dump, so independence was a slippery concept for me.

"Please think about it, Daddy. We all agree that this is import-ant. We'd feel a lot better if you were living with one of us."

"I'll think about it." As soon as they left, I Googled "comfort height toilets." I spent the next hour reading up on the relative benefits of seventeen-inch toilets. It was enlightening.

My Unremarkable Life
Second Birthday and Changing Life Goal

hen the girls were two and Frieda was still with us, I didn't plan to have a birthday party for the triplets. Frieda was away for a week on a family vacation in Pensacola. The new playroom addition funded with the money from Goldie's father was only half done. My new job as a headhunter was keeping me busy working from my home office. I really didn't have time to think about a party. Besides, they were two years old. For them it was just another day to toddle around the house finding new things to turn over or take apart. I was so busy keeping them alive while playing corporate matchmaker that I nearly forgot their birthday entirely.

Lyle, Junior, and Bartholomew did not forget. Early that Saturday they descended on our house, arms laden with presents, balloons, a huge sheet cake, and a case of Budweiser. The girls screamed in unbridled glee when their favorite uncles barged through the front door singing an enthusiastically off-key rendition of Happy Birthday.

Before they had put the gifts down and laid the cake on the kitchen table, the doorbell rang. The front door opened and three mothers from the street came through followed by their platoon of pint-sized terrorists.

I barely knew these women. When we first moved in, they all came by to introduce themselves. I said hello and waved to them hundreds of times since, but I had long ago forgotten their names. After two years, it was too embarrassing to ask.

"Hi, Jeremy," the short, chubby blonde said, "we were having a playdate next door when the children saw the balloons. It's the girls' birthday, isn't it? Mind if we join the party? The kids like your girls and wanted to say happy birthday to them."

I started to object. Whoever heard of crashing a birthday party for two-year-olds? If I had wanted them to come, I would have invited them. Then I remembered I didn't know I was going to have a party until two minutes ago. In my moment of hesitation, the triplets grabbed the other kids' hands and dragged them into the living room squealing at some previously unknown hypersonic frequency.

"No, I don't mind. Thanks for coming." I remembered my host manners. "Can I get you something? Coffee? Beer?"

"Coffee."

"Coffee."

"Coffee," they responded in unison. I went to make coffee while the women and men introduced themselves and the kids tore the living room apart opening the gifts the uncles brought. In the kitchen I stuffed a pile of empty pizza boxes in the trash and hid the week's collection of dirty dishes in the oven. I didn't want the mothers to think I was completely helpless without Frieda. Which I was. When I brought the coffee out, the living room was a disaster area. Lyle, Junior, Bartholomew, and the women were all enjoying a beer and ignoring the mayhem being wrought upon my living room by a swarm of little hurricanes.

I stood in the doorway, coffee pot in one hand, three empty mugs dangling from fingers on my other hand. I felt like I was missing a party in my own house.

One of the women, a tall pretty brunette wearing cut-off blue jeans and a Chicago Bears t-shirt, noticed me standing there like a lost busboy. She took the coffee pot and mugs and put them on the mantel out of reach of the children. "Sorry, Jeremy, we changed our minds about the beer." She giggled. "I haven't had a beer at ten in the morning since college. You throw great birthday parties." She reached into the case and pulled a can out. She used Lyle's churchkey to open the can and handed it to me.

"Darla," she said.

"Excuse me?"

"My name. It's Darla. You've said hello to me a hundred times but never said my name, so I figured you forgot." She held out her hand. "My name is Darla and it's a pleasure to meet you, Jeremy. Again." She held my hand a moment too long.

"Right. Darla. I knew that. Your husband is Robert."

"Richard, but close enough." She took a swig from her beer. "He's out of the picture anyway."

"Richard's gone?"

"Almost a year ago. I kicked him out." She smiled. "Best thing I ever did."

I had no idea how to respond to that. Well, I had an idea, but before I could act on it the doorbell rang again. Junior was closest to the door and went to answer it. He came back with a package and an envelope.

"It's addressed to the girls," he announced. "The return address is Punta Arenas, Chile. Who the hell lives in Chile?" I disengaged from Darla but not before exchanging quick smiles. I'd see more of Darla.

I took the package and envelope. "Hey girls," I shouted to get their attention. "A package for you." I handed it to them. While they shredded the brown paper and ripped at the cardboard box inside, I opened the envelope. There was a card inside.

As I expected. It was from Goldie. "It's from Mommy," I announced. The card was a picture of a llama wearing a brightly colored sombrero. It seemed to be smiling. The scrawled handwriting was painfully familiar. "Happy Birthday, girls. Love, Your Mother." No message for me.

The girls finished destroying the box. Each held a Patagonian dress, bright red and green stripes on the skirt and frilly white collar and cuffs on the top. The dresses wouldn't fit them for at least another year, but it was a nice thought.

"Aw, how cute," one of the mothers said. The girls tossed the dresses aside and went back to ripping the box apart.

Eventually, I ushered everyone to the backyard where the kids could play and eat cake and adults could drink beer and chat. Watching the babies and the mothers at the party, I had an epiphany. This is my life. This is who I am.

I'm not going to be a great mountaineer.

I'm not going to find Bigfoot.

I'm not going to be a fearless explorer.

I'm not going to cure cancer or discover a new planet.

I'm just going to be me.

What a loser.

Then, as if they could read my mind, the girls stopped playing with the other kids and looked right at me. They stared with big innocent eyes, three magnificent elfin beings looking at me. The message was clear. I count. I have purpose. My adventure is my girls. I decided in that moment that I was fine with that. I would be as good a father as I could be. It doesn't sound like much now. But then it seemed like the biggest challenge the world could ever devise. I was a father, dammit.

Over the next few years, Darla and I got together occasionally. Nothing serious. We were both a little lonely but neither of us wanted a real relationship. We were friends with privileges although no one called it that back then. I learned years later that Darla had the same relationship with at least two other guys from the neighborhood. I was happy for her.

I dated a few other women over the years but there wasn't a lot of chemistry with any of them. I guess in the back of my pea-sized brain I still hoped Goldie would come back. Being a father was an adventure. I would have liked to share the adventure with someone.

Acropolites
Jeffrey's Story

The cafeteria was nearly empty. A few nurses huddled around a table in a far corner. A couple with three young children shared a snack with a jovial old man wearing a robe in a wheelchair. The four Acropolites sat at a table near the window where we could watch the butterflies in the garden.

"The girls want me to move in with one of them when I get out of here," I said adding a third packet of sugar to my coffee. I never put sugar in my coffee before, but I found it helped the lousy cafeteria coffee go down better.

"That's a good idea," Junior said with a mouth full of apple pie.

"You should do it," Bartholomew said, "You shouldn't live alone."

"You live alone," I snapped.

"I don't have a choice. You have three loving daughters right here. Why wouldn't you want to live with one of them if they want you?"

"I'm still capable of taking care of myself. I'm not an invalid."

The guys were silent, sipping their coffee and avoiding eye contact.

"What? I'm not an invalid. I can take care of myself."

"We're just saying that after you get out of here, you should consider it."

"OK. I'll consider it." I added a fourth sugar to my coffee. "Jeez, you'd think I was helpless."

Bartholomew patted my arm. "Lord, we know what we are, but know not what we may be."

"Not sure getting old and decrepit is what Hamlet had in mind there."

"It's not. But the sentiment is appropriate. You ain't getting younger, my friend, and things are only going to get worse."

"Look, I know I'm on a fast downhill slide. We all are. But let me dream, will you?"

Roger came up to our table with a tray full of pancakes. "Couldn't help but overhear. Jeremy, all of life is a dream. Most of us just don't know it until it's too late, if ever. But at some moment, lucky people wake up and look around and realize that they are living beings moving though a make-believe word. Like waking up in a dream to realize you are dreaming."

"Thanks for the input, Dr. Phil. I'll consider it." I felt a little bad about snapping at Roger. He's a good guy. "Why don't you join us?"

"Thanks, I think I will." He pulled a chair over from another table.

"What's new in your world?" Junior asked as Roger dug into his stack of pancakes.

"Do you remember Jeffrey?" Roger asked me.

"Of course." Roger had told me about Jeffrey a few days earlier.

"He was an amazing guy. He died last night." Roger chewed another forkful of pancake. "You'd think working in a hospital would put calluses on your heart, keep it from breaking with all the misery and death around you. But it doesn't."

"I'm sorry, Roger." We sat quietly contemplating the pain of losing people we know. My mind drifted back to Roger's story about Jeffrey...

Roger was pushing me through the lobby when he waved at a tall man walking slowly toward the exit. The man smiled and waved back as a woman took his arm. She gave a tired smile to Roger and led the man out the door to a waiting car.

"That's Jeffrey," Roger said watching the man back into the passenger seat and lift his legs into the car one at a time. "And that's his wife, Wanda. Jeffrey is an amazing guy." Roger watched the car drive away. "You were talking about the 'good life' and living with purpose the other day," he said, "that's Jeffrey in a nutshell. A few months ago, I was sitting right here with Monica waiting for Samantha to come out from a treatment. This very tall man walking with his wife and daughter came into the lobby. He was nicely dressed but wore a baseball cap, which seemed out of place. While he was registering at the front desk, a man stormed out of the elevator into the lobby yelling and cursing. He was a small Black man, maybe five-six at the most. Probably didn't weigh 120 pounds. He wore an over-sized tee-shirt and his baggy pants fell down far below his waist exposing grey boxers making him appear young, maybe in his early twenties, but his face was etched with lines that made him look older. His cursing was foul. F-bombs flying everywhere. 'This is bull shit!' he yelled as he blew toward the exit. Then he turned and screamed, 'This fucking place is fucked up. Bunch of fucking losers. Assholes!' He started walking in circles alternating between muttering to himself and yelling at anyone who could hear.

"Hospital rules won't let me confront disruptive patients, so I went to the front desk and called security. Jeffrey walked over to the guy and tried to quiet him down. 'Hey, pal, can you watch the language?' he said approaching the angry man, 'My wife and daughter are over there. I don't appreciate your language.'

"The man glared at him and continued yelling. 'Fuck you, man! Fuck you and fuck everyone.' He continued turning in a circle yelling at the ceiling. 'Fuck everyone in this fucking building.' He stopped and looked at Jeffrey. He shook his head and muttered,

'Fuck you, man, and fuck your wife, and fuck your daughter.' Then he stormed through the double doors and out to the sidewalk.

"I could see Jeffrey was breathing hard and trying to control his temper. He looked like he was going to follow the guy out the door and beat the hell out of him to teach him some respect. His wife must have anticipated his thoughts. She came over to calm him down. 'Let it go,' she said, 'He's gone. Let's get you to your appointment.'

"As they turned to go, through the glass walls we all saw the guy screaming on the sidewalk. People approaching the hospital were afraid to walk by him. His torrent of f-bombs continued. Jeffrey shook off his wife and started toward the door. He was obviously angry. He was going to do something to make this man shut up. His fists were balled tight, and his face was hard and flushed. He pushed the door open and stepped through ready for battle. I ran after him. The heck with policy. I was afraid I'd have to break up a fight before security could get there. The guy turned and looked at Jeffrey with an insane rage in his eyes—a crazed, out of control, animal anger. Jeffrey stepped close towering over him, his arms twitching, ready to throw a punch. But before I could step in, something amazing happened. There must have been something in the man's face, something in his eyes that belied his desperation. Instead of punching him, Jeffrey put a hand on his shoulder and said, 'Are you alright?'

"The little man was taken aback. He, too, was clearly expecting a fight. He was panting hard. His whole body was a knot of muscles ready to unleash his fury. Then he slightly relaxed. Almost imperceptibly. "No, man, I ain't alright." He emphasized the last word—AWL-RIGHT—with a shake of his head underlining the absurdity of the question. 'I'm dying, man!' he yelled. Then quieter: 'I'm dying, man, I'm dying.' Jeffrey put another hand on his other shoulder. The man looked down at the ground. 'I'm fuckin' dying man. Brain cancer.'

"Jeffrey squeezed his shoulders then removed his cap revealing a long scar along the side of his shaved head. He said simply, 'Me too.'

"The man looked at Jeffrey for the first time. His face was still twisted in anger, his eyes narrow slits, a vein pulsing on his forehead. Then he softened slightly. His eyes began to mist. He glanced back at the doors to the lobby and then back at Jeffrey. Then real tears streaked down his cheeks.

"I'm dying and I don't have nobody who cares. I don't have no wife and daughter. You're lucky. I got nobody.' His body released its tension. He sniffed loudly and wiped tears with the back of his hand. 'You may be dying and that really sucks, but you got people. I got nobody.'

"Jeffrey pulled the man to him and hugged him. The man slowly allowed himself to relax and put his arms around Jeffrey. They didn't speak. They stood holding each other on the sidewalk outside the hospital and quietly cried.

"Four months later I was in the room when Jeffrey felt the angry man's frail hand squeeze his, an IV tube delivering a morphine drip to the back of his wrist. Jeffrey gently squeezed back. The man's hand relaxed. One final time. Jeffrey had been with him for every treatment. He wouldn't let the man die alone."

"He was at home. His wife and daughter were with him," Roger said pulling me back to the cafeteria. "The world lost a good one last night."

I didn't say anything for a moment. What could I say? Not knowing anything else Jeffrey had done with his time on earth, in his last months here he proved that his was a remarkable life.

Tasha Reveals
More of Her Story

I held my coffee in one hand and pushed the wheel with my other hand working my way over to Tasha's table near the window in the cafeteria. Even after a few weeks of practice, I was awkward with the chair. I bumped a table with my leg spilling coffee in my lap, but I got there. "You need a cup holder on that thing so you can use two hands," Tasha said smiling with a cheek full of toasted cheese sandwich.

"I can't wait until I get out of this cast and can put full weight on my leg."

"You're getting there. I may have to hurt you to get you all the way, but you'll be dancing the Boogaloo before you know it."

"I'm glad you think so. Sometimes I'm not so sure. This old body of mine doesn't recover very fast anymore."

"Believe me, I've been doing this a long time. I've seen much worse cases than yours. You are doing fine."

I took a sip of weak coffee. Why can't they make decent coffee here? It seems like the doctors and nurses drink a hell of a lot of it. "Mind if I tell you something kind of personal?"

Tasha gave me a skeptical look. "Depends."

"I just realized that other than a rare handshake, you are the first Black person who has ever touched me."

"Really?"

"Yeah. Is that weird? I mean, I have been wandering the planet for seventy-seven years and until a couple weeks ago, I never had physical contact with a Black person."

Tasha smiled. "I'm glad I could add that valuable dimension to your life. I hope your life feels fulfilled now."

"No. It makes me feel like I missed out on something. Something important. I'm an old white guy racist."

"Jeremy Moore, I don't think you're a racist."

"Of course, I'm a racist. I was raised in an all-white neighborhood in southern Indiana in the forties and fifties. My schools were all white. My friends were all white. My parents were racists. My grandparents were racists. Everyone I knew was a racist. They weren't evil people. They just didn't know any better. You can't escape that kind of universal programming. So, yeah, I'm a racist. But I do know better. And I've been trying for the last sixty years or so to not let that inbred racism control me. But it's insidious. The fallacy of white supremacy was extinguished long ago. But the quiet racism of assumptions and expectations bubbles up when I'm not paying attention.

"I mean, I'm a white man from twentieth century America. That alone was winning life's game of rock-paper-scissors. But I didn't even know there was a game. So, now I notice that most of the people being treated in this place are white and old, but most of the people who work here are neither? I should have noticed that the day I was admitted."

"Hey, that's healthcare in America. People who can afford healthcare are mostly white. The people who bust their asses to get through med school are from all over the world - Africa, India, Southeast Asia, South America. The people willing to empty bedpans and clean patients who shit themselves are mostly Black and Latino."

"But I didn't see it. I assumed it was normal. I'm a goddamn racist."

"So, Governor Wallace, you got any problems with me working on you?"

"God, no! I'm grateful you're working on me. I don't think I'll ever walk again without you."

"Well, you keep working on that White Man's guilt of yours. And I'll keep working on that worn-out White Man's body of yours. We both have our work cut out for us."

"That's a deal."

Tasha changed the subject. I was glad she did. "It was nice to meet your daughters the other day. Must be very nice having them so close."

"It is. They love Mount St. Anne. Born here and never left."

"Grandchildren?"

"Yep. Nine of them. And somewhere around nine or ten great-grandkids."

"That must keep you busy."

"None of them live nearby. The grandkids all went off to hot-shot colleges—five to the east coast, the rest to the west coast—and never came back."

"That's a shame. You don't see them much?"

"A few times a year. Holidays mostly. I wish I could see them more but it's good for them to live where they do. Why would any young person want to live here when they can live in Boston or Seattle or New York?"

"I like it here. I prefer the quiet, small-town life."

"That would be Mount St. Anne. Quiet and small. How did you end up here? You've been a lot of places. Why here?"

"The job. When I left the Army, I looked around for a PT position and found this one."

"I'm glad you did."

"Why, thank you, Jeremy. I'm glad I did, too."

"Do you ever miss the Army?"

"Sometimes. I knew a lot of great people in the Army. I know we did important work." A frown crossed Tasha's face. "For a long time, I thought the Army was the perfect place for me." She shook her head. "But I was wrong and now I'm here."

"I'm sorry it didn't work out the way you hoped. But you served your country and that's important. Thank you for your service." As soon as I said it, I knew it was the wrong thing to say. Tasha's face grew dark, her eyes hardened. She stared intently at me. I expected her to cuss me out or something.

"Don't thank me. Save it for the men and women who were in the real battles. I was just a medic doing my job."

"I'm sure you were more than *just* anything. Especially to those boys you took care of."

"Maybe. I loved every one of those young men - and women. I didn't know most of their names or where they were from. I only knew they were brave and selfless, and they were bleeding. I did what I could. Then they were taken away to real hospitals with real nurses. Most of them made it. Some didn't. A lot of the ones who made it lost limbs. Too many have scars no one will ever see."

I didn't know what to say. I felt guilty. I was one of the people whose freedom those soldiers were supposedly sent to the other side of the world to fight for. I was never sure how my freedoms were threatened by small, poor countries thousands of miles away. But so many men and women sacrificed for that cause, it would be cruel to minimize their mission.

"I'm sorry. I shouldn't have brought this up."

"It's OK, Jeremy. It's good for me to talk about the Army. It lets me remember the important things we did. It helps me get past the bad stuff that happened there."

"I really cannot imagine how horrible war must be."

"No one can until they've lived it. But war is war. It's a price brave people are willing to pay to protect our freedom." Tasha's jaw clenched. A vein throbbed in her neck. "But there are other terrible things that can happen. And not everything involves the enemy and grand political purposes." She pushed her chair back. "I need to go. Next appointment in five minutes."

Caring Conversation
and the Clown in the Wrong Room

"I don't care anymore." I was tired and grouchy. Bartholomew looked at me over the newspaper he was reading while we killed time in my room. I should have been in a better mood. Dr. Akufo removed my cast that morning. My leg was fully liberated. I could scratch what itched. My life should have been roses.

"What brought that on?"

"The world is falling apart, and I just don't care. It's my superpower. Not caring lets me rise above the crap and sleep comfortably at night."

"Do you sleep comfortably?"

"No, of course not. The world is screwed up. I wake up at three every night and lie there for an hour staring at the ceiling and thinking about how badly we screwed up the world."

"So, you do care."

"I don't want to care. I can't do anything about insane politicians, or muddle-headed sycophants who believe anything they say. I can't do anything to stop global warming. I can't do anything about structural racism, women's rights to their own bodies, refugees in the Middle East, or terrorist groups in Africa. I donate to the right organizations. I vote appropriately in every election. I really can't do anything more. So, why do I wake up at three every night worrying about abortion rights or elections in some shithole rural state I'll never live in?"

"I wake up at three every night because I have to pee."

"Hell, I have to pee, too. But after I pee, I end up staring into the dark and fretting about the world. Why? Why do I care? My own life is pretty good. In fact, it's damn good. I'll never need an abortion. I'll never fight in some moronic war defending corporate interests. I'll never have to swim across the Mediterranean looking for a safe home. I'll never be shot for driving while Black. I have it made. So, why do I care?"

"Probably a character flaw. I'm sure there's a drug for that."

"There is. Bourbon. But you need so much the cure is worse than the disease."

"I was thinking Prozac. Your problem is you're depressed."

"I'm not depressed. I'm pissed. I'm pissed that the world is so fucked up when it is so easy to fix. We just don't want to fix anything. In fact, powerful forces win when the world loses."

"Depressed, pissed, and paranoid. You definitely need Prozac."

"I need Bourbon."

A clown with balloons and a large paper bag stuck his head through the door to my room. I was happy for the interruption.

"You don't look like Manuelita Cortez," the clown deadpanned through his face paint.

"Wrong room, buddy," I said.

"Sorry," the clown said backing quickly and pulling the balloons through the door.

"Not a very good job with the make-up," Bartholomew observed, "Amateur."

"Obviously. But I'm sure Manuelita will be happy to see him. Remember when you came to the girls' birthday party as Bobo?" Bartholomew had been going through a dry spell in his acting career and started a side business as a professional clown named Bobo. Most of his paying gigs were birthday parties for spoiled rich kids. His appearance at the girls' party was a charity performance.

"I couldn't forget if I tried. I thought I was giving the girls a nice present by showing up at the party as Bobo."

"Yeah, it was a nice thought...."

My Unremarkable Life
The Girls' Tenth Birthday

The country was looking forward to celebrating its two-hundredth birthday in a few months. Back then we still had a few things most Americans could agree on - mindless fireworks, burned hot dogs, cheap beer, and lots of Sousa marching music, among them. Oh, and any excuse for a party.

I had sixteen ten-year-old kids in my backyard celebrating my girls' tenth birthday. Goldie made one of her rare appearances, flying in from California or Belize or wherever she and Cliff were living then. Cliff was off climbing some obscure mountain in British Columbia so Goldie was on her own. The girls were happy to see her. Me? Not so much. She barely spoke to me whenever she visited the girls. We just didn't have anything in common. Except the girls, of course, and she wasn't all that interested in talking about them. But she made the effort to come here for their birthday and I had to respect that.

The noise level from the kids approached the fireworks from Boston Harbor but several excruciating octaves higher. Goldie and a few mothers were sitting together in a huddle of lawn chairs smoking cigarettes and sipping beers. A long folding table was beside them. It was covered in a pink paper table cloth with sixteen paper plates and a large sheet cake. I tried to keep an eye on the screaming tribe of small banshees while snatching furtive glimpses of Marianne Waverly's short skirt and long legs which she crossed and recrossed often. Every time I glanced her way, she was smiling at me. If Goldie noticed, she didn't give any indication she cared. We hadn't been together for years by then. Thankfully.

Marianne Waverly was one of Goldie's old high school friends. Of course, she was way out of my class. I doubt she knew I existed back then, She had been homecoming queen and had a reputation as a world-class flirt. She still looked incredible and her reputation for sexual adventure had only grown. Her former state champion weightlifter husband had a reputation for jealousy and taking it out on anyone he thought was ogling his wife. Fortunately, he wasn't there, but I knew better than to give Mrs. Waverly any indication of interest. But, damn, she was hot and the temptation was killing me. I looked at those tanned legs one more time and she winked at me then turned to the other mothers quietly talking among themselves, oblivious to the noise and to the sexual tension.

My head pounded. I was trying to open one of the new "childproof" bottles of aspirin while holding a can of Schlitz under my arm when the scream-level of the party went to rock concert levels. Coming around the side of the house was Bartholomew as Bobo the Clown with two ponies decked out like unicorns from a Disney movie. The kids went nuts. I felt bad for my friend. Bartholomew's acting career had gone nowhere after his short appearance on Star Trek. He still responded to every cattle call for auditions for television and film roles, but he never seemed to get anything other than non-speaking parts where his handsome face would appear in a scene with the speaking stars. Nothing with a credit. Nothing that paid enough to live on. So he started a business as Bobo the Rent-A-Clown. It paid the rent.

The girls swarmed the unicorns like a cloud of horseflies. The ponies snorted. Bartholomew, flustered by the onslaught of sugar-hyped ten-year-olds, held his arms out to try to block the girls from the animals. It was hopeless. The girls blew right past him.

The ponies looked bored, or maybe sedated. They barely responded to the dozens of sticky hands patting their sides and caressing their necks. "Whoa, girls! Let the little unicorns get into the yard before you scare them. Back off, kids! Back off!" Bartholomew shouted but couldn't be heard over the din. He swatted hands away from the ponies but they came back like horseflies do. Even through his heavy make-up I could see his face flush. His eyes bugged out when one girl grabbed a pony's mane and tried to climb on.

"Back off girls, C'mon, back off, girls! Girls! Girls! GIRLS! GODDAMNIIT, BACK THE FUCK OFF!"

Everything went silent. The words echoed around the neighborhood. A flock of birds flew out of the arborvitae and flapped silently away. The girls stared open-mouthed at the clown. The mothers gaped, smoke curling from their cigarettes. The silence felt like a frozen moment in time. Then the ice broke. Some of the girls screamed. Some cried. My three girls snickered and pointed their fingers at Bartholomew. The mothers yelled. Mrs. Waverly smiled and nodded at me. Bartholomew looked at me with a look of horror juxtaposed on his absurd smiley clown face, I couldn't help it. I laughed. I mean I laughed hard. I laughed so hard I thought I was going to blow Schlitz out my nose. The mothers turned their attention away from the scrum at the ponies and watched me laugh so hard I had my hands on my knees. When I looked up at them and tried to speak, Mrs. Waverly crossed her legs and gave a little wave. The woman was shameless. I raised my hands in feigned surrender trying to indicate my apology for Bobo's flagrant offense. As soon as I did, I realized it looked like a surrender to Mrs. Waverly. In fact, it was. But that is another story. This is a story about the girls' birthday party.

In the midst of all the commotion, Angelica, Mrs. Waverly's brat of a daughter, lit a pack of firecrackers left over from last year's Fourth and tossed it under the ponies. Both animals reared up like the Lone Ranger's Silver and bolted across the yard knocking over girls, folding chairs, and anything else in their way. Bartholomew took off after the ponies with a herd of girls chasing behind. My backyard is not that large and it is mostly surrounded by a tall hedgerow. The ponies broke for the only opening in the far corner. Bartholomew cut an angle across the yard to try to head them off but he tripped over one of the girls and dove face first into the cake on the table. The table collapsed, spilling the plates, lemonade, and cake across the grass. The ponies disappeared through the opening and headed across the neighbor's yard for parts unknown. The herd of kids chased behind with Goldie and a smaller herd of mothers chasing them.

I ran to Bartholomew to see if he was hurt. He slowly raised his head and looked at me, His face was covered in pink icing and rainbow sprinkles. "I hate this fucking job," he said and wiped at the icing on his face.

"You missed a piece," I said scraping a large chunk of icing from his forehead with my finger.

A hand grabbed my hand. Mrs. Waverly was kneeling at my side. "Looks tasty," she said in her husky voice, and licked the icing from my finger. The girls had all gone. The other mothers had all gone. Bartholomew was grabbing napkins and trying to clean his face. No one saw Mrs. Waverly put my finger in her mouth and suck the icing off. She held my finger in her mouth and I felt her tongue slide up and down the length of my finger. She kept her eyes focused on mine. I don't think I was breathing. It had been more than seven years since a woman's tongue made contact with any part of me. I felt like a sixteen year-old in the backseat of his father's car. This was going to get embarrassing fast. Then she pulled her mouth off my finger making a little "pop." She winked and stood up and walked back to her chair. Bartholomew was still wiping his face and missed the whole thing.

"Where did the party go?" he asked.

I pointed to the opening which was immediately behind Mrs. Waverly. "Thataway," I rasped.

"We better get them back here," Bartholomew said jumping to his feet and charging out the opening. It took me a moment to get my shorts adjusted then I stood up and ran after him. Mrs. Waverly, sitting alone in the backyard with her long, tan legs waved as we ran by and licked icing from her middle finger.

Goldie Comes to the Hospital

I was sitting up in my bed absorbed in a copy of Lolita that Lyle had brought me. Nabokov's prose pulled me deep into his beautiful, repellant story - so deep I didn't hear the soft knock on the door. A quiet cough and a harder knock finally drew my attention.

I was sure I was hallucinating. I smelled an oddly familiar hint of lilac. A tall, lithe figure stood in my door. Her silvery white pixie haircut was new. It had a deep blue streak edging her bangs which fell over one eye. Those eyes. Green emeralds peering through mascaraed lids only slightly heavier than I remembered. No smile on her perfectly glossed lips, just a familiar pout accented with deep creases lining her lips.

"Goldie," I managed to say.

"Hello, Jeremy. Can I come in?"

I was sure my room smelled terrible. I looked terrible. Everything was terrible. She came in without waiting for an answer.

"You look…great, Jeremy. The girls told me you looked like hell. You look…yeah, you look great."

"So do you. And I'm not lying like you are. You really do look great."

I couldn't help but stare. It had been years since I last saw her. Many years. Goldie was still striking at 77. She wore a brightly colored floor-length skirt and a white peasant blouse. She showed some signs of age, of course. Her shoulders stooped slightly and the skin on her arms was thin and mottled. Her once cherubic cheeks drooped in pleated jowls. But she looked incredible. At least to my glaucomic eyes.

"You're staring."

"Sorry, I am. I can't really believe I am seeing you."

"Well, believe it." She looked around my room. "Nice place you have here."

"It's OK if you're into Eisenhower-era interior design and stunning views of garbage dumpsters. I call it home."

Goldie looked like she was already trying to find a way to leave gracefully.

"Please, sit down." I motioned to the chair nearest my bed. Goldie took an old newspaper off one of the other chairs and sat down.

"I got your card and flowers," I said. "That was nice. I didn't expect it."

Goldie continued to look around the room avoiding my eyes. "The girls told me about your accident. It was the least I could do."

It really was the least you could do, I thought, but there she was - in my room. That was not a minor thing considering she probably was on the other side of the world a few days ago.

"You came all the way here to see me?"

"I was in the area and wanted to stop by to see how you're doing."

"In the area? I thought you were living in Grenada or Kuala Lumpur or someplace like that."

"Yeah, well, I'm here now." She pulled out a cigarette.

"I don't think you're allowed to smoke in here."

"That's what I like about Grenada or Kuala Lumpur," she made finger quotes around the cities, "you can smoke anywhere and no one cares." She put her cigarette back in the pack. "Naples."

"Naples?"

"I live in Naples now. The one in Florida, not Italy. I moved there a couple years ago." Goldie finally looked at me. "Right after Cliff died."

I remembered getting the email from Goldie. I was one of about twenty people it was addressed to. Dear friends, I am sorry to tell you that Cliff died in a tragic accident in Tunisia. He was competing in a camel race with local Tauregs. As he requested in his will, there will be no memorial service. In lieu of flowers, please consider making a donation to UNICEF or the Fund to Save the Malagasy Sloth—two of Cliff's favorite causes.

Goldie

"I was sorry to hear about Cliff."

"Yeah, well, he had a good life. He died doing what he loved."

"Camel racing?"

"Living. Cliff loved living." Goldie's eyes fell from mine to her hands in her lap. "He had a good life."

"They should make a movie." It was sharper than I intended.

"Yeah, they should make a movie. The big world explorer and his travelling companion."

I thought I saw a tear in the corner of her eye. Was she sad about reliving the loss of Cliff or was she regretting being his partner all those years? Was she sorry she didn't stay with me? Was she second-guessing her whole life and wondering whether she made a mistake those decades ago when she left me for Cliff?

"The best thing I ever did was hooking my wagon to Cliff. I know you don't understand that."

"I don't understand anything you do. Never did. After all these years, you don't need to explain yourself. I know I'll never know who you are."

Goldie stared out the window watching a worker toss plastic garbage bags into one of the dumpsters. Without taking her eyes off the busy worker, she said, "People are always looking for something in life. You keep looking and looking. You don't know what you're looking for, but you know sure as hell you won't find it in the frozen food section of the grocery store or the bucket seat of your minivan or watching the Wheel of Fortune."

"So, you found what you're looking for in Borneo or Mozambique or Bumfuck Kamchatka?"

"Maybe. Maybe I found it out there with Cliff. I don't know. But whatever it is I found, I lost it when I lost Cliff."

"So the movie has a sad ending."

"Not really. It was a pretty good movie." She laughed and dabbed at her eye with a tissue. "It was a damn amazing life." She blew her nose into the tissue. It honked like an angry duck.

"Oh, God, that was disgusting," she said, a shy smile lighting up my room. Goldie was never shy around me. "Anyway, I didn't come here to talk about life or Cliff."

"Why did you come, Goldie? It's been what, fifteen years since I last saw you? You didn't really come here just to see how I'm doing. What's up?" I was suspicious. Who wouldn't be? It was inconceivable that she would come all the way to Mount St. Anne to see me no matter how badly I'd been injured. Did she need money? Was she hoping to get into my will in case I died in the hospital?

"You're right. I came to see the girls. I know I was not much of a mother."

"No argument there."

"I said I know I wasn't a good mother."

"Or grandmother."

"Yes, or grandmother."

"Or great-grandmother."

"Oh, God. I'm a great-grandmother, aren't I?"

"Technically, yes."

"Anyway, I wanted to see my daughters. See if we can be friends. Or something."

"Better late than never. They are amazing women. I am sure you will work something out together."

"It's funny. I have had a good life—more amazing memories than ten lives should deserve. More money than I could ever spend. All because of Cliff."

"What's so funny about that?"

"I lived in fear everyday with Cliff. I was sure he would die a hundred times, two hundred. He was an adrenaline junkie and lived his life always just a misstep away from death. I never felt secure. I worried all the time. And now, when I'm seventy-seven years old and alone, I feel completely secure. I am comfortable. I'm happy." She dabbed her eyes again. "But Cliff left a big hole in my life."

"It's called loneliness," I said.

"Maybe so. Whatever it is, I want to get to know my daughters before…"

"Before it's too late?"

"When you're our age, you never know how much time you have, do you?" Goldie smiled. I thought it was an invitation

"Goldie, listen, I will be out of this place in a few weeks. Maybe we can get together and…"

Goldie cut me off with grunt and a wave of her hand. "I don't think so, Jeremy. I'm going to see the girls, spend a couple of days getting to know them—if they'll let me—then I'm going back to my pickleball court and beachside Mimosas in Florida. Alone."

"I wasn't asking you to move in. I just thought we…"

"Look, Jeremy, there is no *we*. There is only you and me. We had a brief accidental biological encounter when we were both too messed up to know what we were doing. That one minute of stupidity produced three human beings. That is the entirety of 'we.'"

Brief? One minute?

"The fact that they turned out to be such amazing people is entirely your accomplishment. You obviously were a great father. Congratulations. I mean that sincerely. Congratulations. But I just came to see how you're doing. Not to start a relationship."

I was not surprised but her curt rebuff hurt, nonetheless. I thought I was long past the stage where Goldie could cause me any pain. But Goldie was still Goldie. That's when I realized two things. One, I was better off without her and always had been. And two, I was really, really happy to see her.

"Thanks for stopping by, Goldie. It was good to see you."

Goldie stood. I noticed a slight tremor in her hands as she picked up one of the flower arrangements from the table. She read the card aloud. "*Get well, Daddy, and stay off the roof, Love, The Girls.* They call you Daddy? They must be fifty by now."

"Fifty-three."

"Fifty-three and you're still Daddy." She put the flowers down with a sigh. "That's nice. Really. That's very nice. You're a lucky man."

"I know."

She put a tentative hand on my shoulder. "You're a remarkable man, Jeremy." She bent and kissed me on the forehead. "Have a good life, Jeremy." And she was gone.

I stared at the door for a long time. Did I just dream that? That can't have been real. Goldie couldn't have just been here. She couldn't have just said I was a remarkable man. Maybe I should cut back on the meds. Then I noticed the lingering scent of lilac. I breathed it in pulling the aroma deep into my lungs. I coughed like a kid trying his first cigarette.

After I stopped coughing, I stared at the ceiling reliving the last few minutes. I heard Goldie's voice in my head: *You are a remarkable man.* Well, if it is the meds, I thought, I'm not changing my dosage.

My Unremarkable Life
Goldie Calls from Bora Bora

The phone rang early one Saturday morning. I was still in bed. The girls were in the next room sleeping. At the sound of the phone, my heart skipped a beat. The only reason someone would call me that early was bad news. I shook myself awake and picked up the receiver.

"Hi, Jeremy." The familiar voice sounded far away, fuzzy and distant.

"Goldie? Is that you? What's wrong? Where are you?"

"Nothing's wrong. I just wanted to call. I just wanted to talk to someone."

"OK, well, great. Yeah, great. I'm glad you called. Where are you?"

"Bali, I think. Or maybe Tuvalu. Some island in Indonesia."

"You can make a phone call from an island in Indonesia? This must cost a fortune."

"It's OK. Cliff has a fortune. And we're here on expense account, anyway."

"Are you OK?"

"Sure. I'm OK. Cliff is off in the jungle on another island somewhere looking for Hobbits."

I didn't know how to respond to that. I stared at the phone.

"Jeremy, are you still there?"

"Yeah, I'm here. Cliff is looking for what?"

"They call them Hobbits. Some long-lost tribe that supposedly is like a different species of humans. He's with a group from the National Geographic trying to prove the Hobbits exist."

I felt a pang of jealously. My life was all about groceries and housekeeping and raising three Hobbits of my own. No jungles. No National Geography. No exotic tropical island. No expense account.

"Are you still there, Jeremy?"

"Yeah. Sounds like Cliff is doing very well. You must be happy."

"Of course, I'm happy. Why wouldn't I be happy?"

"I'm happy you're happy."

"You don't sound happy. You don't sound like you believe me. I am happy, Jeremy. I'm sitting on a deck overlooking a beautiful lagoon drinking Mai Tais at this all-inclusive resort. It's paradise, Jeremy, and I don't care if you don't think I'm happy. Because I am."

"I am really truly happy for you, Goldie. And for Cliff."

"Bullshit, Jeremy, you think I'm not happy. You think I called you because I'm lonely and miserable."

"I don't think that at all, Goldie. But, um, why did you call me?"

The line was quiet except for the fuzzy buzz sound of 10,000 miles of copper wire.

"Goldie? You still there?"

"Yes."

"So, why did you call?"

"I don't know. Maybe it was a mistake. I was just feeling happy and wanted to talk with someone."

"When will you be back here? The girls miss you, you know."

"I don't know. Cliff said we could be here for months. Then he's supposed to go to someplace in Africa and look for some endangered monkeys or rhinos or something. He wants me to come with him there, too." I heard her sigh. "It's very exciting, you know."

"I'm sure it is." She was miserable. I was tempted to rub it in. She deserved to be unhappy, damn it. "I hope everything works out well for you and Cliff. Send us a post card sometime. The girls would like that."

"OK, thanks. I'll do that. I better go now. This call is costing a fortune."

"I'm glad Cliff can afford it. It was good to talk with you."

"Yeah, tell the girls I…"

"I think I lost you, Goldie. What did you say?"

"Tell the girls I…just tell them their Mom said 'hi'."

"Goodbye, Goldie." I hung up. *Tell the girls 'hi'?*

As if on cue, the door to my bedroom opened and three seven-year-olds crashed into my room and jumped on my bed. "Who was that Daddy?"

"It was Mommy. She's on the other side of the world. She just called to tell me to tell you she loves you."

"She's with Cliff, isn't she?"

"Yes, she is with Cliff. She is happier with him. It's good for all of us."

"Let's make pancakes for breakfast!"

"With chocolate chips."

"And Bosco!"

The girls ran out of my room heading for the kitchen. I once again marveled at their resiliency. How did I ever deserve such incredibly stable, well-adjusted children? Maybe it was just chance—a regression to the mean given the lunatic parents they had.

Acropolites
On Marriage

The Four Horsemen of the Acropolis were gathered in the hospital cafeteria enjoying bad coffee and good pie. It was the day after Goldie's visit.

"Goldie was actually here?" Junior asked shaking his head in disbelief, "That's quite a surprise."

"A shock, actually," I said, "It's the first time she's been back home in years. She still looks good for an old broad."

"How is she doing?" Lyle asked, "I mean, with Cliff gone and everything."

"I think she may be a little lonely right now. They were together a long time."

Junior sighed. "It's hard when you lose your life partner. I feel for her."

"She was with Cliff for more than fifty years," Bartholomew said, "I never got the impression they were all that close. I mean let's face it, Cliff was a self-centered thrill-seeker and Goldie never seemed to have a romantic bone in her body. I wonder what they had in common that kept them together so long."

"Cliff probably liked having a beautiful wife to travel the world with," Lyle said.

"And Goldie probably liked the free ticket out of Mount St. Anne," Bartholomew added, "Not to mention the chance to see places most of us only read about."

"But that's not enough to stay together fifty years," Lyle said.

"You know, they could have loved each other." Junior sipped his coffee. His comment sat on the table like a stale donut waiting for someone to take a bite.

After an empty moment, I bit. "That doesn't sound right, but who knows what's going on in the head of anyone else, especially those two?"

"How about you and Daisy, Junior," Bartholomew asked, "How did your marriage last fifty years?"

"Fifty-two. And to answer your question, it was compromise. We learned to compromise. If I wanted to paint the bedroom beige and she wanted to paint it green, we would compromise and paint it green. If I wanted to go to the mountains for vacation and Daisy wanted to go to the shore, we compromised and went to the shore. See, that's how you make a marriage work, you compromise."

"I don't think that's…" Lyle started to respond but Junior cut him off.

"And chores. We divided up the chores fairly. When she cooked, I did the dishes. And when I cooked, I did the dishes. That's called sharing duties."

"Well…"

Junior interrupted Lyle again. "And then there's learning to understand one another. Like when your wife asks you what you want to do for dinner. You have to understand that she doesn't actually care what you want to do for dinner. She wants you to guess what she wants to do for dinner. But she doesn't even know what she wants to do for dinner. That makes it tricky. *Let's go to the Steak House. No, I'm not in the mood for steak. Then let's go to J.P.'s. No, that place is always too loud. OK, well how about Thai food? Too spicy. Seafood? We had salmon last night. Maybe we should just stay home and order Chinese. That's a great idea.* Of course, I didn't really want Chinese. But see, that's what love is all about."

"Well, I've only been married twenty years, you know," Lyle said. "It is different when you marry in your late fifties. For Barb and me, it's a partnership—like a business merger. She's a CPA, you know. We have shared assets and individual assets. We negotiate everything. We maintain a mental balance sheet of our relationship. So far, the assets exceed the liabilities, so we have positive net equity. That's good enough to get us through another year."

"Sounds romantic," Bartholomew said, "Like my relationship with my agent."

"Yeah, but I hope you're not having sex with your agent at 10:30 every other Saturday evening."

"You know my agent. Would you have sex with him?"

"God no. He's a Republican."

"Hey, watch it. I'm a Republican," Bartholomew said.

"I wouldn't have sex with you, either. Besides, you aren't a real Republican. You just never bothered to change your registration."

"True." Bartholomew forked the last of his pie into his mouth. "Listening to you two, I think maybe I made the right decision to be a bachelor my whole life. I had plenty of companions without the hassle of actually living with someone."

"That's not what we meant, is it, Lyle?" Junior said, "Being married to Daisy was the most important part of my life. Hell, it was my life. I loved her every day and still do."

"To be honest," Lyle said, "there are times when I do think I'd be better off not married. But inertia keeps us going and sometimes it's actually pretty nice waking up beside someone or sitting together on the patio with a glass of wine watching the sunset. Marriage has its moments."

"I was officially married for ten months so I have nothing of value to add to this conversation," I said. "But I will say that seeing Goldie yesterday dredged up some long-lost memories. Of course, none of them involved sharing a glass of wine watching the sunset or sex every other Saturday. Mostly they're just me remembering watching her paint her toenails or staring at her legs while she did yoga in the living room. I remember her being so awkward trying to feed the babies. No breast-feeding for Goldie. She had enough trouble feeding one baby a bottle while I fed the others." I had been over Goldie for a long time. Sitting with the guys and talking about marriage, I realized I was still over her. She wasn't evil. But she was a bad wife and worse mother. I will forever be grateful for the gift she gave me of three beautiful daughters. And for walking away from my life as soon as she did.

My Unremarkable Life
Camping

When the girls were twelve years old, they were starting to get completely incomprehensible to me. They were absorbed with clothes, make-up, the Bee Gees, and some really ugly dolls called Cabbage Patch Kids. The girls said the dolls were a good investment. I was concerned they were becoming too materialistic. I decided to take them for a weeklong camping trip. I recruited Junior to come with me to provide reinforcements. The morning we started the sun was shining, birds were singing, a gentle warm breeze drifted through the trees around our house. A perfect day for camping. We loaded the station wagon with enough gear, food, and clothing to equip a small army for a month and headed to Kentucky. Five hours later we drove into Boone State Park, giant white thunderhead clouds catching the late afternoon sunrays high into the sky.

"Look, Daddy," one of the girls said, "Dunderheads!" Family joke. The first time I explained thunderhead clouds to the girls, I had a bad sinus infection. Long after understanding the correct pronunciation, the girls loved to remind me of that fatherly teaching moment so long ago. The joke never got old. At least not for the girls. "We're going to have a dunderstorm, Daddy!" The girls were hilarious. Of course, the joke was on all of us. We packed everything except raincoats and umbrellas.

Without boys or other girls to worry about, the girls became children again. They ran around the campsite looking for creepy-crawlies under rocks and decaying logs while Junior and I dragged the heavy canvas tent out of the back of the wagon and across the sandy site to a flat area nestled among several serviceberry trees. The tent was thick canvas and weighed at least a hundred pounds. It was large enough to sleep ten people. We rolled the tent out and staked the four corners into the sand.

"OK, girls," I called, "a little help here." They dropped their bugs and worms and whatever else they had squirming in their hands and ran over to us. Junior and I placed the two longest poles into the grommets at each end of the tent. While we held the poles up, the girls used rocks to stake out the guy ropes.

"Just like the circus," Junior said admiring the girls' efficiency.

"But no elephants," one of the girls said as she concentrated on her target. We quickly erected the four corner poles and two more poles on the sides of the tent. Finally, we added two more poles to hold up the canopy at the front of the tent. By the time we pulled all the ropes tight, the sun was setting behind the ridge across the lake. The tent looked like a baggy green hovel that would have embarrassed the worst unit in Custer's army. Nothing like the sharp, roomy display tent they had at the store where I bought it. It was our home now, though. It would have to do.

Junior and I set up five Army surplus cots in the back half of the tent. We reserved the front half for beach equipment and space for games if it rained. The girls grabbed their sleeping bags and duffels from the car and disappeared into the back of the tent. Junior and I set up a folding aluminum table under the canopy. We set our cookstove and kitchen box full of pans, plastic dishes, mismatched silverware, and coffee cups on the table and started to make dinner. The first rumble of thunder rolled in, still far enough away not to raise the alarm but close enough to get our attention. The menu was supposed to be boiled hot dogs and instant macaroni and cheese. A drizzle began to fall, pooling in the saggy roof and canopy. More thunder rolled across the lake and through the trees. The rain began to pick up. Slow drips fell under the canopy.

"Daddy," one of the girls called from inside the tent, "it's raining in here." I ducked inside and found the girls standing under different drips trying to catch the water in their mouths. A fourth drip fell unmolested onto the canvas floor. We repurposed the cook pots and our only frying pan to catch the water and keep the tent dry, leaving us with nothing to cook dinner in. So, dinner that night was peanut butter and jelly sandwiches served under the canopy with rain falling and lightning flashing and dunder pounding in our ears. The girls were happy.

The rain continued all evening. We went to bed early hoping for better weather in the morning. Sometime late that night, I had to get up to pee. I sat up on my cot and put my bare feet into two inches of ice-cold water. I rifled around to find my flashlight dropping it into the water.

"Shit," I hissed.

"Daddy!" one of the girls said reprimanding my language.

"What's up?" Junior asked from the other side of the dark tent.

"We're flooded," I said and splashed my feet in the water to emphasize the point. "I dropped my flashlight." At that point I was temporarily blinded by a bright white light. "Aim that somewhere else," I hissed. One of the girls quickly turned the flashlight to the water on the floor.

"Uh oh," she said quietly.

"Uh oh, is right," I said as two more flashlights came on showing the full tragedy. Shoes and flipflops were floating in the water. Backpacks and duffels were absorbing water soaking their contents.

"Good thing we have cots," said one of the girls, "I'm going back to sleep." Her flashlight went dark.

"That's probably the best plan. If the water gets up to the top of the cots, we'll worry then about what to do," Junior said trying to keep the atmosphere light. I still had to pee, though, so I waded out the tent and relieved myself on the other side of the campsite. It was relatively dry there. In fact, as I looked around the site, the only place with water was the tent. We had pitched the tent in a shallow bowl that slowly filled with cold rainwater.

The next morning the sun was shining in a cobalt blue sky. A warm breeze blew down the lake and across our site. We had clothes, blankets, towels, and backpacks hanging on ropes and tree branches all around out site. The girls were happily wading in the lake trying to catch minnows and crayfish with a small net and an empty coffee can. Junior and I sat in folding chairs sipping hot coffee.

"What the hell is that?" Junior asked pointing toward a large mountain laurel whose gnarly branches roped around one side of a boulder. I looked in the direction he pointed. I didn't see anything. Then the branches of the rhododendron shook. Something was in the bush. "Is it a bear?" whispered Junior. I glanced to see that the girls were well away from the bush focused on their aquatic safari.

"No, too small. It's probably a…" Before I could say "raccoon" a raccoon jumped out of the bush onto the top of the rock and stared at us. My initial thought was "Ha, I was right! Do I know my wilderness or what?" My second thought was, "Why is that animal staring at us? He looks angry." My third thought was "Get a stick, that sucker looks dangerous!" That particular thought came out loud. Junior and I both grabbed the largest sticks from our pile of firewood. Since we had burned most of the good stuff already, the best weapons we had left were thin sticks especially reserved to cook marshmallows—twisted pieces of wood maybe three feet long and less than half an inch across. The raccoon stood up on its hind legs and hissed at us. We leaped to our feet wielding our weapons like Erroll Flynn ready to do battle with the Black Knight.

Junior waved his sword back and forth. "Git! Go on! Git or I'll hurt you," he said sounding uncertain. The animal stopped hissing and turned his beady eyes on Junior. It grinned. Well, maybe it didn't grin. Maybe it just bared its teeth. But it sure looked like it grinned, like it was amused at these silly humans with their marshmallow swords. Like it was pitying our ridiculous hope that we could somehow defeat him. Then the grin left his face and he dropped to all four legs. He crouched down.

"He's gonna charge!" Junior said backing up a step.

"I don't think raccoons charge people," I said trying to de-escalate the situation. "He's probably just trying to scare us away."

"It's working." The raccoon shook its rear end like a dog getting ready to leap but just then the girls walked into camp oblivious to the life-and-death stand-off playing out before them.

"Oh, look!" cried one of the girls. "A cute little raccoon! Look at his little face. What a handsome little animal you are, Mr. Raccoon. Can we keep him, Daddy?"

The raccoon relaxed and sat back on its haunches. It cocked its head to one side and studied the girls.

"No, we can't keep him, honey, he's a wild animal. He lives here."

"He's wild, alright," Junior said with his marshmallow sword still held at a defensive angle. "Wild and mean. Look at him, he wants to kill us."

The girls gave Junior a sympathetic smile. At twelve years old, my girls could be incredibly condescending when faced with what they considered ignorance or naivete. "I don't think he wants to kill us," one of them said. "I think maybe we're camping too close to his house," said another. "He's just telling us to stay on our side of that rock and we can all live happily as neighbors," said the third who reached into a pocket and proceeded to step toward the animal holding out a hand full of Skittles. "We come in peace, Mr. Raccoon," she said softly.

I jumped up and ran toward her before she got in range of the raccoon's sharp teeth and claws. "Stop!" I yelled, "He'll bite you! You could get rabies." The raccoon sat quietly watching the exchange between crazed father and whispering daughter.

"It won't hurt us," said one of the other girls. "Just look at it. It likes us. As long as we stay on this side of the rock." The raccoon seemed to nod its head. It sat up like a large prairie dog and watched the girls.

"Maybe it does like us, but don't feed it. That's dangerous and, besides, we're in a state park, you aren't allowed to feed the animals in a state park." That stopped the girls. They were fearless and always did have a way with animals. But they were also sticklers for rules. If feeding animals in the state park was against the rules, they wouldn't feed animals.

"Sorry, Mr. Raccoon. It's against the rules. But we promise to stay away from your home. We won't come on your side of the rock. Is that OK?"

The raccoon sat back down and seemed to ponder the girls' offer. It made a decision. It hopped off the back of the rock and disappeared into the rhododendron. The girls divvied up the Skittles. They looked at Junior and me for the first time standing with our sabers ready to do battle. "Oh boy! We're going to roast marshmallows!" They looked around the camp. "So, where's the fire?"

A Flower for Samantha
and Jeremy's Heart Problem

Samantha sat on her bed cross-legged cradling Bear in her arms. She was wearing a pale blue hospital gown. Her T-shirt and cut-off blue jeans sat neatly folded on the end of her bed. She wasn't in a hurry to get dressed. She looked serene - if a ten-year-old can actually look serene. Her bright eyes shone as she stared down at Bear and cooed soft assurances. Her face was filled with warmth, love for her Bear. I could imagine Monica with the same look holding Samantha as a baby soothing her with words of comfort, telling her the world was beautiful and her life was destined to be filled with love. It nearly broke my heart. In that moment, Samantha was the most beautiful child I had ever seen - an angel for sure.

Without taking her eyes off Bear, she quietly asked, "Jeremy, what do you think happens to people after they die?" I wasn't sure I heard her. Or rather, I heard her clearly but I hoped I heard her wrong. I was not prepared for that question even though I knew she had to be pondering it for a while. I'd been thinking about death a lot myself. How could I not? I mean I was seventy-seven years old. I was in a hospital surrounded by sick and dying people. I lay awake nights trying to get in touch with that soul the preacher talked about when I was a kid and still went to church occasionally. But it just wasn't there. Much as I wish it were different, it just wasn't there. All we have is the spark that burns as long as our body lives. When the body dies, we are dead. There it is. The Big Sleep and no dreams. No nightmares. No nothing. Das Nicht. All is dark. But I can't say that to a child who knows she will die soon. But what can you say about death when you promised to never lie to her? I didn't say anything. After a moment, she looked up and stared at me with a look of pure innocence. "I want to know. What do you think happens after people die?"

My mind cramped up like a charley horse. It hurt. What did I think happened to people after they die? Nothing. That's what I thought. Nothing. You just die and it's all over. You're gone. You are in the universe for a while then you aren't anymore. Just like before you were born. All is black. Your body rots and disintegrates until each atom and molecule becomes the stardust that existed before it became you. There is nothing after death. That's what I thought happens to people. I promised I would never lie to her.

"They go to heaven," I said. "They go to heaven where all dogs are friendly and vegetables taste like chocolate pudding and it's never too hot or too cold. That's what I think happens to people after they die."

She cocked her head and thought a moment. "I don't think I believe you, but it would be nice." She carefully laid Bear on her pillow and pulled the blanket to its chin. Still tucking the blanket around Bear, she said, "Mom can't talk about this with me. It makes her cry too much. I don't want to make her sad, so I don't talk about it." She smoothed the blanket and turned her full attention to me. "Nobody really knows what happens after we die, do they? I mean, no one can be sure, can they?"

"No, Samantha. I think you're right. I don't think anyone knows. But I do think the world is good. I am sure that whatever comes next will be OK. It will be fine." That much was the truth. That really is what I believed.

"Yeah, that's what I think, too. It's why I am sad I am going to die soon but I'm not afraid. It will be fine. For me, anyway. I know Mom will be sad. That's what I'm saddest about." She slid off the bed and wrapped her arms around my neck. "Thanks, Jeremy. I know you don't really think vegetables will taste like chocolate." She kissed my cheek then waved toward the door. "Now I need to get dressed." I had been dismissed.

As I wheeled my chair out of Samantha's room and down the hall, my heart felt like a bag of sand had been laid on it. I was surprised by the physical reaction to my conversation with Samantha. My heart literally hurt. I became short of breath and light-headed. My hands tingled. I stopped my chair and held tight onto the arms while the painful sensation rippled through my body. Then just as quickly as the feeling came on, it passed. None of the busy people in the hallway seemed to have noticed. The whole episode probably lasted only a few seconds. I shook it off as a foolish old man's overreaction to a young girl's tragedy and slowly wheeled myself back to my room.

My Unremarkable Life
The Girls Learn To Drive

"**N**ow let the clutch out slowly until you feel the car start to move."

CHUNKACHUNKACHUNKA. Stall.

"Slowly!" I said through clenched teeth. "You have to let the clutch out slowly."

"But, Daddy, it's hard." It was 1982. The girls were sixteen and had their learner's permits. It was the scariest time of my life.

"You're a big strong girl. You can control that pedal. Now try again. Clutch to the floor, turn the key. A little gas to get the car started. Good. Now ease the clutch out just a couple of inches."

CHUNKACHUNKACHUNKA. Stall.

"Daddy! Why can't we just get an automatic? All our friends drive automatics."

"Birdie's right, Daddy," Byrne said from the backseat. "Manual shifts are so old fashioned. Can't we learn on your Oldsmobile instead of this old junker?"

"First of all, this is not an old junker. This is a 1965 Dodge Dart with only 45,000 miles on it and in perfect shape."

"Daddy, it's older than we are!"

"And, second of all, I want to be sure you girls can drive a stick shift. One day you are going to be on a date with some guy who has had too much to drink. If he's driving a stick shift car, I want to make sure you can take his keys and drive for him. Now, Birdie, let's try again. Clutch in. Turn the key. Give a little gas. And let the clutch out slo...."

CHUNKACHUNKACHUNKA. Stall.

"Daddy! I can't do it!"

"Yes, you can, honey. Just let me get my teeth back where they belong and we'll try again."

"Daddy, you don't have false teeth."

"I know. Now let's try again."

After a few more whiplash-inducing starts, Birdie finally got the car moving. Shifting into second and third gears was easy. The car was tooling along at maybe 30 miles an hour. Birdie was grinning from ear to ear.

"I'm doing it!"

"See? You can do this, kiddo. Now slow down before you get to the end of the parking lot....Slow down, Birdie.....Use the brake pedal, Birdie....the brake!" I was slamming my foot into the floorboard. Somehow that didn't help. Birdie gave me an "oh, Daddy" smile and eased the car to a stop. She even remembered to push in the clutch.

"That was fun!" she squealed.

I rubbed a cramp in my hamstring and took a deep cleansing breath. "OK, now let's try backing up."

Soon all three girls were taking turns driving figure eights around the parking lot, head-in parking, backing up, and getting a reasonable feel of the clutch. I turned on the radio. Mick Jagger was singing "...I went down to the Chelsea drugstore..."

"Oh, Daddy, find a station that doesn't just play those old fogie songs."

Old fogie? Since when were the Stones "old fogies?" Binkie reached from the back seat and turned the dial. "OOH, the Ramones! I love the Ramones!" Birdie turned up the volume.

"Eyes on the road!" I snapped.

"Sorry, Daddy. I really like the Ramones, too."

"I am glad we have this car, Daddy," Byrne said from the back seat. "Joanie has to drive a little VW bug. The backseat is so small. And the front seats have the stick and parking brake between them. Joanie says it's almost impossible to make out at the drive-in."

"Yeah," added Binkie, "this car has a nice back seat and the bench seat up front leans back to get real comfortable. It's not big enough for a triple date like your Oldsmobile but it will be perfect for a double date. Or even just for one of us." The girls started comparing notes about which boys they wanted to take out and what movies were showing at the drive-in. I remembered my dates in high school in my mother's Nash Rambler. The seat backs could be lowered to make a bed. I never managed to get laid in the Nash but not for lack of trying. I thought about the big Oldsmobile I bought a few years ago when I started dating again. It was awkward in the car but not as awkward as if I had tried to take a date home. I knew what you could easily do in a car with comfortable bench seats. I decided I would trade the Dodge for a VW as soon as the girls got their licenses.

Doctor Visit

and Conversation about Cure

I had my one-month check-up with Dr. Akufo. I was getting used to her intimidating presence, but I still experienced a gnawing chill whenever I had to see her. Probably something to do with my deep-seated need for approval from authority figures. She removed the plastic cast and probed my upper leg and hip.

"Any pain, Mr. Moore?" she asked studying some discoloration around the incision. She removed the sutures a week ago leaving a faint zipper-line running up the outside of my thigh.

"Not really," I answered.

"Not really? What does that mean, Mr. Moore? Do you have pain or not?"

"I don't have pain. I have some discomfort. Stiff muscles, sore joints, the normal sort of pain, I guess."

Dr. Akufo made a note in her tablet. "I'm going to reduce your prescription. I want to get you off the Percocet and onto some over-the-counter analgesics."

I was happy to hear that. Junior would be, too. He was convinced the hospital wanted patients to become addicted to opiates.

"Any questions, Mr. Moore?"

"Actually, I do have a question. What do you know about Stafford's Sarcoma?"

Dr. Akufo removed her glasses and pinched the bridge of her nose. I recognized the stalling tactic. "I take it this is not a hypothetical question."

"It's not."

"You know I cannot talk about other patients."

"Yes, I know. I'm not asking about a patient. I'm asking about a disease. There isn't much on the Internet about it. Is there any chance for a cure?"

"Not much, no. It is a very rare disease. It was only identified as a separate disease a few years ago. There has been very little research on Stafford."

"I hear they have a treatment in Germany."

"Experimental treatment. Very experimental."

"But is it working?"

The doctor finished putting the plastic cast back on my leg. "The research is being done by BioNano, a private company in Stuttgart. They use the patient's own DNA to customize enzymes that can kill the cancer cells. They deliver individual molecules of the enzyme via nano tubes made from boron. It is a very complicated and expensive process with mixed result. The latest report I saw claims fifty percent efficacy in extending life expectancy by a year. A twenty percent efficacy in curing the disease." I doubted it was coincidence that she had done her own research into the disease. She patted my leg, a rare friendly touch. "I am afraid it is not going to be available for our patient, I mean American patients, for years. If ever."

After she left, I Googled BioNano. Buried in their website I found a link to a press release about Stafford and their experimental treatment. It said the company hopes in coming years to develop technology that will decrease the expense of the treatment from its current cost of "approximately one million Euros."

Too expensive, and too late, to help Samantha.

My Unremarkable Life
The Girls Off to College, Bass Fishing

The summer of 1985 was life-changing for me. Coca Cola introduced New Coke which, apparently, I was the only person who liked. I bought my first CD, beginning a complete replacement of my extensive cassette tape collection. And my girls left home for college. Their departure was traumatic for me. It was just another step toward world domination for them.

I was seeing a woman then. Ingrid was a tall, athletic Leo who had more in common with my daughters than with me. She was a vegetarian. She practiced Yoga. She was a morning person who preferred sunrises to sunsets. I liked her anyway. For a year she had been subtly suggesting she move into my house. Neither of us was interested in getting married, but I was too much of a Republican to consider living with a woman without the burden of marriage. I used the girls as my excuse for not asking Ingrid to move in. When I still didn't ask her to move in after the girls left for college, she got the message and dumped me for a personal trainer at the new Sweat and Grunt Fitness Center that opened downtown. I'm pretty sure that was the name of the place. Ingrid and I stayed friends—without benefits—until she and her buff partner left town to go to work for some goofy TV fitness guy named Richard Simmons.

One time while the girls were in college and I was feeling a little empty, I was browsing in Lyle's bookstore just killing time. I found myself leafing through some magazines—no, not *those* magazines. Outdoors magazines. I was scanning an article about professional bass fishing. Lyle was putting some new books on a shelf nearby and noticed the magazine I was reading.

"You should get a boat."

I raised my eyes from the article. "Why should I get a boat?"

"You need something to keep you busy. You've been mopey ever since the girls left."

"I am not mopey. I'm pensive, maybe. Contemplative, probably. Maybe even introspective if you want to push it. But I am not mopey."

"You still should buy a boat. You need a distraction. Tooling round the lake, water skiing, fishing...you know, the bass fishing in Carter Lake is supposed to be the best in the state. You used to like fishing." I did used to like fishing. When I was ten, back when fishing involved a can of nightcrawlers and a push-button reel that created birds' nests every other cast. I spent more time disassembling the reel and untangling line than I ever did with an actual worm in the water. But I enjoyed fishing anyway. I wanted to be Huck Finn, catching monster catfish on the Mississippi or Ernest Hemingway catching giant rainbow trout in the Pyrenees. Mostly I sat on the bank of Marley's muddy pond and, when I was lucky, caught small bluegills with their spiky dorsal fins.

"I don't know. A boat is kind of a big investment. Seems self-indulgent. Besides, where would I keep it? I don't have room for a boat and trailer at my house."

"You can keep it in my lot behind the store. Plenty of room and it's safe." Lyle took the magazine from my hand. "Look at this." He pointed to a picture of a high-powered bass boat skimming across the water, barely touching the surface. It was almost flying. "Wouldn't this be great? We could bomb around the lake or dodge barges on the Ohio. We could take a cooler of beer and spend the day fishing. We'd have a ball in a boat like this."

"We?"

"Tell you what. How about if we buy a boat together? We could go halfsies. It'd be great."

And, so, much to my surprise, two weeks later I found myself carrying an armload of brand new fishing rods, nets, and tackle boxes onto our brand new Skeeter bass boat trailered to the back of my car. It was a beautiful craft. Deep red with silver speckles and deep undertones that seemed to change color every time you looked. A 150-horsepower Yamaha outboard motor. Pedestal seats in the front and rear. Foot-controlled trolling motor. High capacity live well for the giant bass we were destined to catch. It was my new love.

Lyle followed behind with a cooler full of beer and sandwiches. We loaded everything into the boat and headed for the lake. Everything went fine while we were going forward but it got a little dicey when it was time to back the trailer down the boat ramp. I probably should have practiced that before getting in line with about a dozen other boat owners waiting their turn at the ramp. I had backed a trailer before. When the girls were small, I dug up all the junipers and azalea bushes around my house. They had grown ugly and out of control (the bushes, not the girls) and I decided to yank them all out. I rented a chainsaw and an open-deck trailer to haul the shrubs away. Backing up came to me naturally—just look out the back window and make adjustments to the steering wheel as needed. Somehow my brain just knew what to do. I always had excellent spatial reasoning skills. I also always had a severe case of stage fright. My brain would shut down if people were watching.

As soon as I pulled up to the end of the line, a behemoth of a pick-up truck pulled in behind me. The grill on the black monster grinned menacingly in my mirror. Behind the truck a huge cabin cruiser loomed high above the truck's cab. The truck's engine idled with a deep, feral growl.

I watched as each driver ahead of me confidently pulled his vehicle and trailer around to line up with the ramp then, some with an arm across the back of the car seat and their eyes focused through the back window of the vehicle, others using their mirrors, smoothly back the trailer down the ramp and into the water. It looked easy. I was starting to sweat.

As we moved steadily toward the front of the line, I kept glancing at the monster in my mirror. I was reminded of the movie about the killer semi chasing those people down the highway. Apparently, the driver of this truck spent his weekends driving an aircraft carrier around Carter Lake. Behind him the line of trucks and cars with trailers continued to grow.

I became more and more convinced this was going to end badly. What the hell was I thinking? I can't back up a damn trailer. Not with a bunch of guys who are all obviously experts in line behind me watching. Especially Bigfoot behind me. Then it was our turn.

"This should be fun," Lyle said.

My mouth was dry. My stomach hurt. I wanted to pull the car around and just keep going. Maybe the boat dealer would give us our money back. Buying this boat was the dumbest thing I ever did.

"We're up!" Lyle pointed ahead. "Let's show these guys how it's done."

"I'm pretty sure I'm going to show them something." I snapped my neck around to relieve some nervous tension and felt a sharp twinge. I sat there for a moment feeling the muscle in my neck spasm. A horn honked.

"Better go," Lyle said. "The crowd is getting restless."

I slowly eased the car forward, turned a sharp right to bring the boat around behind, and pulled up until the trailer was pointing at the water. I reached for the back of the seat and turned to look out the rear window. Someone stuck a knife in my neck. "I can't turn around. Lyle, you need to do this."

"No way, Jose! This is your car. You drive. Besides, I can't drive a clutch." I silently cursed Lyle's father for his serious dereliction of his fatherly duty. "Use the mirrors. Lots of guys use the mirrors. I was watching."

Now, if you've ever backed a car up with a trailer on it, you know that the rules of Euclidean geometry don't apply. Left is not left. Right is not right. Every little move is amplified a hundred times and always in the wrong direction. Complicate that with having to do everything through mirrors which distort time and space into a Lewis Carroll hallucination-infested world, and I was doomed.

Through the rearview mirror I could see the top of the outboard lined up perfectly with the middle of the ramp. Just back up straight. Don't move anything. Easy does it. I started to back the car slowly. Immediately the outboard motor and the rest of the boat and trailer began a sharp turn to the left. Or right. In the mirror I couldn't tell which was which. I turned the steering wheel sharply to left or right—suddenly meaningless terms—and the boat swung even sharper to the left or right. I slammed on the brakes before the entire outfit jack-knifed.

"Pull forward and try again," Lyle said. "Just turn the wheel the other way next time."

I didn't want to look at the guy in the big truck. I could imagine him laughing then pushing my car and trailer into the trees beside the ramp like a snowplow clearing the lot. I pulled forward to line up the boat and tried again. This time the back of the boat began moving to the other right-left-whatever side. I knew what to do! I moved the steering the same direction I did last time. I figured out it would bring the trailer back to center. Instead, the trailer swung wildly off line.

"What happened?" I yelled, "I moved the steering wheel the same direction!"

"I think you were holding the top of the steering wheel last time."

"Are you kidding me?" I was becoming desperate. "It matters whether I hold the top or bottom of the steering wheel?"

"Apparently it does."

I glanced at the giant black truck. "I can't do this, Lyle. Let's go home. Let's sell this damn boat and go home." Then the driver's door on the black truck opened.

"Oh, shit. The guy is getting out of his truck. He probably has a gun. He's probably going to shoot me for being an idiot." But it wasn't a guy. A petite young woman in cut-off jeans and a halter top climbed down from the truck. She had a wild mane of blonde hair and large hoop earrings. She walked up to my side of the car and tapped on the window. I rolled it down

"Hello," she said, an amused grin on her face. "New boat?" she asked pointing to the trailer with her chin.

"Um, yeah. Just bought it yesterday."

"I guessed. Move over, let me do this for you." Not waiting for an answer, she opened the door.

"Go on, move over. I'll show you how to do this. It isn't hard once you learn the trick."

I slid over near Lyle who hadn't taken his eyes off our pretty new driver. She got in and adjusted the seat so her feet could reach the pedals. She adjusted the rearview mirror.

"This is how you do it." She pulled the car forward to straighten out the trailer. "Grab the bottom of the steering wheel like this, see. Then look over your shoulder and watch the back of the boat."

"I messed up my neck. I can't turn around."

"No matter. Just use your mirrors. Whichever direction you want the back of the boat to go, that's the direction you move your hand."

"But I keep getting my left and right confused."

"I noticed." She nodded to the line of vehicles waiting to put their boats in. "We all noticed. But it doesn't matter. Don't even think about left and right. Just look at the back of the boat and move the bottom of the steering wheel in the direction you want it to go. Go slow and easy and make tiny adjustments and you'll get your boat in the water just fine. Like that."

The trailer was half in the lake and the back of the boat was rocking slightly on the water.

She got out of the car. "Now one of you just ease that boat over to the dock there and you'll be ready to go."

I slid back behind the steering wheel, my knees protruding on either side. "Thank you. Thanks for saving me from a potentially fatal bout of embarrassment."

"No problem. Everyone is a rookie once. Next time, you may want to practice a bit before you come out on a weekend. This is not a good time for amateurs to be clogging up the process."

With that, she jogged back to her truck and climbed in. Lyle ran after her and handed her something through the truck window and jogged back to the car.

"Ahoy, Cap'n, I'll meet you at the dock." Lyle unhooked the boat from the trailer, climbed over the front of the boat and used the trolling motor to back away.

I pulled the car up the ramp and headed for the parking lot. I heard applause from the people in line.

"What did you give that woman?" I asked as I stepped into the boat from the dock.

"Just a little token of our appreciation for her help."

"You gave her a gift certificate to Aphrodite's."

"I did. She seemed to appreciate it. Now stow that cooler and let's get out of here."

Lyle puttered us away from the dock and past the no-wake buoys to the open water of Carter Lake. Once we were on the water, life was good again. We both were too excited to sit in the bucket seats. Lyle said, "Better hold on to something," with a quick nod and grin in my direction.

Do you know the gut feeling of adrenalin from the first hard acceleration of a powerful speedboat? It's something you never forget. At least not if you're a guy. Maximum physical response from a small movement. Speed boats. Sports cars. Women. It's a dream of all men to feel that pounding, out-of-control response to their touch. Most guys won't get that kind of response from women, so we grab for the gusto with high-horsepower engines. Lyle leaned on that clitoral throttle pressing it to its limit. The boat sprang forward like a raging bull out of the chute. I grabbed onto whatever I could to keep from cartwheeling backwards out of the boat. The sheer power of the roaring outboard bored straight into my body. It was like a shared orgasm without the mess. I screamed like a kid on a rollercoaster. The wind broke over the small windshield so hard my cheeks flapped in the wind. Lyle had a crazed smile on his face. "Holy shit!" he yelled, "This is great!" Then he banked the boat into a long curve toward the far end of the lake. We sped across the rippled surface at sixty miles an hour. I couldn't stop smiling. Buying this boat was the best thing I ever did.

Three hours later we were slowly working our way along some sunken tree stumps. I threw a big plastic and steel lure a few hundred times hoping for a big bass. It was hot. The sun was brutal. I could already see my arms were red. I didn't want to think about the back of my neck. And of course, we hadn't had a single bite. Lyle was sitting in the back seat not even pretending to fish anymore. He cracked his fifth or sixth beer of the day. It wasn't noon yet. "Maybe they're in deep water," he said tipping his ball cap low over his eyes. "Or maybe they're napping." He took a long swig. "A nap sounds like a good idea, actually."

I sipped on my third beer. "Tell you what. Let's give this spot another ten minutes then we'll head back toward the deep end of the lake."

"That gives us time for another shot!" Lyle had brought a quart of George Dickel sipping whiskey to celebrate any big fish we caught. When that plan clearly was not going to yield any drinking opportunities, he decided shots were justified simply because. I am not much of a drinker. Never was. Three beers and a couple shots and I'm ready for bed. But Lyle could drink. Many times, I watched him put away a couple of six-packs during a ball game then switch to whiskey or tequila or whatever was available, and he could still function. Sort of.

So it was that after two shots of Dickel, I suggested that Lyle should again drive the boat since I was a little dizzy.

"No problem, amigo!" he said hopping into the driver's seat. "Let's go find us some fish!"

I stowed my rod and took my seat. Lyle looked a little too enthusiastic about driving the boat again. "You sure you're OK to drive?" I asked.

"Of course! There's nothing but open water from here to the dock. What can possibly go wrong?" He grinned a Dickel-infused grin and slammed the throttle down. The mad rush of acceleration again pulsed through my body and any doubts about the wisdom of Lyle driving were overwhelmed by the sheer joy of speed and unleashed power.

We buzzed along the lake at top speed, the trees and bluffs flying past in a blur. Up ahead in a bay off to one side a bunch of dark blobs floated in the water. As we got closer, the blobs turned into about fifty Canada geese lolling in the hot sun. Lyle yelled over the scream of the motor, "Damn geese. Nothing but flying rats." He turned the boat away from the bay but then, in a classic *hold-my-beer-and-watch-this* moment, he winked at me and turned the boat, travelling at full throttle, sharply toward the geese. The boat threw up a massive wave as it curled toward the birds. The geese must have been sleeping. They didn't notice the boat until we were almost on top of them. Then they reacted like scared geese always react. They launched themselves straight into the air in a honking mass of feathers and emptied their bowels. The grin disappeared from Lyle's face a second before we drove through a heavy rain of goose shit at sixty miles an hour. Fifty or more scared geese can produce a hell of a lot of goose shit. I ducked behind the windshield and watched black and white slime explode across the plexiglass. Birds were honking wildly. Goose shit was splattering across every part of the boat. Lyle pulled the throttle back and stopped the boat. Our brand new boat was a disaster. Everything was coated in slimy disgusting goose shit. I wanted to throw up. Then I looked at Lyle.

He neglected to duck. His glasses were completely covered in goose shit. Goose shit dripped from his face. For a moment I stared, too stunned to comment. I wanted to hit him for messing up our boat so thoroughly. But, of course, this was Lyle. And he was covered in goose shit. So, I laughed. I laughed so hard I almost did throw up.

Lyle just watched me letting me have my moment of fun. Then, in a perfectly dead-pan voice said, "If I wasn't too shit-faced to drive before, I guess I am now."

After a couple hours at the do-it-yourself car wash, we got the boat clean. We sold it the next day. Selling that boat was the best thing I ever did.

Life is But a Dream

I was supposed to be using my crutches now, but they made my armpits hurt so I was in my wheelchair when I took a detour on my way to PT. I wheeled toward Samantha's room. I knew she'd be resting before her next round of radiation later that morning. I picked up a single flower from the florist in the lobby, a bright yellow carnation with a long stem to add to the bouquet in her room. As I approached the room, I heard Samantha softly singing, her mother's beautiful voice joining in on the round.

"Row, row, row your boat..."
  "Row, row, row your boat..."
"Gently down the stream..."
  "Gently down the stream..."
"Merrily, merrily, merrily..."
  "Merrily, merrily, merrily..."
"Life is but a dream."
  "Life is but a dream."

I peeked around the door jamb. Monica sat cross legged on the end of Samantha's bed, her back to me. Samantha sat up against several pillows holding her Bear in her arms. Thin wisps of blonde hair hung loosely from under her ball cap. Her skin was ashen and dark circles gathered under her eyes. But she smiled at me over her mother's shoulder looking like a tiny angel.

"Hi, Jeremy!" she said, "Mom and I were just singing.'

"I heard! Very nice. You have lovely voices."

Monica turned around to see me. She looked even more pale and tired than Samantha. Her face was drawn. Her jaw tight. She forced a smile as a tear slid from the corner of her eye. She wiped it with the back of her hand. "Look, Samantha, Jeremy brought you a flower."

I wheeled myself into the room and handed to flower to Samantha. "I always liked Row, Row, Row Your Boat. It's a fun song. You sing it wonderfully."

Samantha beamed. "The last line is my favorite. It always makes me feel better to remember that life is but a dream."

I didn't have a reply to that. This girl and her mother are living in a nightmare, not a dream. But somehow Samantha stays above it all. She is the Dalai Lama and the rest of us mere mortals trying to keep it together in the face of tragedy.

"You keep on singing, Samantha, you and your mother. It makes the world nicer." I patted Monica's arm and smiled weakly. "I have to go. I have a session with Tasha. I don't want to be late."

"Thanks for stopping in to see Samantha."

"And thanks for the flower," Samantha said squeezing Bear tight.

A few minutes later Tasha had me stretched out on a table with my leg somewhere around my neck. It hurt. A lot. "You're making good progress, Jeremy. Your hip rotation is really improving. Can you feel the difference from just a few days ago?"

"Yeah…good," I panted, "I…can…really…feel…the…difference." I felt like the wishbone from a giant turkey.

She eased up on my leg and patted my shoulder. "I know it's uncomfortable, but you can see the progress."

"That which does not kill me…"

"That's the attitude. Now let's work a little on that shoulder then we'll look at your other leg."

Tasha yanked and twisted and pushed various body parts around for another half hour then tossed me a towel. "Let's call it a day. Good session. You'll be home in no time."

"Thanks. I know I should feel good about that. But I keep thinking about Samantha. I can't get her out of my mind. That poor little girl may never go home."

"Everyone in the hospital is pulling for her. She's a rock star here, you know." Tasha wiped the table down and tossed the towel in a hamper. "It's the hardest part of the job, watching people, especially kids, who you know are going to die and you can't do a damn thing to save them."

"I wish I could help her and her mother get that German treatment. It would at least give them some hope."

"You can pray for them, you know."

"I'd rather do something that might actually make a difference for them."

"I believe in prayer. I have to. It gets me through the tough parts of the job."

"You think I'm going to Hell, don't you? Because I don't believe in God."

Tasha put her clipboard down, removed her glasses, and turned her full attention to me. "You underestimate God. Jesus didn't die on that cross just to save believers. He died for all our sins. Everyone's. Even yours."

"So, no one goes to Hell?"

"No one goes to Hell simply for not believing. No one goes to Hell for Adam and Eve's sin. That's what Jesus died for."

"That's a very enlightened view of Christianity. I'm not sure many churches would agree that nonbelievers aren't going to Hell."

"The Church needs believers. God doesn't. I still think you're making a mistake rejecting God and Jesus. But just because you reject Him doesn't mean He rejects you. If you let Him into your heart, you will understand."

"Maybe. But when I'm this close to the end, it seems disingenuous to say I believe. I'm confident in my beliefs. I'm comfortable knowing that someday soon, I will simply stop being. I just hope it doesn't hurt too bad."

"You're a good man, Jeremy. I'll pray for you."

"Thanks. You're a good person, too, Tasha."

My Unremarkable Life
Drug Store Fall

I was walking down the aisle at Schnedeker's Pharmacy trying not to look at the various women's hygiene products I passed by. I needed some foot powder and a new heating pad for my increasingly stiff and sore back. Getting old was starting to pick up momentum. Every morning I would wake up with a new pain-of-the-day. One day it would be a sore wrist. The next day I felt pins stabbing behind my knee cap. The day after that it would be a grinding feeling in my shoulder. The only constant in my body's ongoing parade of discomfort was my back. It was sore pretty much all the time. A heating pad didn't really help but it was nice on cold nights while I watched TV.

Arnie and Beatrice Schnedeker had taken over his father's pharmacy thirty-nine years earlier. If prompted, they would tell about listening to the radio playing over the PA system their first morning as new owners and hearing about Kennedy being shot in Dallas. Arnie was in the back compounding some magic potion, and Beatrice was ringing up a customer who had just bought a large package of diapers when the music was interrupted and the announcement made: "The president has been shot." It was a sad day and an inauspicious debut for the new owners. They told the story a thousand times in the decades since. Now, well into their seventies, they had decided it was time to give up the store and retire to Florida. They put the store up for sale and within a week had competing offers from several large national drugstore chains. After months of negotiations, they had signed the sales papers only two days earlier. This would be their last week in the store before heading to the Sunshine State.

As I worked my way down the aisle averting my eyes from the feminine hygiene products, my foot slipped out from under me and I was launched into an arm-flapping, leg-kicking backflip. I landed hard on my side and heard a nauseating crunch from my shoulder. Beatrice heard me moaning and ran to my side. She was too frail to lift me but knelt beside me. "Are you hurt, Jeremy?" she asked, her tiny blue eyes peeking from behind thick glasses. The deep lines on her face showed genuine concern. "Can you sit up?"

I tried to move but the pain in my shoulder was too much. I just lay on my side and moaned. "I think I need an ambulance."

"Of course! Of course! You stay here. I'll call 911." She pushed herself to her feet." Arnie!" she yelled, "Mr. Moore is down in aisle four." I felt like a janitorial problem more than a medical one.

It turns out I slipped in a puddle of baby puke. As I was lying on the floor waiting for the ambulance, a man who with a large bottle of Brylcreem and very oily hair walked by. "Whoa, are you OK?" He asked standing above me.

"Not really," I said, "but they are calling an ambulance."

"Looks like you have a clear-cut case of negligence, buddy. Do you have legal representation?"

"What? No, I don't want a lawyer," I said through gritted teeth. "It was an accident. I'm fine."

"It's your call, buddy. But here's my number." He stuffed a card in my shirt pocket. "It won't cost you a dime. I work on spec. And I get results. Marvin Xavier Gould, Esquire, at your service." He held out a hand. Reflexively, I tried to reach to shake his hand. I didn't really like the guy and had no intentions of calling him. But it would be impolite to refuse his hand. When I tried to reach out, a burning pain shot through my shoulder and up my neck. "Whoa, you are hurt, buddy. You need a lawyer."

"I need a doctor."

"Yeah, and doctors cost money. Plus all the pain and suffering you are going to go through. Believe me, you need a lawyer and I'm your man."

At that point two EMTs came crashing down the aisle pushing a gurney. They shoved Gould aside and got to work on me. I forgot all about the lawyer until a month later when I got a bill from the hospital for costs not covered by insurance. It was a lot of money. I hated to do it, but I called the number.

"No worries, Mr. Moore," Gould said over the phone. "I'll take care of everything. When we win the case, that's when I get paid. No risk to you."

"Look, Martin…"

"Marvin."

"What?"

"My name is Marvin."

"OK. Look, Marvin, I don't want to cause problems for the Schnedekers. I just want enough to cover my medical bills. Understand? Nothing for pain and suffering. Nothing punitive. They are nice people."

"Got it, Mr. Moore. Got it. Don't you worry one bit about the Schnedekers. I've known them for years. They're practically like grandparents to me. I won't hurt them."

That was the last I heard from Mr. Marvin Xavier Gould, Esquire, except for a form letter each year letting me know he was still working the case. I filed them in the trash along with advertisements for timeshares and offers for credit cards. Fortunately, my shoulder healed reasonably well. The doctors surgically removed my slice, improving my golf game to solidly mediocre. As for the Schnedekers, I received a lovely Christmas card from them each year. Now in their nineties and living well in their condo in Saint Pete, I was happy Mr. Gould, Esquire, was not a very good lawyer.

Lucy Dreams

"**D**o you have Lucy dreams, Jeremy?" It was three days after her last treatment. Samantha sat in her wheelchair looking out over the town. We were enjoying a warm afternoon at the smoking pavilion. We had the rare opportunity to enjoy the place alone.

"Lucy dreams?" I asked.

"Sometimes when I'm dreaming, I know I'm dreaming. I look around and realize that I am dreaming. Mom says those are Lucy dreams."

"Oh, yes. Lucy dreams," I loved that little girl more every time I talked with her. "I don't have them very often, but I have had a few in my life."

"I have them a lot. Seems like almost every night I have one. I like them because I can do things in my dreams I can't do in real life."

"Like what?"

"I can fly in my dreams. I really like to do that. When I know I am dreaming I can just spread my arms and fly." Samantha closed her eyes, leaned her head back and spread her arms wide. "It's fun."

"Sure sounds like it." I thought about this poor kid stuck in her wheelchair unable to walk more than a few steps. Her little body ravaged by the treatments as well as the disease that was steadily killing her.

"Last night I had a Lucy dream. You were in it." Her head was still back, eyes closed. She slowly drew her arms in and wrapped them around herself like she was chilled. "You were in your wheelchair beside me. Just like now. But we were on the street at the top of the hill. I knew it was a dream. I wanted to fly, and I wanted you to fly with me. But you couldn't do it. I put my arms out and rose right out of my chair. You spread your arms out but nothing happened." She opened her eyes and looked at me, sadness in her eyes. "I couldn't help you fly, Jeremy. I really wanted you to fly with me. I asked my brain to help you fly but I couldn't do it. I'm sorry."

"I'm the one who's sorry, Samantha. I'm sorry my dream me couldn't fly. But you know something?" I reached over and tapped her forehead. "You keep using that amazing brain of yours. I'll try harder next time. Maybe I can't fly in your Lucy dreams, but, honey, you make me feel like I can fly every time I talk with you."

That night I had the first lucid dream I could remember since the girls got me into meditation all those years ago. When I realized I was dreaming, I spread my arms out and tried to fly. Even in my dream, though, I couldn't get my fat ass off the chair. I woke up and stared at the ceiling for an hour before I fell back to sleep. If I dreamed any more, I don't remember it.

Acropolites
On Nature and Religion

Lyle sipped his cafeteria coffee, his reading glasses perched on the tip of his long nose like an Oxford don. The Acropolites had been eating donuts and discussing the world's great problems. Having exhausted that topic, we sat in silence until Lyle spoke. "You know what the most important part of your body is as far as Nature is concerned?"

We assumed it was a trick question. No one wanted to bite.

"Come on. Someone guess. What does Nature consider the most important part of your body?"

Figuring he wasn't going to let it go, I guessed, "The brain?"

"Nope." Guess again,

Junior tried. "Heart?"

"Nope. Try again." Lyle was enjoying this. "Bartholomew, you want to give it a try?"

"I have no idea. How about the liver?"

"Your gonads." Lyle sat back and smirked waiting for someone to rise to the bait.

I bit. "OK, I think you lost me there."

"Look, Nature doesn't care about you as an individual. The individual has no inherent value to Nature except in terms of your usefulness to the continuation of the species."

"What are you talking about?"

"Nature. I'm talking about the real world. Life has been doing its thing for hundreds of millions of years. And you know what its thing is?"

"Generating strange subjects for us to talk about?"

"Continuation of life. That is all that counts in Nature. The continuation of life."

"Fascinating."

"The individual is nearly irrelevant in Nature except to the extent it contributes to the continuation of the species. It's the creation of the next generation that is the prime directive as far as Nature is concerned. You, each of us, is just a steppingstone for life to get from the past to the future."

I sipped my coffee. It was cold. "I like to think I matter more than that."

"Of course you do. We all like to think we matter. But Nature doesn't care what you think. As far as nature is concerned, there is no fundamental difference between you and a banana slug. You're both just a collection of molecules arranged to create more collections of molecules. Your brain, heart, liver, spleen, everything that is you—they all exist to allow your gonads to do their job and reproduce. After that, your only purpose, as far as Nature is concerned, is to do everything you can to allow your spawn to live long enough to reproduce again to keep the train going."

"I assume you can see the problem with your line of reasoning."

"Of course. People can't stand the thought that they have no value beyond continuing the species. We have this absurd idea that the individual matters. In fact, lots of us think the individual is more important than the species. It's why we invented religion."

"That again?"

"Think about it. If life is about nothing other than keeping the species going, life is not very fulfilling. But a banana slug doesn't care about fulfillment. No life form on Earth cares about fulfillment except one. Why? Because the brain we grew to support our gonads was so damn successful, it developed all kinds of collateral capabilities like self-awareness, knowledge of death, imagination, and ego. We have this artificial sense that we should matter as individuals. But nothing in Nature supports that concept. So we created religion."

"Interesting thesis," Junior piped up. "Can we get some pie now?"

"Every major religion focuses on the individual. Ultimately, the goal for all of them is personal salvation in some form. Personal salvation. No religion places the species as a whole above the individual. They don't even ask the question."

"But religion is more than personal. It's culture." I said.

"Yes! Of course. It's about creating systems of ethics and norms to allow individuals to live together in a functioning society. Without shared religious beliefs, we'd probably still be competing over wild grasses and mammoth carcasses. But it still supports my point that religion was created because we, as a species, evolved a brain that needed more reassurance and distraction than Nature provides."

"OK. I'm with Junior. Can we have pie now? My gonads have long ago fulfilled their raison d'etre and my brain is dying for some ego-comforting coconut custard."

"Why is it that when I talk to you about important things, I feel like I'm casting pearls before swine?"

"Oink."

Later that evening, when no one was around, I reflected on Lyle's thesis. I often did that after our conversations. I don't know if I bought the idea that religion was created to provide meaning for individuals' lives. I think it was created to control individuals so we didn't kill each other in the tribe. But I did recognize the inherent need most individuals have for finding meaning in their lives. Banana slugs may be content with reproducing and dying as their wont in life. Sentient beings want more, even if there isn't more. It's easier to let someone else tell you what your purpose should be, especially if millions of other people accept the same message, than it is to create your own purpose. It takes courage to reject the comfort of religion, stare into the abyss alone, and accept one's inevitable non-being. In my head, I know that is true. In my heart, I still wish I had an all-powerful invisible friend looking over me and promising me Heaven.

More important, I wished an all-powerful guardian was looking over Samantha. Somehow, that would ease some of the pain of watching her young life end. Maybe that's the real reason we created religion. Not so we can face our own death, but to allow us to survive the immeasurable pain of the death of others.

That night I really wished I believed there was someone to pray to. I'd have been on my knees all night if I thought someone was out there listening.

My Unremarkable Life
Hazy's Death and Funeral

It was February 2003. Colin Powell had just convinced the world that Iraq harbored weapons of mass destruction. Fortunately, it would take only a short war paid for by Iraqi oil money to eliminate the serious threat to American democracy. What could possibly go wrong?

I was struggling to open the front door of my house with both arms full of grocery bags when I heard the phone ring. I had been expecting a call about an internal auditor position at a local bank that looked ideal for one of my clients. In my rush to open the door I dropped one of the bags spilling frozen vegetables and a dozen cans of soup across my stoop. I managed to open the door and shoulder my way in just in time to hear the answering machine beep and the caller's tinny voice begin to leave a message. "Mr. Moore, this is Norman Nutter from Golden Acres..." I dropped the remaining bag on the counter and snatched the phone. Golden Acres was the retirement village my mother moved to several years earlier. It was one of those planned communities in Florida where everyone was from somewhere else, drove golf carts everywhere, and played something called pickleball. It was also one of those communities where sexually transmitted disease was - like the age of the residents - at least twice the national average.

"Hello, this is Jeremy Moore," I panted into the phone.

"Oh, hello, Mr. Moore. This is Norman Nutter from Golden Acres."

"Yes, I heard that. Is my mother in trouble again? Please don't evict her. I'm sure we can work something out. She'll be better, I'm sure."

"Mr. Moore, I'm not calling to report another rules infraction by your mother." Mr. Nutter hesitated. "I'm sorry to have to say there's been a terrible accident."

"Accident? What do you mean, *accident*?"

"I'm so sorry, Mr. Moore. She and Mr. Wiggerstine were, um, engaged in some …amorosity…in the pool during a rainstorm late last night. A lightning bolt hit one of the poles for the water volleyball net." He hesitated again.

Amorosity? Is that what they call it now? "Is my mother OK?"

"Mr. Moore, I am terribly sorry to tell you your mother is dead."

The words seemed to come from a different world. They didn't make sense. My mother was dead? That can't be right. "My mother is dead?" I asked seeking clarification.

"It appears Hazy, that is, it appears your mother and Mr. Wiggerstine experienced no pain."

"No pain?" I repeated trying to make sense of this.

"Um, yes sir. They were still…engaged…when the pool man found them this morning. It took the coroner a while to separate them."

"Wait. You're telling me my mother was having sex in a pool and she was hit by lightning?"

"Well, yes, I'd say that is accurate."

"Wow. I mean…wow."

"You may be relieved to know that they both looked happy."

"Excuse me?"

"Yes. When we discovered them in the pool, they both had smiles on their faces. Well, not exactly smiles. More like wide-mouth, screaming, rapturous grins."

"Not a bad way to go, is it?"

"That's not really mine to say, Mr. Moore." I heard a muffled sob or maybe chuckle. "But all in all, there are worse ways to go."

A week later we had Hazy's funeral. After the obituary appeared in the local newspaper, I began getting cards from people expressing their sympathy. Nearly all of them were from men. Cards were coming in from all over the county. I was stunned. I knew my mother had a lot of friends, so to speak, but I had no idea how many. The small family graveside funeral we hoped for turned into something a bit more.

It was cold. A slight drizzle fell. Besides the girls and their husbands and, of course Junior, Lyle, and Bartholomew, a couple dozen people, all old men and mostly strangers to me, came to the burial. Most of them looked to be well into their 80s. A few used canes or walkers. One sat in a wheelchair, a plaid blanket over his knees and a stuffed toy elephant in his lap. I recognized a gray and withered Brainfart. I also recognized a former congressman, a local TV weatherman, the retired police chief, and the truck driver Mom brought home those many years ago. In the back of the group was a guy with dark glasses and hat pulled low who I swear looked like a famous rock-and-roll star from New Jersey. They each held a single long-stem rose in his hand. The men gathered around the grave quietly talking and sharing flasks. From what I could overhear, they were sharing stories about my mother. Soft laughter occasionally rose over the sound of the rain. The preacher asked for quiet. He was a young minister recently hired to replace the long-time preacher who gave the Christmas sermons my mother and I so religiously attended every year of my childhood. Of course, neither of us had been in that church since I was confirmed. The preacher had no idea who my mother was.

"Dear friends," the preacher began, "thank you for coming to share this sad but very special moment with Hazel Moore's family and friends." He launched into a boilerplate commentary on a life well-lived and the joy Hazy was now experiencing at the side of her Redeemer in Heaven. He said my mother had been loved and loved well. Someone behind me whispered "amen." I gave a short eulogy and then invited people to come up and say something about my mother. That's when things got interesting.

The first person to speak was a huge man who had pushed the man in the wheelchair up the hill to the gravesite. He was over six feet tall and nearly as wide. He looked vaguely familiar. He carefully stepped to the side of the grave and nervously wrinkled his felt fedora with both hands. The rain stopped.

"Hazy was a good woman. She saved my life. I was struggling with the whiskey and living in a flophouse when she found me in a bar. She saw something in me. We had some good times." He looked up shyly at the other men. "If you know what I mean." They all smiled and nodded. "But more than that, she made me feel good about myself. She introduced me to Benny over there," he gestured toward the man in the wheelchair, "who hired me on at the circus. Got a job. Got sober. Had a good life. Thanks to Hazy." He dropped a rose onto the coffin.

The next speaker was the retired police chief. "Hazy was a good woman. She saved my life. My wife had left me and took my kids. Can't blame her. I wasn't a good husband or father. I thought about ending it until I pulled Hazy over for doing 40 in a 25 zone. She sweet-talked me out of a ticket and into a date. We had some fun," the same shy look around, "and she showed me how to be a better man. Got back with my wife and kids, got a few promotions, ended up chief. I owe that to Hazy, my amazing Hazelnut." He dropped his rose onto the coffin.

It went on like that for nearly an hour. Speaker after speaker shared their stories of my mom changing their lives. The stories got louder and raunchier as the flasks emptied but they all had the same theme. My mom, Hazel Moore, was an angel. I never knew it. I knew she had lots of men "friends," but I never realized she had real, loving friends who were deeply grateful she was part of their lives.

After everyone had spoken and the funeral was breaking up, the cold drizzle began again. A shy little man I hadn't noticed before came up to me. He carried a case of Jack Daniels. "Mr. Moore, I'm Norman Nutter. We spoke on the phone."

"Yes, Mr. Nutter. Thank you for coming all the way from Florida for my mother's funeral."

"She was a good woman," Nutter said. I expected him to tell another story of my mother changing his life. Instead, he handed me the Jack Daniels box. "While we were cleaning her apartment, we found this box in the back of a closet. The note on the top says to send this to you in the event of her passing. I wanted to deliver it in person." A tear slid down his cheek. "I wanted to tell you personally that Hazy was a good person and you should be proud."

The box was heavy. Though not heavy enough to be full of whiskey bottles. Nutter started to say more but words didn't come out. He shook his head and walked quickly away.

"Thanks for bringing this, Mr. Nutter," I called to him. He waved a hand over his shoulder and continued skittering away through the soft rain.

I opened the box. No liquor but what appeared to be a collection of relics of my childhood. Baseball cards, a badly worn catcher's mitt, a raccoon cap missing the tail, some other toys and gewgaws from that mythical time. And books. Dozens of paperbacks from my childhood bedroom. They were all there—London, Verne, Zane Grey, Golding, Poul Anderson, the entire Tolkien trilogy. It was the Alexandrian Library of my youth. My mother kept my books and childhood relics for more than sixty years. I looked for a note. Something to explain why. Nothing. I guess that was my mother. She didn't say much. She just did things. More selfless things than I could ever imagine.

I stood in the rain long after everyone else left. I felt like I had finally met my mother.

Tasha, Monica, Samantha,
and The Blood Moon

One evening Tasha surprised me and stopped by my room. She had never done that before. I was sitting in my wheelchair finishing the last of my meatloaf and mashed potatoes dinner.

"Care to go for a walk?" she asked, "Monica and Samantha are waiting in the pavilion. There's a lunar eclipse and the moon is turning red. Samantha wants you to see it."

I shoveled in the last cold blob of coagulated gravy and potatoes. "Let's go. I'd never pass up that kind of offer."

I was glad Tasha offered to push the wheelchair. I was still sore from our PT session earlier in the day and I had been noticing some difficulty breathing when I exerted myself. It was starting to get to me, the idea that my body was not recovering well. I'd been moping around for a couple of days, and I suspected Tasha noticed and wanted to get me focused on something other than my injuries and malfunctioning body.

Monica and Samantha were talking quietly as we approached. The moon was an orange hanging low in the sky. Samantha had a blanket tucked around her legs. She held Bear on her lap.

"Look, Jeremey," Samantha said when we pulled up beside her and Monica. "Isn't it amazing? The moon is moving into Earth's shadow and turning red."

"I remember watching a lunar eclipse when I was about your age. I used to sneak out of my bedroom window and lie on the roof over our porch to watch the sky at night. One night when the moon turned red like this, I thought the moon was having a brownout."

Tasha laughed. "I remember brownouts. Suddenly all the lights in the house would dim and the TV would flicker."

"I was sure that was happening to the moon. I was so happy when Southern Indiana Gas and Electric restored full power and the moon brightened back up."

"That's not what made the moon get bright," Samantha smirked. "It was the sun."

"I know that now. But when I was your age, I wasn't as smart as you are. I didn't know about lunar eclipses."

We stared at the moon for a long time. I thought Samantha had fallen asleep. Tasha and Monica quietly talked to one another. I daydreamed. The memory of lying on the roof at night watching the stars and dreaming about life was bittersweet. It was such a beautiful time of life. It was a great world for a kid. Everything seemed possible. I don't know if I ever felt happier than I did lying on my back in the dark thinking.

"Jeremy, you fell asleep." Samantha woke me from my reverie.

"No, I didn't. I was thinking."

"You were snoring."

"That was heavy breathing. I breathe heavy when I'm thinking."

"What were you thinking about?" Monica asked.

"I was thinking it would be fun to ride my wheelchair down Mount St. Anne Hill."

"I think that would probably be a bad idea," Tasha said.

"But it would be an adventure," I said. "Start at the hospital and just roll down the hill all the way to town. It would be a heck of a ride."

"You should do it, Jeremy," Samantha said clapping her hands together in excitement. "It would cheer you up."

"I didn't know I needed cheering up."

"You do! You've been kind of grumpy. Maybe a fun ride would make you happier."

"I'll have to think about that. Besides, I didn't know I've been grumpy. I'll work on that."

We sat in silence contemplating the moon and the hill and what it means to be happy. Samantha broke the silence.

"Will I be able to see the moon when I'm in Heaven?"

Monica flinched. "Oh, honey, you won't be in Heaven for a long time." Samantha started to respond but Monica cut her off. "It's getting cold, Samantha, we need to get you back to your room." She stood and began pushing Samantha's wheelchair toward the doors of the hospital. "Thanks for a wonderful evening, Tasha, I'm so glad you thought about the eclipse. It was beautiful. And thanks for joining us, Jeremy. See you tomorrow."

Samantha called over her shoulder, "Goodnight, Jeremy. Goodnight, Tasha. See you tomorrow."

When they were gone, Tasha lit a cigarillo and sighed. "Poor Monica. I can't imagine being in her situation. I guess I'd be in constant denial, too. It's just impossible to comprehend."

"Miracles do happen, I suppose."

"We can hope. Monica can hope."

"I guess there's no chance of getting Samantha into the German treatment, is there?"

"Seems impossible. It's a million dollars or more and even then, it may not work. No insurance will cover it. Monica told me she already expects she will have to sell her house just to pay for the bills insurance doesn't cover here. It's not fair."

I had no response to that. It wasn't fair. But who said life is supposed to be fair? Life sucks and then you die, right? But, dammit,

Samantha and Monica deserve so much more than life has given them.

Tasha snuffed her cigarillo out and dropped it in the urn. "I better go. Got the early shift tomorrow. Want me to take you back to your room?"

"No thanks. I think I'll stay here and watch the moon for a while." Tasha left. I wished I had a blanket. I was suddenly cold. The moon continued to darken, the orange-red turning blood red.

When I got back to my room, I couldn't sleep. I could not resign myself to the idea that Samantha was going to die - soon if the prognosis was correct—and there was nothing I could do to help her. There was no way I could send Samantha to Germany let alone cover the cost of the treatment if she got there. I decided then that if I couldn't help Samantha, maybe I could help Monica. I pulled out my laptop and Googled "how to write your own will."

My Unremarkable Life
The Last 17 Years

After Mom died, I suddenly realized that I was an orphan. It was a weird thought to be an orphan at sixty years old, but there it was. Not that Hazy was a big part of my life by then. We talked on the phone a few times a year. I'd see her for a day or two whenever she was in town between romances and travel. But she was always there somewhere, a presence in the world that I realized too late was comforting. It never registered before but as long as my mother was alive, I felt as if I was a generation away from death. Not anymore. Now no one stood between me and my own mortality.

I put my life on autopilot. I had long before forgotten my dream of living a life worthy of an action novel, but I still had some modicum of joie de vivre. Even that began to wane. For the next seventeen years my life was on cruise control set five miles an hour below the speed limit. I settled into a routine. Work during the week. Yardwork and golf with the guys on the weekend. Eating frozen dinners or Chinese takeout and watching Jeopardy and Wheel of Fortune every night. Holidays with the girls and their families. And the long, steady submission to time as my body slowly eroded. It sounds bleak. It wasn't. It was life as most of us experience it once we make peace with the world.

So, there I was a year ago - in the hospital rehab looking back on my life wondering where it went and trying to ignore the inevitable which lay somewhere in front of me.

Tasha's Real Story

D r. Akufo told me I would be released in a day or two. My strength was returning. I was able to walk short distances on crutches. I could take a crap on my own. I was finally getting out of there. So, why wasn't I happy?

I needed some air. Dinner wasn't sitting that well. I wheeled myself through the hospital to the front entrance and started across the parking lot to the overlook shelter. It was almost always empty after dinner as the day shift workers had left and the evening shift hadn't been on long enough to take a break. I liked the shelter. It afforded a view of most of the city below and of the hills to the east beyond. I was told it was a nice place to watch the sunrise, but I was never out there that early. The shelter was a flagstone patio covered by a wooden roof supported by four columns of stone. It had been built by the CCC back in the thirties as a public overlook. The hospital bought the whole hilltop to accommodate its rapid expansion back in the fifties and retained the overlook for patients and visitors to enjoy.

A pale gibbous moon was just rising over the hill as I approached the shelter. I smelled Tasha's cigar before I saw her leaning against one of the stone columns staring out over the city. She sipped from a flask.

"Nice night," I said, announcing my arrival and breaking Tasha's reverie.

"Yes, I guess it is." Tasha was unusually soft-spoken. She was contemplative and I was interrupting her.

"I'm sorry. Maybe you want to be alone," I said starting to turn away.

"No, it's good," she said, "I appreciate the company." She offered me a corona cigarillo. "Want one? They're pretty good with a little Jack."

I wasn't sure a cigar and bourbon would help my unsettled stomach, but Tasha's friendly offer was too important to pass up. This was a rare opening. I pulled a slim cigar from the pack. She handed me a Bic lighter.

I took a few puffs and let the smoke curl out of my mouth into the evening air. She handed me the flask. It was nearly empty. I took a small swig and handed it back. We both stood quietly watching the lights come on across the city below. The grid of streets stretched between the hills like a giant bedewed spiderweb across a dark lawn. It was quiet except for the occasional pop-pop-pop of a semi using its jake brakes coming down the highway into town. I was intensely aware of Tasha's presence. She towered above me in my wheelchair. Taller even than at the PT table where she so often intimidated me. I sensed her strength but also some underlying sadness. She took a swig from the flask.

"Tonight is my tenth anniversary."

"Wait. You're married?"

Tasha laughed. "No, Jeremy, I am not married. It's the tenth anniversary of my discharge from the Army. Seems a lot longer ago than that."

"How long were you in the Army?"

She chuckled—a bitter resignation evident in the sound. "I tell people I had ten amazing years in the Army. Unfortunately, I served for twelve years."

"I imagine it was tough. Iraq was a nasty place to be."

"Yes, it was. So was Afghanistan. But that wasn't a problem. I was prepared for war. I could handle war. I could handle being shot at, dodging IEDs, patching up wounded soldiers and getting them back to base hospitals. I could even handle the sight of wounded children crawling among the rubble of bombed villages crying for their dead parents. It was hard but I could handle it. It was war."

"Sounds terrible."

"It was. But the Army is a team. A family. That's what my dad said when he urged me to enlist. 'Soldiers have each other's backs - always. The Army takes care of its own. It is an honorable and faithful group of men and women who will always be there for you.'" She stared out across the city but seemed to be looking at something much farther away. I could barely hear her whisper, "God, he was wrong. He was so damn wrong." She shook her head and took another drink from the flask.

I'm not the brightest bulb on the Christmas tree but I was smart enough to know that anything I said at that moment would probably be wrong. I had no idea what to say or do. So I did the only thing I could think of. I held my breath and waited.

"I was raped."

Three words spoken without emotion. No anger. No fear. No sadness. A statement of fact. A simple statement that shot through my body like a lightning bolt.

"I was raped." Tasha repeated in the same flat voice. She held her cigar close to her mouth and stared at something far away. I was paralyzed knowing no matter what I said, it would be insufficient or ignorant. So, I watched Tasha take a slow puff on her cigar and said nothing. She was not looking for a reply. Watching her, I understood that she was not starting a conversation. She was opening to me, and my role was to listen.

"He was my commanding officer. Big guy. Tough as hell and I respected him more than any man except my father."

Tasha didn't say anything else. It was obvious what happened. I wanted to reach out and hug her. Maybe just touch her hand to let her know I cared. But my paralysis continued. I didn't want to do anything that would make things worse. Finally, I said, "I'm sorry, Tasha."

She didn't reply. Her eyes stayed focused on something in the distance. Her posture as erect and statuesque as ever. But I sensed a tremor in her body. She was fighting to stay in control.

"I was raped twice. Once by a man. And again by the Army. I can handle the first. Just a bad thing that happens to women all the time. But the second was different. You don't expect the organization you love with all your heart to turn on you so viciously." She took another sip and looked at me for the first time. A quick glace to see how I was reacting. I nodded slightly, my eyes blurring.

"Yeah, so, I haven't talked about this much since I got out of the Army. My analyst thinks I should try to…" she made quotation marks in the air with her fingers, "…*externalize* my experience. Therapy, she says.

"I was a medic on a Medevac team in Mosul. My third tour - once in Afghanistan in the early months of the war, then in Baghdad right after the invasion. Those were intense tours with so many casualties - mostly Afghan and Iraqi troops and civilians, but too many American soldiers, too. My third tour was during the surge when we were desperate to put down the insurgency that threatened to undo everything we'd accomplished in Iraq. The work was brutal. So many mangled bodies. Young men with horrendous injuries. My job was to helicopter into the action with the Medevac team and get the casualties out of the field and into the hospital as soon as possible. Usually, we would have these men in surgery in less than an hour after they were injured. It was amazing. We were amazing."

Tasha closed her eyes. A tired, soulful smile curled the edges of her mouth. "I was so damn proud to be a soldier in the United States Army."

The corners of her mouth dropped. A deep frown lined her chin. "I was so stupid."

"I never told anyone outside the Army about that night." She shook herself and took a drag on her cigar. She held her head back and let the smoke rise out of her mouth. "They told me not to report it. They said it is just a fact of life for women in the armed forces, a condition of employment. I should have listened. The first thing the investigating officer said to me when he began the interview was did I know the penalty for making false charges against an officer? The first damn thing. He said that even if I was being truthful, if a court-martial disagreed with me, I would be charged and probably court-martialed myself. I went ahead anyway. I believed in justice. I believed in the Army my dad told me about. When it looked like I might be able to convince someone about my story, the rapist said it was consensual sex. He was married. He was written up for fraternizing with an enlisted person. I was charged with adultery - he was married but only I was charged with adultery - and discharged from the Army. Ten years ago today."

I waited to see if she would say any more. She remained focused a million miles away. "I wish I knew what to say," I finally said.

"It's OK Jeremy. I learn so much from the people here at the hospital. People like Samantha. If she can handle her problems with so much dignity and joy, I think I can forgive the world for the demons it unleashed on me. I have to move on." She took a hit on her cigar but it was out. "I needed to tell someone, and you were unlucky enough to show up when I was ready to talk. Thank you for listening. And thank you for not saying anything stupid."

She looked at the stub of her dead cigar. "Guess I'll head home and get some sleep. You want me to wheel you back?"

"No, I'm good. I want to sit here a while and look at the moon."

"See you tomorrow, Jeremy. Be ready for some productive time in therapy. Our last session, you know."

"I know. I'm going to miss you."

I watched Tasha walk across the darkening parking lot. I realized my teeth were clenched, my jaw tight as a vise. How could something like that happen to someone like Tasha? How could it happen to anyone at all? I hoped all the bastards who let her down so horribly would rot in Hell. Then I remembered I don't believe in Hell. The bastards got away with it. Fuck. The bastards usually get away with it.

I started back toward the parking lot and my room when I felt the now familiar pain in my chest, a fluttering spasm that stopped me cold. My arms tingled. I couldn't breathe. I thought I was going to lose consciousness. Then, just as before, the pain subsided. I sucked in cool evening air and waited for the feeling to come back to my arms. I slowly made my way back to my room.

Acropolites
Death is Easy

The next morning the guys stopped by my room. Bartholomew had a paper grocery bag full of clothes for me. "I couldn't find a suitcase," he explained, "But here are the clothes you asked me to get for you for your grand exit. It must feel good knowing you'll be in your own bed soon."

"Yeah, it will be nice." I wasn't very enthusiastic about my own health.

Junior dropped a small stack of mail on the chair by the door. "I wasn't sure you'd want this to wait until you got home. You got a gas bill, a flyer for new windows, and a letter from some attorney," he said waving an envelope at me, "Mr. Martin Xavier Gould, Esquire. Looks official."

"I doubt it. I hear from that hack once a year or so. Toss it on the table with the rest of the junk. I may look at it later."

"Ready for some pie?" Lyle asked.

"Sorry, guys," I said, "I'm not really up for the cafeteria right now."

"Are you OK?" Junior asked, concern etched in his face. He knew that me skipping pie and coffee was a bad sign.

"I'm fine, I guess. Samantha is not doing well." I didn't want to mention my conversation with Tasha. I didn't want to violate that confidence. I wasn't about to mention my chest pains. I'd never hear the end of that. "She's lost use of her legs. The disease is accelerating."

"Christ," Lyle whispered.

"Isn't there anything they can do?" Junior asked.

"They're doing everything they can. There isn't much they can do except fight the symptoms. The closest thing to a cure is a new experimental treatment in Europe that no US insurance will cover. It's expensive and usually doesn't work." I felt a tightening in my chest. "That little girl is the strongest person I know. But I don't see how she wins this fight."

"It's not fair," Bartholomew said plopping down into the chair by the door. "Here we are, old men with our lives almost entirely in the rearview mirror, and there's this child who has barely started to live. Anyone of us would trade places with her in a heartbeat. But that's not the way the world works."

"Nothing's fair about death," I said.

We sat in silence contemplating our own mortality and the tragedy of a life ended before it hardly begins.

"Dying is hard," Lyle said to no one in particular.

"Dying is easy. Watching someone else die is hard," I said. I'd been thinking about death a lot lately.

"How can you say dying is easy? I get that it's harder to watch someone else die. But dying is hard."

"Dying is easy for a lot of people. For believers, it's eternity in the kingdom of heaven and a chance to be reunited with loved ones who die before them. For nonbelievers like me it's Das Nicht, nothing. The big sleep. Either way, it's easy."

"What about Hell? Don't you worry about Hell?"

"No one who really believes in Hell actually thinks they will go there. Hell is for other people."

"So, you are not afraid of dying."

"Of course, I'm afraid of dying. It might hurt and I don't do pain well. But I'm not afraid of death." I had never articulated that before. It surprised me when I said it. But I didn't fear death. I was ready for death. I was surprisingly ready.

Samantha's Dream

It's just there. All the time. From the moment you first come to understand death, the awareness of your own mortality becomes an integral part of your psyche. It's everywhere, always, like the Cosmic Background Radiation that permeates the entire universe. Every direction you look the radiation signal is there pulsing, static, enigmatic, and universal. But like the CBR, awareness of our mortality is a quiet signal easily ignored and forgotten. Until the noise of living subsides and the signal comes out of the background.

Then our existential angst begins to strengthen, sharpen, take on a physical presence. No longer remote and abstract, it becomes personal and concrete. This is when life becomes most precious.

We were sitting in our wheelchairs in the lounge near the nurses' station eating cookies and drinking chocolate milk. The TV on the wall was showing the Weather Channel with the sound off.

"I had a dream last night." Samantha twisted an Oreo cookie apart and inspected the white center. I noticed her hair no longer fell from her green ball cap.

"A Lucy dream?" I asked.

"No. I didn't know it was a dream until I woke up." She licked the cream from the cookie and popped the black disc in her mouth. "You were in it."

"I hope it was a happy dream."

"It was. Sort of. We were flying kites in a big field on a hilltop. Just you and me. The field was covered in bright yellow flowers. The weather was perfect. We ran across the field and the wind took our kites higher and higher. When we looked up at the kites, they were wheelchairs, funny-looking wheelchairs flying in the sky on the end of our strings. That's when we realized that we could both run just like normal people. No chairs or crutches." She twisted apart another cookie.

"That does sound like a happy dream. I'm sure it will come true someday soon."

Samantha looked at me through narrowed eyes. "You think we will make our wheelchairs fly like kites?"

"Well, maybe not that part of your dream. But the part where we run across a field of flowers on our own legs. I'm sure that part will come true."

"Mom was there in my dream, too. She was watching us and laughing so hard. She was very happy. That doesn't happen much, you know. Then she started yelling at us. I couldn't tell what she was saying. She waved her arms and kept yelling. We kept running and laughing." Samantha frowned, black Oreo crumbs on her dimpled little chin. "She sounded angry. Or maybe worried. But I just kept running anyway." She put the last of her cookie down on the table. "Then you tripped and fell. I knew you were hurt. You didn't say anything, but I knew you were hurt. But I kept running. I held onto my string and got pulled into the sky. I was flying. I went higher and higher and you and Mom were just tiny specs on the ground."

"Sounds exciting."

Samantha turned those deep brown eyes on me. "Do you think my dream is about dying, Jeremy? Do you think it means I died and left you and Mom behind?"

That kid could ask the toughest questions. Dreams don't mean anything. They're just your brain chemistry doing weird stuff in your head. I believed that. But I also knew this little girl had a disease that was going to kill her. Maybe soon. What do you say to a kid who knows so much more than you do about what it means to see your own mortality standing right in your face?

"I think it means the opposite," I said, "I think it means you are not just going to walk and run, you are going to be amazing."

Samantha looked unconvinced. "That would be nice." Then her face went pale white, and her eyes rolled back into her head. A raspy moan escaped her slack mouth. Her tiny body spasmed causing her back to arch and her hands to ball into tight fists.

"Nurse!" I yelled staring at that little girl in horror as seizures rippled through her body. "Oh God, nurse!" I screamed. "Somebody help!"

Strong hands pushed my chair from behind clearing the way for two nurses to get to Samantha. "It's OK, Jeremy," I recognized Roger's voice. "The doctor is on the way. The nurses will take care of Samantha. Let's get you out of here and let them do their work."

I stared at Samantha as Roger turned my chair around and wheeled me out.

I never saw her again.

Samantha's Last Chance

We sat in an overheated waiting room outside surgery. Junior, Lyle, and Bartholomew huddled in a corner drinking coffee. Monica was squeezed between Tasha and Roger on a vinyl bench holding hands and quietly praying. The girls stopped by to deliver sandwiches and provide their emotional support. We had been there for four hours.

Every time a door opened or someone in scrubs walked by, we held our breath expecting the worst. Finally, one of the surgeons came in. Her face was hidden behind her mask and glasses, but we could tell she was not bringing good news. Monica looked at the surgeon and broke into loud sobs.

"Samantha survived the surgery, Mrs. Bradshaw. We are moving her to the ICU right now."

Monica ran to the surgeon and hugged her. "Thank God!" she gulped through her sobs.

The doctor held her at arms' length. "Mrs. Bradshaw, Samantha survived the surgery, but she is in a very deep coma. Her brain is incapable of maintaining life functions. She is on life support."

Monica stared at the doctor's eyes. "But she's going to be OK, isn't she? She's going to wake up, isn't she?"

"Mrs. Bradshaw, we were able to remove several tumors that were pressing on her spinal cord. But there is another one. It's inoperable and, as I am afraid you know, nonresponsive to treatment."

"What does that mean?" Tasha asked as Monica slumped into her chair.

"I'm sorry, it means we do not expect Samantha to regain consciousness. She will survive only as long as the machines can keep her body alive."

We were stunned into silence. Our little girl was gone.

"Can I see her?" Monica asked wiping her nose on her sleeve. She squared her shoulders and held her head up. "I have to see her."

"Of course, Mrs. Bradshaw. The nurse will gown you up." A nurse magically appeared and took Monica's arm.

"Come with me, Mrs. Bradshaw. We will have you with your daughter in just a few minutes." The doctor turned and left, Monica and the nurse closely behind. The rest of us stood watching Monica walk toward a nightmare none of us could imagine.

"You all should go home," Tasha said breaking the silence. "Jeremy, Roger can help you back to your room. I'll stay here and let you know when I hear anything." I was grateful someone took charge. I was paralyzed. I needed someone to tell me what to do.

Back in my room my heart was dying. My brain felt like it was an unbalanced washing machine on high spin. I couldn't concentrate. Nothing made sense. I had known so little tragedy in my life. I had never lost anyone so close to me. Even my mother's death paled in comparison to the pain of Samantha's. I didn't think I could survive this kind of pain.

Roger realized I was in serious distress. "Jeremy, you just lay down on your bed. I'm going to get a doctor." A moment later a young Latino doctor I had never seen before was at my bedside checking my vitals.

"Mr. Moore, your heart is racing and your blood pressure is quite high. I'm going to give you a shot to help settle things. I know you've had a terrible shock. This will help you sleep."

The next thing I knew, it was 7:30 the next morning. The sun was shining. Puffy white clouds drifted in the blue sky. Birds flitted around outside my window. Then I remembered. I was appalled at the damn birds. For God's sake, *don't they know the world is ending?*

That was a terrible day. I stayed in my room. I couldn't get myself to eat. I had a few phone calls from the girls and the guys checking up on me, but I told them I was not feeling well and wanted to just sleep. No updates about Samantha. I stared at the ceiling for hours. Late that night Tasha appeared at my door. She was crying.

"Monica just told the doctors to pull the plug."

"No!"

"She couldn't let her daughter suffer any more." She leaned on the doorjamb. "I pray that God will look after both of them."

It was too much for me. I snapped. "How can you believe in God if little girls can die like this?"

"I can't explain God's purpose. I just believe in His wisdom. It is hard sometimes. But I know that everything is His will."

"I can't accept that. Little girls don't die because God has some grand plan we can't understand. Little girls die because they get sick. Sometimes science saves them. Sometimes not. God is not a factor."

"Whether science saves a little girl or not, it is God's will that decides."

"I'm sorry, Tasha. I don't like your God."

"It's OK, Jeremy, God doesn't care what you think. He loves you anyway."

I was too tired to argue. I stared at the ceiling thinking about the little girl and her mother.

Tasha must have read my mind. She came into my room and put her hand on mine. "Samantha was a strong girl. Monica is a strong woman. She will get through this somehow." She squeezed my hand then turned and walked away.

A strange calmness came over me. I got out my bed for the first time all day. I changed into the clothes Bartholomew brought me - gray slacks, white button-down shirt, paisley tie, black sports coat, brown wingtips. I looked at my crutches by the door. I got into my wheelchair and headed for the door.

Jeremy's Big Ride

I wheeled past the cafeteria and garden. I wheeled past Cardiology, Oncology, Neonatal, Diagnostic Imaging, Geriatrics, Gastroenterology, OB-GYN. I must have wheeled past dozens of people, but I didn't notice anyone. I rolled through the lobby and out the double doors to the sidewalk. It was cold. I didn't care. I rolled my chair to the top of the hill overlooking the city. Progress Avenue stretched out below me, a long steep slide. Samantha and I had sat there just a day ago. It was a thousand years ago. The world had changed into something unrecognizable. I was lost.

No matter how hard I tried, I couldn't make sense of what had happened. All my beliefs about life and death, God, Heaven and Hell—everything I thought I knew at the core of my being—were suddenly just the glib postulations of an ignorant man. I knew nothing. No one knows anything. We can decide what we want to believe or not believe, but it doesn't matter. We don't know and we never will know. But we can't live in that kind of universal ignorance. We have to live as if we know. We have to live in our make-believe reality. No matter how sure we are about our reality, it's all smoke and mirrors. Life is but a dream.

I closed my eyes and spread my arms. I took a deep breath of cold night air.

And I laughed.

I laughed at life.

I laughed at death.

I laughed at mayflies.

I laughed at old men.

I laughed at pain and loss.

I laughed at God.

I laughed at my life.

Camus was right. Life is absurd.

A white flash of pain and sudden acute awareness shot through my body. A cold breeze washed across my face. I was rolling toward the brink of Progress Hill. I wasn't afraid. I was exhilarated. I was powerful. I was in charge. I could be and do anything I wanted. I decided I would fly. The wind on my face pushed tears from the corners of my eyes. My wheelchair picked up speed. I was accelerating down the hill, gravity exercising its will on me. I surrendered to the pull of the planet. I rolled faster and faster. I felt the wind grab my wide-spread arms. The wind would not let gravity have its way. I felt myself lifted from the ground, chair and all. I was leaving the solid ground and being drawn higher and higher into the night sky. Pale silver clouds surrounded me in a diaphanous fog before I shot through the tops of the clouds into a black sky alive with a billion stars. Far in the distance, a sharp mountain peak pierced the clouds, an island in an ocean of foam.

I leaned to one side and my chair veered off its course and fell back into the fog. I broke through the clouds and found a dense forest before me. I saw a small clearing with a single tree in its center. I could make out movement around the base of the tree. As I approached the tree, a large bear was circling the trunk and occasionally roaring at something in the branches. Someone yelled for help. I flew down to get a closer look. The bear saw this weird creature zooming out of the sky. It reared on its hind legs, swatted at me once then ran off into the woods. I landed my chair and a creature climbed down from the tree. It was a tall man wearing a full-length fur coat. When he stepped out of the shadows, I saw he was no man.

"Bigfoot?" I asked tentatively.

"Thank you for saving my life, Jeremy. I've been waiting for you a long time." The beast smiled. "Want to take a picture?" Then he pulled a cell phone from somewhere in his fur, wrapped a long hairy arm over my shoulders and snapped a selfie. "National Geographic will love this. You can have the phone. Lousy service out here anyway." Then Bigfoot loped off into the woods.

Before I could process what just happened, the forest disappeared. The ground fell out from under my chair. I heard a loud roar—thousands of people chanting my name. "Jeremy! Jeremy! Jeremy!" A stadium full of fans appeared. My chair circled down to the playing field where the Yankees were playing the White Sox. I was in the on-deck circle. Whitey Ford was on the mound. A batboy handed me a bat and pushed me toward the plate. I stared out at old Whitey. He stared back. Then he threw his best pitch. I closed my eyes and swung with all my might. The crack of the ball on the bat was the best sound I ever heard. As the ball sailed over the left-field fence, I was again transported skyward in my chair.

The clouds swallowed me again. My heart was calm. The wind was cold, but I was warm. I flew down into a town where a large circus tent was illuminated from inside. I flew into the tent. A beautiful trapeze artist vaulted herself into the air and did a triple somersault. I grabbed her ankles as she flew by, did my own somersault, and tossed her to a burly man in tights holding onto another trapeze with his knees. The two aerialists winked at me. The ringmaster below saluted me while the crowd cheered. I rocketed out of the tent back into the dark sky.

I flew back up through the clouds into the starry night. The peak was close now. I flew over it. Below I could see three climbers approach the top. I dropped closer. It was them. It was us - Hillary, Tenzing, and a very young me. I stood on the summit with an ice-axe in one hand and a large crescent wrench in the other. The world spread out below me, wave after wave of sharp peaks disappearing into the misty horizon. Young me saluted old me as I flew past.

The clouds swallowed me once more, engulfing me in whiteness without dimensions. No up or down. No left or right. No forward or back. Just there. I was lost but I was OK. I was fine. The clouds opened one more time. A hill covered in a field of yellow flowers spread below me. Junior, Lyle, and Bartholomew were tossing a Frisbee around. The triplets were showing Roger how to do a yoga pose. Tasha and Monica were sitting on a blanket holding hands and watching butterflies flutter among the flowers. I drifted down near them, but they didn't react. They couldn't see me. I became frightened. Why couldn't they see me? And where was Samantha?

A fierce updraft grabbed me and shot me high into the sky back through the clouds and into a bright sunlit sky. The sun was blinding. I saw a small dot against the sun. It was moving toward me. Or maybe I was moving toward it. As we approached, the dot became a person, then a child, then a girl in a hospital gown and bright green baseball cap.

"Samantha!" I shouted seeing her. She waved. Her blond curls illuminated the edges of her beautiful face. She smiled.

"Hi, Jeremy, you finally learned to fly in your dreams! Let's race!" And off she went soaring through the sky toward the sun. I chased after her. Unlike our wheelchair races in the hallway, I had no chance of catching her. She looked over her shoulder to make sure I was coming. I heard her singing.

Row, row, row your boat, gently down the stream.

She flew straight into the sun.

I wasn't going to lose her again. I flew after her. I willed myself to go faster but I couldn't catch her. She was too fast. She was too young. She was too damn young. She shouldn't be here. She should be back on that hill with her mother picking yellow flowers and chasing butterflies. She should not be here with me.

At that moment, I flew into the sun. A final white-hot flash tore through me. Everything went black.

The next morning the Mount St. Anne police found me at the bottom of Progress Hill sitting peacefully in my wheelchair, deader than a stump.

A Year Later

For nearly a year I have wanted to tell Samantha's story. My story. But I had to wait. I needed to know the ending. Now, finally, I know.

The Mount St. Anne Cemetery stretches across fifty acres of rolling hills. Ancient oak trees, still bereft of leaves, dot the property. Gray clouds are low in the sky. A chill mist floats on the breeze. I am looking down on a flat headstone near the base of one the oaks. A small mound of flowers obscures the name on the stone. Three figures in hooded raincoats kneel beside the grave saying a silent prayer. I recognize Monica when she looks up toward the sky like she's searching for something. She turns back to the grave when an ebony hand with brilliant orange nails pats her on the shoulder. Monica and Tasha kneel and place flowers on the grave. The third figure kneels beside the grave, head covered by a bright green ball cap. Tiny hands place a bouquet of white and red flowers on the gravestone knocking the other flowers to the side, revealing the name.

"Jeremy Moore."

Samantha pulls her hood back and waves toward the sky, directly toward me. I feel her eyes lock on mine. It is the happiest moment of my entire life. She turns to Monica with a smile while tears mix with the rain on her cheeks. Tasha pulls Monica and

Samantha into a bear hug. As the three of them walk away, holding hands, I hear Samantha's sweet voice singing.

"Row, Row, Row Your Boat…"

This is what happened that terrible day a year ago: After the doctors pulled the plug, the room got very quiet except for the hum of the air conditioner and the erratic beep, beep, beep of the monitor. Monica held Samantha's hand. The doctors and nurses quietly slipped out of the room to leave the mother and child alone.

Roger and Tasha were waiting in the hall outside the room. Everyone was weeping, even the usually stoic doctors.

Finally, the beep, beep, beep stopped. A heavy silence seemed to fall on the whole world. Monica put her head on Samantha's little chest and sobbed. Her tears fell onto her daughter's gown. Her heart shattered. She wanted to scream at the world, curse God. She wanted to die herself and be with her daughter.

Samantha's body spasmed. Monica gasped. Samantha let out a raspy breath. The monitor beeped once, stopped, beeped again. It kept beeping. Monica screamed Samantha's name. The medical team ran back into the room. Everyone stared dumfounded at the monitor except Monica who watched her daughter's face as color returned and her eyes opened.

Samantha survived the episode but she was still very ill. Monica was desperate. Samantha had another chance, but she needed the new treatment, or she would die. Soon. Monica couldn't go through that again. A week after the scare in the hospital, Monica got a thick envelope in the mail. It was from Marvin Xavier Gould, Esq. It contained my will naming her sole beneficiary. At the time the will was written, my total estate was less than $200,000 but I thought it would help her with unpaid medical bills. The envelope also contained a letter from Marvin Xavier Gould, Esq., indicating the decades-old case against the pharmacy had been settled. The court found the big chain that bought the store two days before I slipped was responsible for all outstanding obligations of the original store plus compensation for pain and suffering plus interest. The company was in negotiations to merge with a mega-giant chain and didn't want minor irritations like my suit to compromise the process. After twenty years of fighting it, the company had settled for $5 million. Marvin Xavier Gould, Esq. got forty percent leaving $3 Million for Monica.

Samantha got the treatment. It worked. That remarkable little girl was alive.

My departure from the world seemed to bring luck to all my friends. Bartholomew got the part. He was even nominated for an Emmy. Critics called his performance as the old gay former football player brilliant.

Lyle made a pile of money when Oprah mentioned the XTC3000 on her program and he sold his three-state distribution rights. He used some of the money to buy a first edition *Moby Dick* only to find an original letter from Herman Melville to Nathaniel Hawthorne tucked into the pages. The Smithsonian offered him $250,000 for the letter. Anyone can stop by Lyle's bookstore to see the letter displayed under glass in the coffee shop.

Junior met Angela in church. Angela owns a large horse ranch in Kentucky that she and her long-dead husband built up from a few acres, a barn, and one old quarter horse into one of the most successful horse ranches in the state. They were married in the same church in Mount St. Anne where Goldie and I enjoyed our short-lived nuptials.

Speaking of Goldie, she came to my funeral. She didn't speak but it was nice to see her there. The girls (who donated the money they made on their XTC3000 investment to a safe house for battered women) convinced Goldie to stay in town for a week and try their latest health and self-improvement initiative. She enjoyed it so much, she sold her place in Florida and moved back to Mount

St. Anne where she attends the girls' programs religiously and is even learning how to be a great-grandmother.

Tasha and Monica, two amazing women, are now a couple. They dote over Samantha and they are affectionate with one another. They realized their feelings for each other in Germany when Tasha volunteered to accompany Monica through the difficult months of Samantha's treatment. Tasha has learned to trust the world again. Monica has learned that miracles do happen.

And then there's Samantha. After the scare in the hospital, the doctors were able to stabilize her well enough to be able to travel to Germany. Samantha spent another month in the hospital in Berlin undergoing the most advanced medical treatments in the world. Four other children with Stafford Sarcoma were also being treated there. She became friends with them. When they weren't knocked flat by their treatments, the children could be found racing wheelchairs, eating snacks in the cafeteria, singing songs, and upending the staid culture of the Berlin hospital. She stays in contact with her friends through whatever social media is de rigueur for young kids today.

Finally, there's me. My funeral was nice. People spoke there. They told stories. Some were even true. They told jokes. Most were funny. As funerals go, I thought it was a good one.

I was remembered as a good man who lived a remarkable life.

I can live with that.

THE END

If you enjoyed this book,
please consider leaving a review
at Jeremy Moore on Amazon

Afterward

This book is not an autobiography. It's not a memoir. I am not Jeremy Moore. I'm ten years younger and better looking. But we have a few things in common. As a young person, I did hope for a life that would make a good book. That didn't happen. Some of Jeremy's unremarkable life experiences are based on loose historical fact. I do have a fear of heights. My earliest baseball experiences still haunt my dreams from time to time. I was on stage crew in high school and spent well-deserved time in detention. I did buy a hatful of pot from a guy on a horse on the Rio Grande. I did drive my grandfather's pickup truck wildly across the mudflats not knowing a guy was hanging onto the tailgate. I have never been to Rose Polytech, but college roommates will recognize Bogart. And, yes, I did watch a good friend become completely shitfaced on his bass boat.

The story of Jeffrey and the cancer patient is true.

Many of the Acropolites' conversations are based on bourbon-inspired discussions with old friends, especially Chuck, over the years.

Pretty much everything else is a product of my imagination.

Tasha's character was inspired by a documentary premiered at the Sundance Film Festival in 2011. *The Invisible War* is a heartbreaking look into the tragic experiences of women in the military. Sadly, Tasha's story is far from unique.

I made up Stafford's Sarcoma, so I hope you didn't bother to Google it.

Special thanks to Alison, Jan, and Chuck for being beta readers of my first completed draft and telling me it didn't suck. Their corrections, suggestions, and admonitions infinitely improved the book. Asking someone to read your novel isn't like asking them to listen to a new song you wrote or an NFT cartoon cat you just drew. It is asking someone to invest hours of their time in focused concentration while you climb inside their head and stumble around trying to tell a story. I am amazed and grateful that these great people did that. And then they did it again when they read the final draft. Thank you! Thank you! Thank you!

Made in the USA
Middletown, DE
08 July 2022